Snowy Mountain Christmas

SHARON SALA

sourcebooks casablanca

Published by Sourcebooks Casablanca, an imprint of Sourcebooks
P.O. Box 4410, Naperville, Illinois 60567-4410
(630) 961-3900
sourcebooks.com

Cataloging-in-Publication Data is on file with the Library of Congress.

Printed and bound in Canada.
MBP 10 9 8 7 6 5 4 3 2 1

Chapter 1

Ozark Mountains: Late November

Mystery author Trey Austin had just spent two weeks prowling through the Ozark Mountains in Arkansas. He was looking for a place to stop for the night when he saw a sign on the side of the road that read Food and Eats Ahead.

As he passed the city limit sign, the name of the town was right below it, but half of the sign was broken off, and all there was left to read was ETTA. He drove past a diner that had long since closed and then checked into the only motel. He barely got the bed turned back before he fell into it half-dressed and passed out.

It was midmorning before he woke up, and it was too late for breakfast. In the light of day, the motel looked even worse, so he checked out and went across the street to the diner he'd seen last night. It wasn't until he sat down, opened the menu, and saw the daily special that he realized today was Thanksgiving.

A few minutes later, a waitress appeared with water and a notepad.

"You want the Thanksgiving special? It's real good. Phoebe makes corn-bread dressing just like my mama."

"Sure, why not?" he said, and then stared out the window.

A stray dog walked by, so skinny Trey could count his ribs, and he watched as it jumped into the bed of an old blue Ford truck. A few minutes later, a man came out of the store and headed for the truck, saw the dog in the truck bed, leaned over, and petted him. But when he opened the door to the cab and motioned for the dog to get in with him, the dog chose not to budge, so the man drove away with the skinny dog happily riding in the back.

Trey's eyes narrowed at the sight, thinking, *At least that dog knows what it wants*, then he looked away.

Minutes later, the waitress came back with a plate full of sliced turkey, corn-bread dressing, and mashed potatoes with a good slathering of gravy on all three and a little ramekin of cranberry sauce.

He didn't think about the fact that he was spending a holiday alone. He'd spent nearly every holiday of his life alone, surrounded by people hired to take care of him or to educate him, or by choice.

He ate without thought. The food was good. The diner was noisy. The waitress kept coming by to refill his glass of sweet tea, and on her last trip by, she left his ticket. When he finished, he laid down a handful of bills on the table, including a good tip, and headed out the door.

Today, he was going home to Phoenix.

He refueled before he left town and, as he went, began admiring the landscape and the vivid colors of autumn Mother Nature had painted on the leaves. He looked his fill as he drove, knowing he wouldn't be seeing the likes of this in Phoenix.

One hour passed, and then another, and he was beginning to think he'd missed the turn he'd meant to take, because he had spent the better part of an hour on a graveled county road, trying to find a connecting road to get him back to a main highway.

His GPS was set, but he feared being this deep in the Ozark Mountains was messing it up. The dead tree he just passed looked like the one he'd seen fifteen minutes earlier. And to add to the frustration and drama of the day, the sky was getting dark. A thunderstorm was imminent, and there wasn't a house in sight to stop and ask for directions.

Trey was approaching a fork in the road and was almost certain he should go right, but the GPS was telling him to go left, so he did, and drove into the oncoming thunderstorm.

Within seconds, the blowing rain shifted his visibility to only a few yards ahead. The windshield wipers were ineffectual against the downpour, and the graveled road was quickly becoming a quagmire. He kept looking for a place to stop and wait it out without blocking the road, but the road was too narrow, and there was nowhere to turn around without getting stuck. With loud claps of thunder overhead, followed by intermittent cracks of lightning, it was all he could do to stay focused.

Then all of a sudden, it was as if the world blew up in his face. Lightning struck a tree just to his left with such explosive force that he instinctively turned his head away from the flash and flying debris.

But as he did, he swerved, then overcorrected, and before he could regain control, the car began to roll.

He was still conscious when the windshield popped out, but he never knew when the driver's side door broke off, or when he landed upside down in a flooding ditch. The last thing he remembered was driving rain in his face and then everything going black.

For the past seven days, Marley Corbett had been on what she called a "gathering mission," traveling through little hidden-away places in the Ozark Mountains, talking with the locals in the hills, cooking with them, baking with them, and when she could, coaxing ancestral recipes from them to add to her menu at the lodge. She was only twenty-seven, but she was the fourth-generation owner of Corbett Lodge, located on Pikes Peak, just above Colorado Springs.

The older women she'd been visiting had been intrigued by the grit and determination of the petite young woman with blond hair and blue eyes, but it was her love for food and cooking that won them over.

She'd spent the better part of two weeks on the road, sometimes sleeping in the spare rooms of the women she'd gone to visit, and other times in whatever motel she could find. Some places had been downright dismal. Some had a measure of charm that even age had not been able to displace.

But this morning, the visits had all come to an end. She was finally on her way home. She'd just left Dollie Porter's home, laden down with jars of pickled beets and pear honey jam, and a stack of Dollie's recipes to go with the others she'd been accumulating.

She had a long drive back to Colorado but was under no time constraints. The lodge had been closed for renovations since the day she left, but she'd received a phone call last night, telling her the renovations had been finished, and now she was anxious to get home. Christmas was coming, and she couldn't wait to get the tree up in the lobby of the lodge and start shopping for gifts.

As she drove, the little hand-carved Santa Claus she had hanging on her rearview mirror was swaying back and forth. She'd bought it at an Ozark craft show last week and was taking it home to hang on the Christmas tree.

She thought back to the people she'd met on this trip, and the wonderful food she'd had, and the generosity of the elders in sharing their recipes. She was excited about incorporating them into her new menu, and daydreaming as she drove, when she began to see storm clouds gathering. And the farther she drove, the darker it became. There was no way around it. She was about to drive into a thunderstorm. And when she did, it was a full-force deluge.

Ditches on both sides of the graveled road were filling up from the rain and rushing in sudsy torrents. Her windshield wipers were on high, and she was praying that roads here didn't flood. She'd slowed down drastically just to be able to still see the road and was anxious to get back to the main highway when she drove up to a fork in the road.

She knew the right fork was the one she needed, but even through the downpour, she could see the angel, bright and shining, blocking her path. The hair crawled on the back of her neck. She was no longer alone.

All of her life, Marley Corbett had seen and talked to angels, and she knew there was one with her at this moment, and the message to her was clear. She was meant to take the left fork instead, and so she did.

Rain was blinding, and the wind was blowing it sideways. She thought about stopping to wait for the storm to pass, but she knew she was on this road for a reason, and so she kept driving.

Then, through the curtain of rain, she began to see something up ahead. As she got closer, she realized it was a wrecked car. But when she drove up on it and saw the driver still inside, she realized why she'd been sent this way. Someone was in danger!

A dark Land Rover was resting upside down in a ditch, lying lengthwise like a hot dog in a bun. The front of it was angled slightly downward, leaving the back end up out of the rushing water. The windshield and the driver's side door were completely missing, which exacerbated the danger to the man in the front seat.

She could see him inside, motionless and hanging upside down, still strapped into the seat. But the rising water rushing through the front half of the car was far too close to the top of his head. If she didn't do something fast, he was going to drown!

She quickly pulled her red Jeep over to the side of the road and jumped out on the run. Despite the all-weather jacket she was wearing, she was soaked to the skin within seconds. She leaned into the car and put her hand on the man's neck to feel for a pulse. The steady thump beneath her fingertips told her he was alive, but not for long if she couldn't get him out. His head was only inches from being submerged.

It was disorienting to step into rushing water, knowing she was standing on the inside of a roof, but she wasn't very tall, and there was no other way to get to him. She tried to unfasten the seat belt, but it wouldn't give. It appeared to have been jammed from the pressure of his weight.

"My knife," she muttered, then climbed out of the wreck and ran back to her car to get her Swiss Army knife, then ran back and climbed inside.

The rushing water made it hard to keep her balance as she began cutting the straps on the seat belt, but it was tricky. She knew the moment he was released he was either going to fall into her arms and trap both of them in the water or go headfirst into the water anyway. Timing was everything.

Okay, guys. You got me here. Now, you're going to have to help me, Marley thought, and began sawing through the heavy straps until she felt them beginning to give way.

In a panic, she threw the knife out into the road and slipped her hands beneath his armpits and locked them around his shoulders. As his head fell forward against her neck, she leaned backward, and using her body as a lever and his weight as the fulcrum, she pulled him toward her so hard that they fell out of the open doorway together, trapping her beneath him.

The rain in her face was like being shot with ice pellets. She couldn't tell if it was actually beginning to freeze into sleet, or if it was just so cold it felt that way, but she had to move and began using her upper body strength in an effort to roll him off.

It didn't work. He didn't budge.

Then she heard the voices.

Try again.

"Then help me!" she cried, and gathered all her strength and shoved. When he rolled off of her onto his back, she immediately crawled onto her hands and knees, gasping for breath. The rain stung. The wind was brutal. But he still wasn't safe.

She was finally free, but the man's feet were still in the water, and if she didn't do something fast, he was still in danger of drowning face up in the storm.

"God give me strength," Marley whispered, then grabbed him by both arms and began dragging him the rest of the way out of the ditch and up onto the road, struggling and slipping over and over, until she had finally pulled him clear. Then she grabbed her knife out of the mud and ran back to the car for her umbrella and cell phone.

He hadn't moved when she returned and once again felt for a pulse as she knelt behind his head. To her relief, it was there, steady and strong. She immediately shifted her position, putting her back to the wind to use her body as a windbreak, then began the struggle to open the umbrella without it blowing away.

Finally it popped open, and before the wind could catch it, she pulled it all the way down to the top of her head and leaned over so that his face was completely protected. Once she was settled, she made a call to 911, offering up another prayer for it to go through.

After only a couple of rings, she heard a voice.

"911. What is your emergency?" the dispatcher asked.

Marley began rattling off info and, as she did, heard the panic in her own voice.

"I just drove up on a wreck in the middle of a severe thunderstorm. The car was upside down in the ditch and the ditch was flooding. The driver was hanging upside down by his seat belt, about to drown. I got him out of the car, but he's unconscious, and I don't know where I am. I know I was on a rural road about fifteen miles southwest of a home where an old woman named Dollie Porter lives, driving northwest. I came to a fork in the road, took the left fork, and that's where I found him. Can you get a GPS location from my phone?"

"Yes, ma'am. Don't hang up. I'm locating now and dispatching police and ambulance. Does the victim have any open wounds? Can you tell if he has any broken bones?" the dispatcher asked.

"There was blood in his hair and on his face before I got him out of the car, but it's all washed away. I see a bleeding cut on his forehead, but I can't tell if there are broken bones. His breathing is steady. He has a strong pulse. But it's storming so hard now that it's all I can do to shelter him." Just as she said that, a strong gust of wind almost yanked the umbrella out of her hands, and she began to panic. "I can't talk anymore. I need both hands to keep this umbrella over his face."

"Yes, all right, but don't hang up. Leave this line open so we'll still have a direct connection to your GPS," the dispatcher said.

"Okay. I'm putting it in my pocket now," Marley said, and then grabbed onto the umbrella with both hands and held it steady, protecting his body as best she could.

But the cold was as brutal as the rain, and it wasn't long before she began shaking. To keep herself from an all-out meltdown about her own misery, she began to study his face.

Even though she was looking at him upside down, it was obvious beneath the mud, blood, and soaking wet that he was striking. A strong jaw. Black eyebrows that arched like wings in flight, high cheekbones, and a Roman nose that might have been broken once. She could see the sensual curve of his mouth, but wondered what his voice would sound like, and while she could see his black, rain-soaked lashes, she wondered what color his eyes were, and if there was someone somewhere who loved him, who was frantic for his safety. In an effort to take her mind off her own misery, she began to talk to him.

"Hey, stranger. This is a terrible way to meet, but stay with me, okay? You're not alone. I'm right here with you, and I'm not going anywhere. Help is on the way. I'm not going to give up on you, so don't give up on me. My name is Marley, but everybody calls me Bug. I grew up in the mountains in Colorado. Are you from Arkansas? Is someone worrying about you? Wondering where you are?"

The wind popped the back of the umbrella so hard she almost lost her grip. "Whoa, that was close," she said, and pulled it down farther. "So, since you're not the talking kind, I'll tell you about me. I'm not married. Never have been. Dan and Lisa Corbett were my parents. I lost them four years ago in a car crash. Worst day of my life. I don't have any siblings. Just friends…good friends. Dear friends…but no family anymore. What about you? Brothers and sisters? Great parents? You'll have to tell me about them someday." Then she stopped to take a breath and realized she was crying.

"I just want you to know, I've got you. You're not alone, and since the angels made sure I found you, then I know you're going to be okay."

Rain kept blowing under the umbrella, and she paused to wipe it away from his face. Her hands were colder than his skin, which had to be a positive thing.

"I like to read. Do you? I read everything. My absolute favorite mystery writer writes under the name Chapel Hill, but nobody knows who he or she is. Isn't that the best? A mystery writer whose identity is a mystery?"

She thought he was trying to regain consciousness because his eyelids were beginning to flutter, but then he went still again. She knew he must be miserable in the cold, on the gravel, but there was no way to shelter him beyond what she was already doing, and her misery was giving way to despair.

She leaned forward, her forehead resting against the top of his head as she willed herself not to cry. There were no more stories left in her, and he wouldn't open his eyes.

"Don't die," she kept pleading. "Please don't die."

But time kept passing, and she was so close to all-out panic that she couldn't think. It had taken the better part of an hour just to get him out of the car, off of her, and up onto the road, and that was before she'd even called 911, and that was nearly thirty minutes ago. She was about to lose hope when she began to hear sirens.

"Oh my God! Oh, honey! They're coming. Help is almost here. They're going to get you out of this awful storm and make you well. I knew the angels wouldn't have sent me here just to watch you die." She began cupping his face and patting his cheek. "You're going to be okay."

She knew when the rescue units took the left fork because the sirens were getting louder. And when a county sheriff's car finally rolled up, followed by an ambulance, and behind that, a wrecker, Marley breathed a huge sigh of relief. She leaned over until her mouth was next to his ear.

"Help is here," she whispered.

Deputy Curtis Stone was on the move when he got the call about the wreck. It was already raining, but he drove into the core of the storm before he reached the location, and when he did, he was stunned at the sight.

A big Land Rover was upside down in a ditch, and through the rain, he saw a young woman huddled beneath the umbrella she was holding over the victim. Stone couldn't see her face, but he could see that she'd positioned herself to take the brunt of the storm to protect him.

He jumped out on the run.

Marley looked up as a uniformed officer in a rain slicker came running toward her. The relief of knowing help had arrived was overwhelming, and she choked back a sob.

"Miss, are you okay?" the officer asked.

"Yes, but he's not," she said.

Moments later, the EMTs rolled up and came rushing toward

them. Two of them helped her up, then moved her out of the way as they began working on the victim, leaving her shaking so hard she could barely stand.

She watched them checking the man's vitals and still stood nearby as another EMT came running with a stretcher. There was a moment when she knew her job was over, but leaving now felt like she was abandoning him.

She staggered as she turned away, so cold and miserable she didn't know she'd just walked out of one of her shoes. Her entire focus was just getting into the sanctuary of her Jeep.

It was the sirens that woke him.

Trey had already begun regaining consciousness, but the sudden blast of sirens was as strident in his ears as the alarm by his bedside.

Part of the time he knew he'd wrecked. And in those lucid moments, he kept hearing a sweet voice—and sometimes he thought she was crying—and wondered if she'd been hurt too, and then he'd pass out again. He'd even had a brief glimpse of her face just as help was arriving. She'd looked away as he opened his eyes, and he wanted to tell her something, but he couldn't remember what it was, and then he slipped back under again. It wasn't until they'd moved her and the umbrella away and the cold rain hit Trey's face that he really came to, but by then, the woman was gone.

He'd heard her voice. He knew she'd been there. But he couldn't think enough to speak. He turned his head and caught one fleeting glimpse of a rain-soaked blond about half his size before the medics surrounded him.

His last glimpse was of her getting into a red Jeep, and then his little angel was gone.

After that, the voices came.

Men's voices. Loud voices.

Someone issuing orders. Someone else responding.

Then he was conscious of hands, so many hands, rolling him onto a stretcher and then out of the rain into the back of the ambulance.

At that point, he passed out again.

Deputy Curtis Stone stood watching as they loaded the victim into the ambulance and drove away. Then as he turned to wave the wrecker to come in, he glanced down and saw one little red shoe in the mud. The woman had been wearing red shoes!

He picked it up, looked around for her car. It was gone, and he realized he'd never asked for her name. Aggravated at himself for the oversight, he took the shoe to his cruiser and bagged it, and then went back to help clear the road. As he walked back to the site, he sidestepped a big puddle and then noticed a large tree on the side of the road that was split down the middle.

Upon closer inspection, he could see char marks on the green wood, and the ground beneath the tree looked like it had exploded from beneath. His eyes widened as he looked back at the location of the wreck. Lightning had recently struck this tree, and now he was curious to find out if this was what had caused the man to wreck.

He still had a trip to make to the hospital. He didn't know if he'd get a statement, but he had to ID the victim before he could close out his report.

As soon as the tow truck left with the wrecked vehicle, Deputy Stone headed into Clarksville to the Johnson County Healthcare Center with the victim's personal effects: a phone from inside the console that hadn't been submerged, a suitcase, and a duffel bag that had been in the back of the Land Rover.

By the time the ambulance arrived at the hospital, Trey was fully conscious. He knew from listening to the EMTs that he had a gash on his head and a large contusion on his rib cage, likely from the seat belt. He didn't remember much after the car began to roll until he heard the woman's voice. Even then, he hadn't fully understood what she was saying, but he'd felt her hand on his face and known he was no longer alone. Then in the ambulance, he keyed in on the medics talking about her during the ride.

They said she'd been huddled over him, using her body as a windbreak and holding an umbrella to keep the rain out of his face. They were theorizing the various ways she might have been able to get him out of the car by herself. She wasn't very big, they'd said, and that she'd cut the seat belt trapping him to get him out.

But nobody mentioned her name, and he didn't know if she was okay. Had she hurt herself getting him out of the car? And how the hell had she dragged him out of the ditch and onto the road? He was six feet, two inches tall and weighed in at a buck ninety-five.

Now, he was in an ER with staples in his forehead and a portable X-ray hovering over him, taking pictures of his head and chest. Moving was miserable, but it happened anyway, and then they were gone.

He closed his eyes and sighed, wishing himself to a place where pain did not exist. After a few moments of silence, he heard footsteps and then a man's voice, questioning the nurse.

"How's he doing?"

"Waiting for X-rays, sir. BP and pulse rate are a little high, but likely due to pain," the nurse said.

"Is he conscious enough to question?" the man asked.

Trey opened his eyes enough to see who was there and saw a uniformed officer with an armful of bags. His bags.

"I'm conscious, just trying to ignore a blistering headache," Trey said.

The deputy put the bags against the wall.

"I'm Deputy Stone with the Johnson County Sheriff's Office. I worked your wreck and got your belongings from the car before it was towed. I won't bother you long. Just a couple of things to finish my report. I need your name and address, and whatever you can remember that caused the wreck."

"Trey Austin. Phoenix, Arizona. I was doing some research in and around the state this past week and was on my way home. My GPS was acting up, and I was pretty sure I was lost when I drove into a thunderstorm. It was a lightning strike that caused me to swerve. One minute I'm driving and then what sounded like an explosion and a blinding flash just to my left. I lost control, then overcorrected. I remember the car beginning to roll. I don't remember anything after the windshield popped out until I heard a woman's voice. I couldn't wake up enough to talk to her, and kept drifting in and out of consciousness. Is she okay?"

Deputy Stone shrugged. "Unfortunately, she drove away before we knew it."

"You didn't even get her name?" Trey asked.

Stone shook his head. "All I got was a shoe. It was stuck in the mud. And I see I accidentally brought it in with your things."

"It's her shoe?" Trey asked.

"Yes, for sure. I saw her wearing them when we helped her up."

"Helped her up? Was she hurt?" Trey asked.

"No, just freezing, and she was on her knees in the gravel when we arrived, holding an umbrella over you. I think she was so cold she was just stiff," the deputy said.

"God," Trey muttered, and then saw the little shoe inside an evidence bag. "Do you have any reason to keep that shoe?"

"No. It's not evidence of anything but a Good Samaritan."

"Can I have it?" Trey asked.

"Yeah, sure. I'll put it in your duffel bag if you want so it doesn't get misplaced," Stone said.

"Thanks," Trey said. "I'll need a copy of the accident report and info as to where the car was towed before I leave."

Stone glanced at the nurse. "Are you admitting him?"

"I'm sure we will. At the least, he's concussed and a long way from home. He'll have to get better to be able to travel," she said.

"Okay then, Mr. Austin, I'll drop it by sometime tomorrow. Take it easy and try to get some rest," he said and left.

Trey glanced at the suitcase and duffel bag and hoped his laptop was still dry and intact. They'd all been in the back of the Land Rover. He'd packed it within layers of clothing in his suitcase, and the bags didn't look like they'd been submerged. But in a worst-case scenario, everything was saved to the cloud as well as a duplicate file he'd sent to his home office in Phoenix.

A short while later, Trey was moved to a single room in the medical center, wearing a hospital gown that was far too short, and hooked up to a number of machines. He was just so glad to be dry and warm, and with enough naproxen in him to alleviate the pounding headache.

He drifted in and out of sleep, thought about calling his parents, then opted against it. All he knew was that they had flown to Lucerne, Switzerland, before Thanksgiving and were staying until after Christmas, maybe the New Year, but they never spent holidays together, and Trey was used to their absence in his life. He didn't know why they were the way they were, but he knew why he didn't miss them.

His parents hadn't raised him. The nannies and housekeepers they'd hired had been the ones who wiped his tears and bandaged up his cuts and scrapes, and when he was ten, his parents sent him away to boarding school. Coming from a wealthy family had drawbacks, and for him, that was the big one. His parents were the reason he existed, but after graduating college, he'd made his own way in the world without them.

The next day, Deputy Stone came by as promised with the accident report, the name of the towing company, and the tow yard. Trey contacted his insurance agent and let him deal with the rest of it and waited impatiently to be released.

Just before Marley drove away from the wreck site, she reset her GPS. She drove slowly through the continuing rain, with the heater on blast until her shaking stopped. Her hair and clothes were beginning to dry by the time she reached the access road to Interstate 40. She took the westbound on-ramp and drove until she was out of the rain and didn't stop until she'd reached Fort Smith. That's when she realized she was missing a shoe.

"I liked those shoes," she muttered, then got out, stuffed the muddy one under the front seat, got another pair from her suitcase, and put them on before refueling.

She went inside the large truck stop and headed straight to the bathroom, washing up as best she could, then brushing the tangles out of her hair before returning to the store area. She made a quick sweep through the refrigerated section and bought a bottle of sweet tea, then went down the candy and chip aisle for some snacks before getting back on the road.

She ate while she drove, but the farther she went, the more exhausted she became. The trauma of the day was catching up. By the time she drove across the border into Oklahoma, she started looking for a place to stop. She drove until she reached Sallisaw, then stopped at a hotel and checked in. She made it all the way up the elevator and into her room before coming undone.

Maybe it was the quiet, or the comfort of not being wet and cold, but as soon as Marley locked the door behind her, she sat down on the side of the bed and began to cry. A few random tears quickly turned into harsh, ugly sobs, and she cried until the overwhelming feeling of fear had completely left her.

No tears needed. You saved him.

She sighed. The angels were talking to her again. "I know. But I was so scared. Please let him be okay."

She waited for an answer she didn't get and then went to wash her face. Her eyes were red. Her skin was pale. The last thing she needed was to get sick this far from home, so she went down to the restaurant in the lobby, absently scanned the menu, and when she saw they served breakfast all day, she ordered her childhood comfort food—scrambled eggs, bacon, and toast. She ate with appreciation for the simple meal that it was and felt better when she went back upstairs.

A long, soaking bubble bath later, she crawled between the sheets and closed her eyes. When she woke up again, it was morning. She spent one more night on the road, and on the morning of her third day, she was heading west. Tonight, she would be home, happily wandering the renovated guest rooms of Corbett Lodge and sleeping in her own bed.

Chapter 2

The sun had gone down by the time Marley reached Colorado Springs. To her delight, the city had already decorated the streets and the streetlights with Christmas decor. Some businesses had huge red bows on their doors, while others had opted for wreaths or colorful blinking lights around their windows and roofs. All they needed was a little snow and it would be a Christmas wonderland.

Although it was already dark, it wasn't late, so she stopped at a supermarket to grab a few things to take home and was going down the deli aisle when she felt a hand on her shoulder. Before she could turn around, the hand had slid all the way down her back to her hips.

Horrified at the familiarity, she turned, saw who it was, and shoved him backward, shouting without caring who was listening.

"Jared Bedford! What's wrong with you? Get your hands off me!"

Jared took a step back and held up his hands. "Don't be so touchy, Bug. We've been friends all our lives. I was just trying to say hello."

"Friends? We have never been friends, and you have no concept of boundaries. I put up with this all through high school to keep my father from going to jail for breaking your neck, but no more! If you ever put your hands on me like that again, you'll be sorry."

There was a crowd of shoppers gathering, but Jared wasn't

backing down. He shoved a hand through his straw-colored hair, then narrowed his eyes down to green slits.

"What are you going to do? Your daddy's dead, and I'm not scared of you."

Marley was in shock. This was the most blatant act of crossing a line he'd ever pulled. Suddenly, she was afraid, but she couldn't let him see it. Instead, she leaned forward and lowered her voice just enough so that he was the only one who could hear her.

"You mistake my size for helplessness. I don't need my daddy to pull the trigger on that shotgun I keep loaded at the lodge. If you ever put your hands on me like that again, I will make you sorry."

The grin froze on Jared's face. He glared at her for a few moments and then made a quick pivot and strode off. When he did, the crowd dispersed, but it was a frightening, embarrassing homecoming she hadn't expected. And now she was going to go back to that big empty lodge alone, and Jared Bedford likely knew it.

She quickly finished her shopping, loaded up her car, and drove out of the parking lot, then circled a couple of blocks to make sure he wasn't following her before leaving the city. After that, she headed up the mountain, while paying close attention to the dark road behind her, watching for headlights. And when she saw the Corbett Lodge sign, she quickly took the turn and drove onto her property.

The drive was barely a hundred yards up into the woods, and the security lights lit the way as she pulled around back into her garage. The lights came on inside the moment the door went up, and even as she was getting out of the car, the doors were going back down.

She exhaled slowly, releasing the tension she'd been feeling.

It was like being tucked into bed.

She was home.

The routine of putting up groceries, unpacking her suitcase, bringing in the canned goods she'd been given, and storing her new recipes were enough of a distraction that she forgot about Jared.

She began thinking of the man from the wreck. Was he healing, or was he succumbing to injuries she didn't know he'd had? The thought of spinal injuries exacerbated by being moved had been on her mind, but she also knew he would have drowned if she had not moved him.

She ran upstairs to see the renovations and was delighted by the changes. The hardwood floors were gleaming. The new tile in the bathrooms looked elegant, and the walls in the guest rooms had been freshly painted with a color called pale sage.

It fit the ambiance of the lodge so well. Now all she had to do was put the rooms back together again, but not tonight. That was something for another day.

She went through the lodge, checking to see that all the doors and windows were locked, and the public bathrooms were empty, and that everything was in its place. Then she set the security alarm and went to work, putting her dirty clothes in the hotel washing machine and carrying her empty bags up to the attic.

Her stomach growled as she was descending the stairs, and she realized she hadn't eaten since morning. She'd been gone so long that there was nothing to eat in the fridge without cooking, so she opted for popcorn and a can of soda, took them to the family quarters at the back of the lodge, and locked herself in for the night.

It felt wonderful to finally crawl into her own bed, but when she fell asleep, she dreamed of the wreck again, and of the man. And in the dream, when she cut him free from the seat belt, the flooded ditch suddenly became a river, and they both fell into the water. The last thing she saw was his dark head face down in the water, being swept out of her grasp.

She woke up sobbing. It was almost 6:00 a.m. as she threw back the covers and showered and dressed, ready to do anything to forget the nightmare.

Trey Austin was released from the hospital the same morning that Marley woke up at home. He was leaving with bruised ribs, sore muscles, and staples in his forehead. For now, the recurring headaches had precluded a flight home, so he had rented a car, and it and the rental agent were waiting for him just outside the lobby entrance when they wheeled him out.

The orderly loaded up his bags into the SUV, and the rental agent handed over the keys.

"Safe travels," he said. "Just contact our office in Phoenix when you're ready to turn it in, and they'll pick it up at your residence."

"Many thanks," Trey said, and then slid behind the wheel.

There was a moment right after he started the engine, when he first put his hands on the steering wheel, that he felt a brief spurt of anxiety, remembering being inside a rolling car and thinking, *Is this the day I die?* But the moment quickly passed. Grateful to be back on his feet and with a set of wheels beneath him again, he set the GPS and drove away.

He knew his energy level was going to be slow and low, so he paced his travel accordingly. Once he hit the interstate, travel went smoothly, and it was mostly just a long, straight shot to Phoenix, but he was tired. He stopped midway and stayed the night in a motel in Amarillo, Texas, just off the interstate.

The room was ordinary but clean, and he was tired and hungry. After he ate, he came back to the room and went through his luggage, elated to see everything in the suitcase dry and intact, including his laptop. When he went through his duffel bag, he found the little shoe again, still safely tucked into an evidence bag—still muddy with scratches and nicks in the leather at the toe.

He kept looking at it inside the bag, wondering why the toe would be so scratched, and then flashed on what they'd told him about her down on her knees in the gravel, keeping the rain off his face. If it did that to her shoes, what must her knees have looked like? He had a lump in his throat as he put it back down and continued digging through the bag.

He'd already found his cell phone and charger while he was in the hospital, but he hadn't gone through anything else. Now, he was seeing how thorough Deputy Stone had been in recovering his things from the wreck. He'd even had the foresight to grab the remote control to his garage that had been clipped to a visor, along with everything that had been in the console and the glove box. His thoughtfulness in gathering up Trey's belongings had not gone unnoticed.

He went to bed that night exhausted and hurting, then slept fitfully, dreaming about the wreck and the woman's voice telling him over and over to hang on, that help was coming.

He woke before daylight, grabbed some coffee and doughnuts from the free breakfast at the motel, and was back on the interstate just as the sun was coming up behind him. He stopped twice. Once for fuel. Once to stretch his legs, and for food and water so he could take his meds. He needed the pain pills, but he couldn't take them on an empty stomach.

His phone dinged now and then, signaling text messages, weather alerts, Amber Alerts, and twice with alerts that the interstate lanes ahead were blocked off to one lane as highway patrols and tow trucks were clearing wrecks. Even the thought of another wreck made him break out in a cold sweat.

It had been dark for hours when Trey passed the Phoenix city limit sign, but he was back on home ground, driving beneath streetlights already festooned with Christmas decor and within the familiarity of his surroundings. He shuddered, thinking how close he'd come to never seeing another Christmas.

By the time he reached the gated community where he lived, he was as exhausted as he'd ever been. He opened the garage door with his remote and drove inside. Moving on autopilot, he dragged his bags into the house and down the hall to his bedroom, adjusting the thermostat in the hall as he went.

Everything looked the same—his big four-poster bed, the reading area near the window. He could tell the furniture had been polished, a sign that the cleaning service had been here, even when he was not. But it didn't feel the same. He didn't feel the same. For the first time in his life, he'd faced death and come out on the other side, thanks to a tiny angel who'd performed a small miracle on her own to save him.

He stripped, showered, then crawled into bed. He'd used up his last bit of energy just getting his things inside the house, and when his head hit the pillow, he rolled over and passed out.

It was the grinding sound of the trash truck that woke him the next morning. He thought about rolling over and going back to sleep, but he was hurting too much to relax. He had to get food so he could take the pain relievers and made himself get up.

After he'd shaved and dressed in a pair of sweats and an old black T-shirt with a Phoenix Suns logo on the front, he made coffee and toast. He found a near-empty jar of strawberry preserves and scooped out what was left onto his toast. The food settled his stomach. He popped the pills and then went back to lie down.

As his head pain abated, he drifted back off to sleep into a recurring nightmare he had every time he was sick, or in pain.

The maids were whispering in the hall.

Trey heard the voices, but he couldn't make out the words, and then someone shouted, and the door to his bedroom flew inward, hitting the wall with such a thud that his little night-light lamp fell off the dresser, shattering into a million pieces.

"My light! My light!" Trey cried, and leaped out of bed.

Before anyone could stop him, he'd run across the glass.

The pain was so startling that he froze, and the look on his father's face was so threatening, he was afraid to cry out.

"Who put that lamp back up? I told you to get rid of it. He's ten years old! He's too big to need to sleep with a damn light!" Anders shouted. "Tend to his feet. Someone clean up this mess!"

Trey was frozen in place, pretending he couldn't feel the broken bits pushing deeper into his flesh.

"I did it, Daddy. I put the light back up," Trey whispered.

"After I told you not to?"

"But, Daddy, it was just a light. I need the light."

"No! You don't need the light. You're an Austin! You need to be tough!"

"I am tough, Daddy. My feet are bleeding but I'm not crying. I like the light, because I need to see."

Anders opened his mouth, and then stopped and looked at the blood pooling beneath his son's feet and walked out of the room.

Trey woke with a gasp as the memory of that pain was still fading in his head, then rolled out of bed. He glanced at the clock. It was nearing noon. He'd been asleep for hours.

He went to the bathroom to wash his face, hoping to wash away that dream. Even after all these years, he still remembered parts of the aftermath. The trip to the ER in the middle of the night. The nanny had gone with him in the ambulance. The trip home just before daybreak in the family limo with both feet swathed in bandages. It took the better part of two weeks before he could walk without pain. And by the end of the month, he was on his way to boarding school.

He looked up at himself in the mirror as beads of water were still clinging to his face. The child he'd been had turned into this man. Some days he thought he got who he was. Other days, he accepted that he was as close to a hermit as a man could be, with no desire to change his stripes.

He frowned at his reflection, then turned away, dried his face, and left the room. His bags were still against the wall in his bedroom, so he plopped them onto his bed and began sorting through the clothes as he unpacked.

One pile for laundry.

Another pile to go to the cleaners.

He set the little red shoe, still in the evidence bag, on his reading table and then carried the laundry to the utility room. The familiarity of his own things in his own house felt like luxuries, and as he continued the business of laundry, the nightmare passed.

Careful of the staples in his head and the bruising on his chest and ribs, he finally sat down to order food through DoorDash, made some coffee, then opened his laptop to check email. He hadn't checked it since the wreck because reading made his headaches worse, but that was then and this was now, and it was time to get back to business.

He had four emails from his literary agent, Meredith Bernstein, all relating to needing a delivery date for his new contract. And when he hadn't answered the first, Meredith had followed up over a period of days with three more emails, each a little more urgent, until the last which was dated earlier this morning.

Trey! Respond or I'm calling the police to make a welfare check on you!

He smiled, knowing she meant it, and began typing a response. Meredith didn't mess around.

M—

Had a wreck in Arkansas. Spent three days in the hospital,

then took me a couple of days to drive home. I just arrived home late last night. I'm okay. Regarding the new contract, let's do a next-year delivery date of November first. That gives me the rest of this month to heal and nine months to finish the novel.

The next email he opened was from his mother, Gloria. It was nearly ten days old.

Trey darling. It's snowing huge feather-size flakes. The ski slopes are wonderful. Dad and I had dinner with some royals last night. Such fun!

Mom

Trey read it twice, telling himself not to make a thing out of the fact that she hadn't followed up to check on him for not responding, or even asked what he was doing for the holidays. He knew he was looking for something between the lines of what she'd said, but it wasn't there.

He sent a reply as random as her message.

Have fun. Don't break anything.

Trey

After that, he went through the rest of the email, deleting spam and paying bills that had come due.

The positive part of his job as a writer was that the only person who knew his identity was Meredith, and she was sworn to secrecy.

The world knew his work by the pen name Chapel Hill, and that's the way he intended to keep it. He didn't correspond with readers. He didn't appear at conferences. The identity of Chapel

Hill was as mysterious as the mysteries he wrote, and oddly enough, the fact that no one knew his true identity boosted his sales.

When DoorDash arrived, he retrieved his food and carried it to the kitchen, turned on the TV for the sound of other voices, took the pain meds, and ate in silence. He was gathering up the food containers when his cell phone rang. He glanced at the caller ID, turned off the TV, and then answered.

"Hey, Meredith. I swear I'm okay."

"Oh my God! Why didn't you call me? Who was with you? Where are your parents?"

"You couldn't have done anything. Nobody was with me. They're in Lucerne, watching it snow and dining with royalty."

He heard a delicate snort and grinned as Meredith unloaded on him.

"Did you even call them? You didn't, did you? You need a keeper!" she muttered.

"Of course, I didn't call them. They sent me off to boarding school when I was ten. I've been doctoring my own wounds and fighting my own battles ever since, except for the time when I first signed with you and got mugged in New York. You came to the hospital to check on me."

Her voice softened. "Well, of course I would. And I'm sorry, just the same. How did you wreck? Were you hit by another car?"

"No, just missed getting struck by lightning though," he said, and proceeded to tell her the story, all the way down to the little shoe he'd brought home with him.

"That's not random. She was there because you needed her to be," Meredith said.

"I'm not as fanciful as you, but after all that happened, I tend to agree with you," he said. "If she hadn't found me, I would have drowned, hanging upside down in my car. It would have been a very ignominious death. One most unworthy of the grisly mysteries I write."

Meredith groaned. "Do not say that, even in jest. You're my favorite client, but don't tell."

He sighed. "Thank you for being a friend."

"You're welcome. You can send me a box of See's Candy and I won't send you a Christmas fruitcake."

Trey laughed. "Deal."

She hung up.

He was still smiling as he finished cleaning up, then locked the house, set the security alarm, and went to lie back down. The silence made his life seem even more empty, so he turned on the TV, then closed his eyes and fell asleep.

For Marley, coming back to the renovated guest rooms was a bit like moving into a new home. Before she left, she and Wanda had packed everything away. The first thing she'd done when she began stirring was to run up to the attic and get the wreath they always hung on the front door. They weren't going to be open for business, but this was also her home, and Christmas was her favorite time of year. She got it and the door hanger and then took them both downstairs, got a folding chair from the office, and then carried everything to the front door. Being short had its drawbacks, and hanging a wreath on a big door without a ladder was one of them. The folding chair would have to do.

Once she had it hanging, she stepped back on the porch to see if it was centered. Satisfied with the pine boughs and the pine cones tucked within, she fiddled with the big red bow at the bottom, then straightened the tiny red cardinal that had been perching on the same sprig of pine for the past five years and called it done.

After returning the chair to the office, she headed upstairs to begin unpacking and sorting, laying aside some things to donate that no longer fit with the new decor, and making a list of what needed to be replaced.

Officially, the lodge would reopen on New Year's Day. But Christmas dinner was held here for her close friends and people on the mountain who had nowhere else to go. It was the grandest time, and she was already thinking about gifts.

The lodge also held an annual New Year's Eve party. It was tradition in the area, and people made reservations months in advance to make sure they were on the guest list. With a guest limit of one hundred and fifty to stay within the fire code of the premises, it was first come, first served.

The lodge also had a dozen rooms to rent, and they were all booked for the night as well, so there was a lot for her to do before reopening.

Jack and Wanda Wallis were Marley's lifesavers, and the nearest thing to a family she had left. They were working at the lodge when her parents, Dan and Lisa Corbett, were running it and before Marley was born. Years later, when Dan and Lisa were killed in a car wreck, the Wallises became the backbone of the lodge, leaving Marley to come to grips with her grief.

Even now, four years later, her parents' absence had left a huge hole in Marley's heart. She missed the sound of their voices. Her dad's booming laugh. Her mother's tender touch.

There was no one left in Marley's life to remind her of her childhood foibles or to bring her homemade butterscotch pudding when she was sick. Marley had become an orphan at the age of twenty-four, and some days, the burden of this lodge seemed insurmountable. But on other days, she knew it was the lodge that had saved her.

It had given her a purpose, and with that, had come a deep-ingrained knowing that, if this place was to survive a fourth generation of existence, she was the only one who could make that happen.

While she'd been gone, Jack had been on-site every day, happily wrangling the work crews. This morning she'd sent a text to let them know she was home, and she was still upstairs moving boxes when she heard Jack call out.

"Hey, Bug! Where are you?"

She had been Ladybug to her family and friends since she'd taken her first steps, and over the years that got shortened to Bug. Now she answered to that name as readily as she did to Marley.

She ran out into the hall. "Up here!"

"We thought you might need some help," Wanda said as they shed their coats and started up the stairs.

"And you thought right! I missed you," she said as she hugged them both.

Jack gave her a pat on the back. "We missed you, too, honey. So, what do you need me to do first?"

"Help me get boxes into the right bedrooms. They're labeled according to room numbers, and then after that, would you please get the fire going in the great room? Oh, and keep a watch out for Craig. He's on his way with a delivery of firewood. And you do not help him unload. He's bringing help. You just show him where it goes. And if you see Jared Bedford anywhere on the property, let me know. He hassled me in the supermarket last night. Felt me up in the deli aisle and laughed about it when I had a fit, and made innuendoes about me being alone since Daddy died, and what was I going to do about it."

Anger washed all over Jack's face, and then he remembered Bedford had been part of the renovation work crew, which added a whole other layer of concern.

"I'm going to have myself a talk with that man," he muttered.

"No need. I told him I kept the shotgun loaded at the lodge and I would have no problem using it," Marley muttered.

"Oh my God," Wanda said. "You should have called the police."

"And said what? That Jared Bedford put his hands on my butt, and I threatened to shoot him for it? I think he just likes to harass me. We're just going to pretend the creep doesn't exist and carry on," she said.

Jack didn't argue, but he didn't like it. He took off up the hall without another word, leaving Marley and Wanda on their own.

Marley tucked a stray lock of hair behind her ear. "The rooms look so good. We need to change all the bedspreads. I ordered them before I left. Do you know if they came?"

"Well, there are twelve large boxes in that little storage room across from the public bathrooms, so I'm guessing that it's them. We can donate the old ones! But first, the dust covers need to come off the beds. We have twelve rooms to put back together. If you have other stuff you need to do, I can do everything but change out the spreads. I'll have to wait until Jack can carry them up here for me," Wanda said.

Marley hesitated. "I do need to confirm the wholesale delivery today and pay some bills, and then I'll get the dolly and bring up the boxes in the guest elevator."

"Then go do what you need to do. We knew you'd be overwhelmed with all that needed to be done, and we got tired looking at each other."

Marley laughed. "Whatever the reason, I'm glad you're here," she said, and headed downstairs on the run.

"Slow down, girl!" Wanda shouted.

"Yes, ma'am," Marley said, and not only slowed her steps, but used the handrail as she went.

Jack and Wanda had been married for more years than she was old, but they were still so funny and cute together. It made her long for a relationship like that, but it had been six years since she'd had any semblance of one. Once her father died, her quest to save the lodge and keep it solvent had taken over every aspect of her life, and in her heart, Jack and Wanda had replaced the family she'd lost.

She went to her office and began double-checking orders, paying bills, and fielding phone calls. It was business as usual. She could hear Wanda singing, "I saw Mommy kissing Santa Claus," and smiled.

A short while later, she heard Jack come thumping down the stairs and start banging around the fireplace.

The lodge was alive again. The only downside to her life was the recurring nightmares about the dark-haired man from the wreck.

Every night, she either dreamed she was trying to save him, or that he'd gotten lost and she was trying to find him. The obsession was weird. She didn't even know his name, but she'd formed some kind of a bond with him for the time she'd been with him.

Part of her thought it was because she'd been the only one responsible for keeping him alive until help arrived, and maybe she was still holding on to that feeling. It wasn't healthy. It didn't make sense. But she didn't know how to turn it off.

A couple of days after Trey was home, he checked in with his regular doctor, who was properly horrified at what Trey had experienced. After checking the healing wound on his forehead, he contacted the hospital in Arkansas and asked for all the records to be sent to him, then sent Trey home with orders to keep his social life low-key and to come back in a few days to get the staples out.

Word about the wreck was also beginning to spread within Trey's small social circle. The first time Trey walked into his favorite coffee shop, the little barista who usually served him saw the staples and freaked.

"What happened to you?" she cried.

He touched the staples and shrugged. "It was only a matter of time. My brains fell out, and as you can see, it only took four staples to tuck them back in, which doesn't say much for the size of my intelligence."

She shook her head, frowning as she made his usual order. "That's not funny, Trey."

"You're right. I sure wasn't laughing at the time. I had a wreck and I'm healing just fine."

She set his coffee on the counter and waved away his money. "This one's on me."

He lifted the coffee cup as if to toast her. "Thank you," he said, and left the coffee shop with a smile on his face.

Later that same day, his insurance agent sent a Christmas poinsettia to the house and followed up with a call, informing Trey that they had totaled his car and he'd be receiving a check for the value. That meant he needed to turn in the rental car and go car shopping—something he certainly hadn't planned on doing, but stomping through dealerships wasn't on his preferred list of things to do, so he sat down with his laptop and started researching vehicles. He knew what he didn't want. Now he had to see what they had on hand that suited his style and needs.

It had to be an SUV or the like. With four-wheel drive. And leather seats. And all the bells and whistles of communication, including a GPS tracker. He was always alone, and this wreck had brought home the dangers of no one knowing where he was or how to find him.

He had a running list of possibilities and the locations in the city, and decided to keep the rental car until he'd done his shopping. And then he saw a van pull up into his driveway and remembered today was the day for his cleaning service. He got up to let them in, but when he opened the door, they came in carrying food in covered containers.

"What's all this?" he asked as the trio of women from TLC Cleaning surrounded him.

"We heard about your accident," Tessa said.

"We brought food. Enchiladas and homemade tamales," Leslie added.

"I brought cake. Tres leche. Your favorite," Connie said as they swept past him and put the food on the kitchen island.

"You three are my favorites! The ultimate TLC trio. Thank you so much!"

"You're welcome. Go sit. We're going to clean now," Connie said.

Since they were about to get down to business, Trey grabbed a cold drink from the refrigerator and went back to his laptop, happy with the sound of people in the background and thinking about the meal he'd be having tonight.

A couple of nights later, some of the guys from his gym stopped by with two six-packs of beer, on the pretext of wanting to hear about the wreck. But they soon tuned in to the Sports Channel and then proceeded to drink most of it themselves.

Finally, their designated driver herded them out, leaving Trey with a lot of pats on the back and best wishes. He was glad they'd come, but even happier they were gone. He'd done all the male bonding moments he cared to do in college, but in an odd way, their friendship still validated him. All the while, that muddy shoe was still in the evidence bag on top of his dresser, reminding him of the valiant little soul who'd saved him.

The day he went to the doctor's office to have the staples removed, he hadn't thought much about the procedure. He pulled staples out of papers every day. Surely, it was no big deal.

Only he was wrong. It wasn't excruciating, but it also wasn't particularly pleasant, but it was over, and their absence seemed to finalize the end of his ordeal.

When he got home, he went into his bedroom to change clothes and, as he did, glanced at the shoe again. The urge to actually hold it in his hands was so strong that he carried it to the kitchen and, for the first time, took it out of the bag.

Once he did, the need to clean it followed, which he did carefully, almost reverently. Now it sat on top of his dresser as a memento of the event. A small, red leather shoe, missing the person it belonged to.

It sat there for a day before the unsettled feeling returned. He knew he was never going to be satisfied until he'd seen her face-to-face, and the only way that could happen was if he could find her.

His first instinct was to just tell the story and get it out to the general public. Even if she didn't see it, maybe she'd told someone about the wreck and they would see it, and they would notify her, and—

That's where his imagination ended. He sighed. He didn't know what would happen after that. It would be up to her to respond, but he'd never know if he didn't try.

He took a picture of the shoe. Titled the story, "Searching for Cinderella," and then told of the wreck, his rescue, how brave she was, and how diligently she waited for help to come while sheltering him from the storm. He told of how the little shoe was left behind, and how desperately he wanted to meet the woman who'd saved his life. At first, he'd thought about not posting his name and picture, but if he didn't, people would likely assume it was a guy trying to lure innocent women into his grasp. So, he posted a snapshot of himself with the fresh scar on his forehead, and the directions as to how to contact him via an email address he set up especially for this project, then posted it to every social media site he belonged to.

After that, all he could do was wait and hope his parents stayed in Europe and didn't see it. In every scenario that went through his mind regarding their reactions, none of them were good.

To his surprise, the story went viral, and before long it was being shared on other sites and was picked up by newspapers and more than one national news outlet, and that's when the responses began to pour in.

Trey was inundated with wannabe Cinderellas, and lying Cinderellas, and offers to *be* his Cinderella if he couldn't find the real one. But none of them rang true, and no matter how many pictures he looked at, and how many stories they spun, none of them looked right, or had the right answers to his questions. He wasn't giving up, but he was beginning to fear that she just didn't want to be found, because the entire nation had become involved in the quest.

Newspapers were running the story, "Searching for Cinderella."

A famous shoe company offered a lifetime supply of their shoes to the real Cinderella, should she ever be found.

And every night when Trey went to bed, he dreamed of her voice, saying...*Hang on, honey. Hang on...help is coming!*

Chapter 3

The guest rooms at the lodge were all put back together. The cleaning service she used for the lodge had come and gone, and Marley was looking forward to getting the lodge back open, but there were still things to do before that happened.

This morning, she'd had Jack bring up the last of the bushels of apples she'd been storing in the basement, and now she and Wanda were in the process of making apple butter. They had two automated apple peelers going and two big pots of applesauce and spices cooking down into the thick, brown jam it would become, and a table full of sparkling-clean canning jars ready to fill with the finished product.

Wanda had the radio tuned into a station playing Christmas songs and was singing "The Little Drummer Boy" with the singer on the radio. Jack was outside clearing off the light snowfall they'd had last night from the sidewalks and the steps on the covered porch spanning the length of the house, and Marley was at the stove, keeping an eye on the pots of simmering apple butter, stirring it now and then to keep it from sticking.

"This smells so good," she said as she dipped a spoonful out of one of the pots and put it on a saucer to cool. It wasn't just to taste, but to test the cooled consistency of the spicy jam to see how close that pot was to being done.

"It sure does, Bug. One of your hot biscuits and a spoonful of your jams is the way to a man's heart," Wanda said.

"I've fed a whole bunch of men in my life, and not one of them has stuck," Marley muttered.

"That's because you keep shooing them away like pesky flies," Wanda said.

Marley laughed. "Maybe it's the name. Maybe a Bug and a fly can't be friends."

Wanda giggled and then cored the apple she'd just peeled, cut it into quarters, and dropped it in yet another pot to cook down in the consistency needed to turn it into sauce.

Marley glanced over her shoulder. "How many left to peel?" she asked.

"Less than a peck," Wanda said. "We're making good time, honey. There will be jars of apple butter cooling and sealing all over the kitchen."

"There's nothing more satisfying than hearing those lids pop as they seal," Marley added. "In a day or two, we'll get them down into the basement and on the shelves with the rest of the jams and jellies."

"Your daddy putting in that freight elevator from the kitchen to the basement was the handiest thing he ever did here," Wanda said.

"Agreed," Marley said, and tested the spoonful of cooling apple butter with her finger. It was already beginning to set up. She grabbed a clean spoon and took a little taste, then rolled her eyes. "Umm, perfect. Let's get some jars. This is ready."

It was hours later before their last pot of apple butter had cooked down and been canned. Jack and Wanda had gone home with a pint of fresh apple butter, and Marley was kicked back in front of the fireplace with a plate of buttered toast and a little dish of the spicy jam she'd saved back. Nutritionally, it was lacking in protein, but it was satisfying to her soul.

She was watching the evening news as she ate, while waiting for the weather report. She quit eating when she ran out of toast, then got up and carried her dishes into the kitchen and stayed to make herself something to drink and, as she did, missed a rebroadcast of the "Searching for Cinderella" story.

By the time she came back, they'd gone to a commercial break. She plopped down with her glass of iced tea just in time to see the weather report. Satisfied that there were no imminent warnings, she decided to drive into the city tomorrow and do a little Christmas shopping.

Trey's television was on, but he wasn't paying attention to the program. Instead, he was staring into the flames in his fireplace. The fire was real. The logs were not. They were made of refractory cement. He knew because he'd looked it up once. But it was as warm and pseudo cozy as being alone at a fireside could be. He was consoling himself with a shot of bourbon because he was getting nowhere with his search. In the past five days, he'd gone through thousands of Cinderella emails to no avail and was at the point of accepting this might not work after all.

Finally, he downed the last of his bourbon and headed for bed. Just before he turned out the light, he glanced at the shoe and realized he had it turned in such a fashion that it appeared to be moving away from him. In a flight of fancy, he turned the shoe around until it was pointed straight at him.

"Okay, little angel. Do your thing. Walk this way."

Then he turned out the lights and crawled into bed.

Marley was so tired when she went to bed that for the first time since the wreck, she slept without dreaming, and woke as the first rays of sun were sweeping across the mountain.

"It's morning, Ladybug. Up and at 'em," she muttered.

It was her homage to her father, who'd always been the one to wake her when she was a kid, and ever since she'd come back to the lodge, it had become her personal ritual. After that, she threw back the covers and headed for the shower. Jack and Wanda would be here later, and she wanted to be ready and waiting when they began boxing up jars of apple butter to move to the basement.

She dressed quickly and headed to the kitchen to start a pot of coffee, then while it was brewing, made herself a bowl of cereal and opened her laptop to check emails as she ate, eventually winding up reading through social media instead. She rarely had time to indulge, but this morning she opened Facebook to check out the comments on the Corbett Lodge page, then began scrolling through the random posts.

And that's when she saw the picture of the red shoe, saw the photo of the man from the wreck, and read the story beneath it. The hair was standing up on the back of her neck, and her heart was pounding, and then she read it again with tears in her eyes.

"Oh. My. God."

Her first instinct was to answer. She wanted to hear his voice. To see the color of his eyes. She thought they were dark, but she wasn't sure. It was obvious he'd healed, or he wouldn't be involved in this search, but there was a moment when she hesitated, and as she did, she heard a voice.

You have to do this.

Still shaken, she carried her dishes to the sink and loaded them in the dishwasher. Before she could gather her wits, she heard Jack's truck coming up the drive and closed her laptop. This was for later, after Jack and Wanda were gone.

They came in through the back entrance as usual.

"Morning, Bug. Are you ready to get at this?" Jack asked.

"I need to be ready. There isn't an empty surface anywhere in the entire kitchen," Marley said.

"I'll go down and get the dolly and the boxes," Jack said. "We'll have this done in no time."

"After this is finished, if you'll bring down the Christmas tree from the attic and set it up in the center of the lobby like always, I would appreciate it. I want to go into the city while the weather is still holding and finish my Christmas shopping."

"If you want, we can decorate it, too, while you're gone," Wanda said.

Marley sighed. "That would be a huge help. I'm too freaking short for anything."

Jack grinned and tugged at the ponytail of the hair she'd piled high on her head. "That's why your daddy called you Ladybug. Because you were so little and cute. Don't worry, kiddo. We've got you."

"I'm coming with you to the basement," Wanda said.

Jack winked. "Awesome. Great place to sneak a little kiss."

Wanda rolled her eyes. "You don't have to sneak anything from me. We live together."

Jack laughed and swatted her backside as they headed down the hall toward the freight elevator.

Marley watched them going with a combination of jealousy and joy.

"I want that, too. What do I have to do to make this happen?" she muttered, then remembered the angels had already told her to answer the man who was searching for her, just like they'd sent her to save him. "I know, I know, you already told me. But you know how I am. Sometimes I need reinforcement before I act."

But the whole time they were moving apple butter to the basement, all Marley could think about was that man—Trey Austin. At least now she knew his name. It didn't dawn on her that he might have been conscious enough to see her, but now the tease of reuniting with a total stranger was both enticing and daunting.

It was just after 10:00 a.m. when they finished, and Jack and Wanda immediately headed for the attic to get the Christmas decor, while Marley changed clothes and drove into Colorado

Springs. The decorated storefronts made the season even more festive, and she was soon caught up in the delight of shopping. Christmas dinner at the lodge wasn't for the public. It wouldn't be a big gathering, but it would be with people who meant the most to her, and the ones on the mountain who had no other place to go. It wasn't charity. Just a gathering of friends and a few lost souls.

A new pocketknife for Jack. A bottle of Wanda's favorite perfume. A pair of heavy-duty gloves for Craig, who cut and sold firewood for a living. A new turtle figurine for a friend who collected them, a new cookbook for another friend. Packets of beef jerky for two of the old-timers. Skeins of yarn for the two knitters in the group. But the gifts were always personal—something she knew they would like, something they would use or treasure. She skipped lunch to finish shopping and, as she was coming out of a shop, saw Jared Bedford watching her from the other side of the street and stopped.

Jared grinned at her and flipped her off.

She didn't react. She just stood there staring until he finally walked away. Only then did she return to her car with her purchases. After that, she grabbed a Subway sandwich to go, and headed home.

She still needed to deal with the man who was searching for his Cinderella. She knew it was her shoe. She knew it was the man she'd saved, but was he her real Prince Charming, or did he already belong to someone else? There was only one way to find out.

The first thing she did when she got home was dump her purchases in the kitchen, then hurry into the great room to add a log to the fire before going to get a closer look at the tree in the lobby.

Immediately dwarfed by the size, she looked up at the angel on top and smiled.

"There you are," she said softly.

It was the same angel that had been on her grandparents' Christmas trees, and then her parents', and now hers. Seeing it was almost like having them with her again, if only in her heart.

The tree itself was ablaze with twinkling lights, while the limbs were entwined with gold and silver garlands and four generations of ornaments, including a ladybug ornament commemorating Marley's first Christmas.

She remembered the Santa ornament she'd brought back from the craft fair and ran to get it, then searched the tree for the perfect spot and hung it, then stepped back for a broader view.

"Welcome to the tree, little Santa," she said, and then turned to look about the room.

Jack and Wanda had made it beautiful, even adding holly garlands on the staircase and more garland and candles over the mantel on the fireplace. But her tummy was rumbling, a reminder she still hadn't eaten, and her sandwich was waiting, so she went back into the kitchen, her footsteps echoing in the empty lodge.

She turned on the TV in the kitchen for company, and the entire time she was eating, she was also thinking of how to respond to the man with her shoe.

It was nightfall before she finally sat down at her computer, uploaded a selfie she'd just taken of herself, and instead of going down the list of questions she should have answered, she just started writing, as if she was talking.

> Hello, Trey Austin. It's me, Cinderella, a.k.a. Marley Corbett. I'm sorry I didn't see your story earlier. I don't get online much, and I've been busy. I sent the photo as requested, but I didn't know that you'd even seen me, and other than a drowned rat, I can't imagine what I must have looked like in that storm.

Until I saw the picture of the shoe, I'd completely forgotten about shoving the matching one beneath the seat in my car. In fact, it's still there, and except for what might have fallen off, still caked with mud.

I'm so happy to know you are okay. After the deputy moved me out of the way and the EMTs took over, all I could think about was getting into my car and out of the storm. It was so very cold.

I think I was in something of a daze myself because I didn't realize I'd lost a shoe. I just started the car and drove away. It wasn't until I stopped for gas in Fort Smith that I saw it was gone. So, Prince Charming, I guess your search is over.

I am including my phone number for your convenience.

She read it through again, then hit Send before she changed her mind.

She had no idea how long it would take to get an answer, or if he'd already given up and gotten over the need to find her. But she had no control over what happened next. Either he'd contact her, or he wouldn't.

She'd already wrapped the little gifts she'd bought today and placed them under the tree, and she was ready to call it a night, so she went through the lodge locking up, turning on night-lights, and setting the security alarm. She left the tree lights blinking and, as she started down the hall to her room, paused and turned around.

Everything was in shadows.

The fire in the fireplace had burned down to embers.

The fire screen was in place, but the faint scent of woodsmoke lingered in the room.

A faint blue glow from the full moon was coming through the windows, turning the room into a land of familiar shapes and shadows, while the Christmas tree blinked a good night.

"Night, Mom. Night, Daddy. Miss you," she whispered, then turned her back on the day.

Jared Bedford was sitting in his apartment, well on his way to getting drunk. Marley Corbett had stared him down, and he'd turned tail and walked away. He didn't know what made him angrier. The fact that she wasn't afraid. Or that he didn't have the guts to follow through on all his threats.

He upended the beer he was holding and drank what was left. That little bit of liquid courage rallied his ego.

He would, by God, follow through, and soon. He just needed to find the right time.

After the time he'd spent inside the lodge, he already knew how to make it look like she'd just disappeared, and he knew where he was going to hide what was left of her when it was over.

Trey had waffled all day about attending an early Christmas event at a local country club, and almost talked himself out of it. Then at the last minute, he dressed for the event and went anyway.

His choices were to either participate in the life he'd been given or accept that he was becoming a hermit, happy only when he was lost in the storytelling of another mystery. At any rate, attending the event would solve trying to figure out what to have for dinner. And instead of driving himself, he called an Uber. Just in case he was tempted by a glass or two of wine.

To his surprise, upon arrival he was actually glad he'd gone. He was met at the door by Frank and Carrie, the host and hostess, and immediately became the topic of conversation.

"Trey! So glad you are up and about and felt like coming! Have you had any luck finding your Cinderella?" Carrie asked.

"Regretfully, I have not," Trey said.

"No matter. There are plenty of young women here who would gladly step into those shoes," Frank said, and then laughed at his own pun.

"Enjoy the evening," Carrie said.

"Thanks, I will," he said, and snagged a glass of wine from a waiter's tray as he moved through the crowded room.

The muted murmuring of guests overlaid the music coming from somewhere up above their heads. He saw people who were vaguely familiar, and some who were total strangers.

Quite a few had already separated into little groups, while the pretty people moved around the room like colorful peacocks, strutting from place to place.

As the evening went on, the event would have been perfect but for the steady stream of single women who had no qualms about telegraphing what they wanted from him.

They didn't really know him, but by single status alone, and the fact he was the only child of extremely wealthy parents, they saw him as a "catch." He was satisfied with that false narrative. His pseudonym, Chapel Hill, was the wall behind which he lived and breathed.

The evening ended with a serve-yourself buffet, and then the hunt began to find a place to sit and eat without being propositioned.

A friend from the gym rescued him from two clingy women and invited him to a little corner table with him and his wife. When Trey finally sat down with his plate, he moved a holly ring and candle to the side to set his plate down and breathed a sigh of relief.

"Thanks, Gary. I owe you."

Gary's wife, Addy, laughed. "It's your own fault for being so damn pretty and, I might add, also single."

"I was born with the face, but being single is by choice," Trey drawled.

The conversation shifted to other things. He picked at his food, using it as an excuse not to talk. He mostly just listened and nodded in all the right places until he was ready to call it a night.

The party was still going strong when he called for an Uber. He said his goodbyes and left the party. A few minutes later, he was on his way home.

His Uber driver was a regular and knew Trey wasn't a talker, so the drive home was quiet, although the streets were busy. The headlights coming toward them from the opposite direction looked like a string of pearls, and the Christmas decor on the streetlights and in the windows was a vivid reminder of another holiday he would only spend alone. But after the lively evening, Trey welcomed the silence. A short while later, he entered his house and reset the security alarm behind him.

He was home, but not yet ready for bed. He needed to unwind a bit, and after changing his party clothes for sweats, he grabbed a bottle of water and his laptop and kicked back on the sofa.

He hadn't checked his Cinderella email all day, so he opened the email and started down the list of new messages. The first thing he looked at was the picture they'd sent, and then the questions they'd answered. It was easy to spot the shams. But it was also depressing. Every failure was a step farther from finding her.

He was fifteen minutes in when he opened the next email. And the moment he saw the face, then read the message, his heart skipped.

"It's you! Oh my God, it's you!"

His heart was hammering. He looked at the time stamp on when he'd received it and realized it was hours ago. He glanced at the time. It was late. He didn't know where she lived. He didn't know what time zone she was in. But she'd given him her phone number, and he couldn't bear to wait another second to hear her voice again, so he reached for his phone.

Marley had been in bed watching a movie when she fell asleep. She was dreaming about making a snowman with her dad when her phone began to ring.

She woke with a start, saw the TV still on, and at first thought the ringing phone was from the television, until she realized it was the phone on the charger beside her bed. She hit Mute on the TV and saw Out of Area on the screen and knew before she answered that it would be him.

"Hello? Is this Marley Corbett?"

"Yes, this is Marley."

"This is Trey Austin, the guy you pulled out of the wreck. I'm so sorry to be calling this late, but I was at a Christmas party and just got home to find your message. I've been looking for you for so long that I couldn't wait another second to hear your voice."

Marley liked the sound of his voice. "That's okay. As I said in my letter to you, I had no idea you were looking."

"I'm in Phoenix," Trey said. "I need to see you face-to-face to thank you from the bottom of my heart for saving my life. I'll come to you. I'm bringing back your shoe. I'll trade it for a hug. Where are you located? Is there a place nearby where I can stay? I don't want to intrude upon your life. If you're married, then bring your husband to feel safe. But I need to do this."

Marley hesitated. This is where her trust of angel messages had to come into play. The unknown was always a little scary at first.

"I'm not married," she said, and thought she heard him exhale, as if he'd been holding his breath.

"Neither am I," he said.

She shivered. This was really happening.

"I live just outside Colorado Springs," she said.

"I can drive that in a day. Can you recommend a place to stay?"

She hesitated again, and then plunged headfirst into the unknown of what this might be.

"I own and run a kind of B and B called Corbett Lodge. It's fifteen minutes up the mountain from the city. You will be my guest. And, for the moment, my only guest. I've had the lodge shut down since before Thanksgiving for renovations in the guest rooms. I'm reopening to the public on New Year's Day. I'll send directions to your phone."

"Thank you, Marley, thank you! Not sure what time I'll arrive, but I'll get a couple of hours' sleep and then head your way."

"There is a snowstorm predicted to hit this area. They said it should arrive around midnight tomorrow night… Oh…wait, it's already tomorrow. Pack extra clothes just in case we get snowed in. It wouldn't be the first time."

"Thanks. I'll pack and leave at daylight," he said. "See you soon, and thank you again."

"Safe travels," she said, but he'd already ended the call.

She glanced at the clock again. The sun would be up in a few hours, and her first guest in the renovated lodge was on his way.

She quickly sent him directions, turned off the TV, and set her alarm for early rising. Even after she'd turned out the lights, she lay there thinking they'd met in a thunderstorm and would likely be meeting again in a snowstorm. Why all the chaos?

Trey was so excited that he barely slept.

He was packed and on the road before daylight, his GPS set with directions she'd given him to the lodge, and his sat phone on the seat beside him. He didn't want to be caught without cell coverage, and he didn't know how reliable coverage was, but he was about to find out.

It was I-40 to I-25 all the way to Colorado Springs, and then through the city and up the mountain, and he needed to get there before it began to snow. That was his plan. He didn't know what Mother Nature had in mind.

The alarm Marley set last night went off at 7:00 a.m., but she was already in the shower. It was still beeping when she exited the bathroom to get dressed. She turned it off and turned on the TV to catch the morning weather report, and then got jeans and a sweater from her closet and got ready for the day. After putting her hair up in a messy bun on top of her head, she headed for the kitchen and began stirring up batter for blueberry muffins while she was waiting for the coffee to make, wondering if Trey Austin was already on the road. She hoped so because the predicted snowstorm into this area was moving faster than expected, and she couldn't help but worry.

As soon as she had the muffins in the oven, she went to the fireplace to stir the embers and start a new fire, adding kindling until it caught. Once she had a good blaze, she added a log and went back to check the muffins. They were done.

"Perfect," she said as she took them out and set them on a cooling rack. A couple of minutes later, Jack and Wanda walked in the back door. "Morning! Your timing is perfect. I just took blueberry muffins out of the oven."

"Don't mind if I do," Jack said.

Wanda rolled her eyes. "I just fed him."

Marley laughed. "Oh, I don't doubt that." Then she thought of the visitor on the way and needed to let them in on what was happening. "Before you two get busy, come sit with me. I have something I need to tell you."

Wanda frowned. "Are you in trouble, honey?"

"No, no, nothing bad. Come sit and I'll explain."

"I'm gonna need coffee, too," Jack said.

As soon as they were at the kitchen table, Marley took a quick sip of her coffee and then folded her arms on the table and leaned forward.

"Have either of you heard anything about the story that's been all over social media and the news about the man looking for Cinderella?"

"Yeah! I heard that on the news last week. The guy with the shoe, right?" Jack said.

She nodded. "So, that man is on his way to the lodge. He's supposed to arrive some time tonight if he doesn't get caught in the snowstorm somewhere."

"Why didn't you tell him it was closed?" Wanda asked.

"Because I'm the woman he's been looking for. I'm his Cinderella."

Wanda gasped. "What? What on earth do you mean?"

"I'm the one who pulled him out of the wreck. I'm the one who saved his life." And then she began to explain how it had all happened, and how she'd driven away without knowing she'd left a shoe behind.

"Oh my lord, Bug! Why didn't you tell us about this before?" Wanda asked.

Marley shrugged. "I don't know. I didn't know his name, and then they took him away, and I guess I didn't think I'd ever see him again."

"You're something else, Bug," Jack said. "Did you see the wreck happen, or—"

"Oh. Right. I didn't tell you that part. No, I didn't see it happen, and if I had stayed on the road I'd meant to take, I wouldn't have found him," she said.

"What made you change your route?" Jack asked.

"It was raining really hard, and I was coming up to a place where the road forked. I knew I was supposed to take the right fork, but all of a sudden there was this huge bright light within the rain, completely blocking the right fork. I knew it was an angel blocking my way, and that I was to take the other road, so I did and found him."

Wanda sat, staring at Marley. "I don't know how you came to have this connection, but you've been this way all your life. It used to freak Lisa out, listening to you tell what you'd seen and what you'd been told. She thought it was your imagination for the longest time, until she realized you were telling her things about people who died before you were born and telling her things that were going to happen before they did. Dan just accepted it as part of who you were."

Marley nodded. "I know. I was little. I didn't know how to explain anything. I just kept telling her it was the angels talking. She took me to multiple doctors because she wanted a rational explanation. I think she would rather I had been a little crazy than accept the reality of my life. But this is how I came into the world, and I apologize to no one for it. Anyway...the man's name is Trey Austin. He is driving up from Phoenix, and he will be staying here for a day or so. Longer if we get snowed in."

"Are you afraid? We can stay here, too," Jack said.

"Jack, every person who's stayed in this lodge was a stranger. Every family. Every couple. Men and women. Besides, the angels already told me it was okay. And you and Wanda can't get snowed in here with me. You have your own home and pets to care for."

"Well, I can always get here on the snowmobile if the need arises," Jack said.

She grinned. "Yes, mister, I know that. Now, let's get the morning stuff out of the way and then you two go home before the snow gets here, okay?"

"Deal," Jack said. "I'll move a good bit of wood in for the fireplace and then bring up a couple of ricks to the back porch. Oh, and I'll make sure you have gas cans filled for the generator, just in case."

"What do you want me to do?" Wanda asked.

"I thought I'd put Mr. Austin in the first suite at the head of the stairs, so would you fill the mini fridge with bottled water and soft drinks, and make sure the toiletries are in the bath, and a bath mat and fresh towels in there as well? I'm going to bake cookies for the room."

They got up from the table and headed in different directions, while Marley carried their coffee cups to the sink, but then she paused and turned around. Before she did anything else, she needed to get that shoe out from beneath the car seat, so she grabbed a bag from the utility room and headed for the garage.

Trey had been on the road for hours, briefly stopping once to refuel and the next time to make a pit stop and get some food. He kept the radio in his car tuned in to the weather channel on Sirius XM, and his eye on the busy interstate.

But it seemed the farther he drove, the more road construction areas he drove through, which kept slowing him down, and that just led to frustration.

Now that he'd found the woman he'd been looking for, he felt impelled to hurry. It didn't make sense, but he kept thinking if he didn't get there on time, then she might disappear, and she'd be lost to him again. Logically, he knew a stranger shouldn't matter this much, but she did.

He drove while the sun was setting in the west. After that, it was dark and headlights all the way. It was just after 9:00 p.m. when it began to snow. At best guess, he was a little over an hour outside of Colorado Springs.

At first, it was just tiny windblown flakes momentarily spotlighted by headlights that blew into the windshield, lasting only as long as it took for the wipers to clear them away. The farther north he drove, the heavier the snow fell, but the interstate traffic was still keeping the highways clear.

About thirty minutes outside of Colorado Springs, the snow had begun to accumulate and drift across the interstate, and at times, it was difficult to see the road, so he got behind a semi and followed the taillights, knowing that trucker knew this route far better than he did.

When the truck finally reached the city and pulled off into the lot of a big motel, Trey kept driving. Now he had the streetlights and Christmas lights to see by, and again, enough traffic in town to keep the main roads open.

He stopped to refuel at a gas station that was still open and had to brace himself against the wind and blowing snow as he filled up.

It wasn't until he left the city and started up the mountain that he ran into snowpacked roads with no ruts and poor visibility. He was relying solely on the GPS to keep him from getting lost, and grateful the new Land Rover he was driving had four-wheel drive and snow tires.

What should have taken him less than fifteen minutes stretched into thirty because he'd slowed down to watch for the sign. She'd sent him a picture of the Corbett Lodge sign that was plainly visible on the west side of the road, but tonight, nothing was visible beyond ten feet in front of his headlights.

Then, just when he feared he might have passed his turn, he saw the CORBETT LODGE sign and took the turn. He couldn't miss it now. This road led straight to the lodge. All he had to do was stay out of the ditches.

Chapter 4

It was nearing midnight, and Marley was bordering on panic.

Trey Austin hadn't called or sent her any messages about being delayed. But the snowfall was so heavy, she couldn't see beyond the porch. She'd been pacing from room to room, from window to window, seeing nothing beyond the faint glow of barely visible security lights.

She kept envisioning him trapped in the storm somewhere along the route, then telling herself that life wouldn't deal him two blows like that within the same month.

She didn't question the validity of their emotional link. It was obvious he felt it, or he wouldn't have been so adamant to meet her. And she'd held him in her arms for what had felt like a lifetime before the ambulance arrived. They'd survived a traumatic event together. It was to be expected.

Then, as she was standing at the windows, she heard a voice.

Turn on all the lights.

"Yes! Of course!" she cried, and began running through the downstairs, turning on every light switch, and then up the stairs to turn on lights in the hall, and then lights on the upstairs balcony that ran the length of the house, and back downstairs to the garage, and turned on all the outer lights around the shed and the parking lot, and then ran back to the front windows in the lobby. She still couldn't see much beyond the blizzard, but all of the lights and blowing snow had turned the lodge into a pulsing, glowing orb.

She was convinced that if they'd told her to turn on the lights, that meant he must be near and needed something to guide him in. She was staring into the white void, waiting, hoping for headlights to appear, when suddenly there they were.

Relieved beyond measure, she watched the lights as the car approached the lodge, then stopped. The headlights went off. She saw a shadowy figure emerge, waited until he was coming up the steps, and then ran to the door and flung it open.

Trey was driving blind, relying on the shadowy shapes of trees on either side of the road as a guide. From her message, she'd indicated the lodge was close to the main road, but in the dark, in a blizzard, close felt like a hundred miles. All he could do was keep moving.

When he finally saw a glow in the distance, he guessed he was almost at his destination. The closer he drove to it, the larger the glow became, until he realized she hadn't just left a candle burning in the window to light his way. She'd lit up the whole place to guide him. Emotion washed over him at the thoughtfulness of the gesture.

The moment he reached the lodge, he wasted no time getting out, but as he did, he actually staggered from the wind and snow. He grabbed his bags from the back seat, ducked his head against the blizzard, and trudged through the knee-deep drifts piling up around the porch. It wasn't until he felt a tread beneath his feet that he realized he was finally at the steps.

He looked up just as the huge door swung inward, and then he saw her, bathed in so much light he didn't think she was real.

"Careful on the steps!" she called as he started up, and then suddenly she had him by the arm and was leading him inside, into a place of warmth and beauty.

Marley was taken aback by how big he was standing up beside her, when she'd only known him lying down and unconscious. What did register was that he was covered in quickly melting snow and appeared exhausted from that drive.

"I was so worried about you," she said.

He couldn't stop staring at her. Standing beneath the lights of a huge crystal chandelier with all that glorious hair framing her face, she looked like an angel. Then he looked down and saw the snow melting at his feet.

"I'm getting snowmelt all over your floor."

She laughed, and the sound rolled through him like music. "When it snows up here, everybody melts on the entryway." She held out her hand. "Welcome to Corbett Lodge."

He dropped his bags and clasped her hand as if he'd been reaching for a life preserver. "I was afraid I'd never find you, and now that I have, I am at a loss for words."

"You're safe. I'm never at a loss for words. Come to the fire and take off your boots. They're probably full of snow. The drifts outside are piling up."

He followed as if she'd tethered him to her, took off his coat, then his boots, and stood them by the fire before he turned to sit down and found himself looking into the bluest eyes he'd ever seen.

"I have so many questions. All I remember is nearly getting struck by lightning, then swerving. I have very little memory of any part of the actual wreck."

Marley was focused on his eyes. They were so dark they were almost as black as his hair. And the sound of his voice was a deep, raspy rumble that made her feel it inside, the same way thunder did when it rolled across the mountain.

Then she heard him mention lightning and gasped. "Lightning! I wondered what caused your accident."

He heard her talking, but the words barely registered, and he knew he was staring. "The day of the wreck…how did you find me? How did you ever get me out of the car? You're half my size."

Marley leaned forward, her elbows on her knees. "Oh, I didn't find you by chance. The angels did it. If they hadn't stopped me at that fork in the road, I would have taken the one on the right. But there was this huge white light in that road blocking my way. I thought maybe a bridge was out up ahead or something like that. I always pay attention to their messages, so I took the left fork and, within minutes, drove up on the wreck. That's when I knew they'd meant for me to find you."

Trey's head was spinning. He interrupted her, certain he'd misunderstood. "Did you just say 'angels'?"

She glanced up, forgetting that usually freaked people out, and was afraid she would see that look on his face, but it wasn't there.

She shrugged. "Sorry. Everybody who knows me takes this for granted. I hear angels' voices. Sometimes the messages guide me. Sometimes they warn me. Can't explain it. I was born this way. Anyway, back to you. I was frantic when I realized there was a person still inside the car. The windshield was missing, and the driver's side door was gone. I could see you hanging upside down, so I knew your seat belt must still be fastened. I jumped out and started running through the downpour. You were alive, but unconscious and very close to drowning. The water in that ditch was deep and rising."

Riveted now by her story, he set aside the subject of angels.

"How did you get me out?"

"I climbed in with you and tried, unsuccessfully, to unfasten your seat belt. I think your weight was pulling against it, so I ran back to my car and got my Swiss Army knife."

He zoned out on the phrase "Swiss Army knife." *How many women did he know who carried one of those?* Then he realized she was still talking and picked up the conversation.

"Ran back to cut the belt. I knew you would fall when it began to release, and I knew I wouldn't be able to catch you or keep you from going headfirst into the flooded ditch, so when I crawled inside to cut the belt, as soon as I felt it give, I grabbed you and leaned backward, pulling as hard as I could. Your weight propelled us both out, but then I was trapped beneath you, and I couldn't wake you up, and all I could think about was that no one else knows what's happened or where we are."

"I fell on you?"

She waved away the concern. "You didn't hurt me. But it took a good deal of effort before I managed to roll you off. Our feet were still in the flooding ditch, so I got myself up and out, then pulled you up into the road, only to realize you had a good chance of drowning anyway, just being face up in that deluge. That's when I began to panic. I didn't know how badly you were hurt. I didn't know if, by moving you, I might have injured you more, but it was done. I ran back to my car again to get an umbrella, then got down on my knees behind you to form a windbreak and held the umbrella over the both of us to keep the rain out of your face and called 911." She sighed. "I didn't know where we were, but I knew the road I'd been on. They followed the GPS location of my phone to find us. I kept talking to you, but you never woke up."

"I heard your voice…more than once," Trey said. "I wasn't conscious enough to know what was happening, but I remembered you kept saying, 'Hold on, honey. Hold on. Help is coming.'"

Marley's eyes welled. "Oh…I didn't know you'd heard me."

"The sirens. I heard the sirens," Trey said. "That was what woke me. I had a faint glimpse of you right before a deputy moved you back. I saw you walking away, and then nothing. I didn't know if you were okay. I didn't know anything…and then the deputy found your shoe. When I asked for it, he gave it to me. It was the only connection I had to the woman who saved my life, and I knew I would never rest another day of my life without finding you and thanking you face-to-face. So, thank you, Marley Corbett. Thank you for being my angel. Thank you for saving my life."

He reached across the space between them with his hands outstretched.

Still a little teary, she gripped them firmly. "We'll both thank angels, because if it hadn't been for mine, I would never have found you."

"I don't know what to think about you," he said softly.

"There's nothing to think about. I'm just the Cinderella you were looking for."

That's when he remembered the shoe and opened his bag. "Now that you mention it, I have something that belongs to you," he said, and pulled it out.

She smiled, and then kicked off her left shoe and extended her foot. "Do your thing, Prince Charming."

He knelt before her and slipped the little red shoe on her very small, slender foot. "A perfect fit!"

Marley pointed to a muddy little shoe on the floor beside the firewood.

"And there's its mate."

Trey saw the mud-caked shoe and sighed. The final proof. Before he cleaned up his shoe, it had looked just like the muddy one.

And then, as if on cue, the old grandfather clock in the hallway began to strike the hour. When it did, they looked at each other and smiled, thinking of the clock striking midnight in the fairy tale.

"Midnight. Talk about timing," Trey said.

"Well, I'm not going to turn back into a cinder maid because I already am one, and there's no coach about to turn into a pumpkin, just a blizzard having its way with the mountain. And I am being terribly remiss in not getting you to your room so you can rest. Are you hungry? There's always food already made here. How about I show you to your room and then you come down to the kitchen?"

"Are you sure that wouldn't be too much trouble?" he asked.

"I'm sure," she said, and quickly took off the shoe and put her other one back on. "Leave your boots. They'll dry by morning. Grab your things and follow me."

Trey picked up his coat and went back to get the luggage he'd left sitting, while Marley ran to get a key from the front desk. They started up the staircase just as the clock struck twelve. He paused at the landing and looked down into the lobby at the blazing fire, the flickering lights of the Christmas tree, and the garlands of greenery hanging everywhere, then up at the huge wooden beams in the ceiling and the massive logs that made the walls of the great room below. This princess already lived in a castle; it was just made of wood. Then he realized she was already gone and hurried to catch up.

Marley was holding the door open as he approached. She stepped aside for him to enter, then followed him in, giving him the quick rundown of amenities.

"You get yourself settled and comfortable, and then follow your nose. The hallway to the kitchen is on your left as you come down the stairs. Oh…is this too late for coffee? I can do hot chocolate or—"

"Don't go to the trouble to make coffee unless you want some, too. I'll drink anything but matcha tea."

She laughed. "Understood. I'll see you downstairs," she said, and pulled the door shut behind her.

By the time she reached the kitchen, she already knew what she was going to do—toast the blueberry muffins she had left over from this morning and scramble some eggs with diced onion, chopped ham, diced red and bell peppers, a few bits of diced pickled jalapeño peppers, and a handful of shredded Fontina cheese. By the time Trey came down, the eggs were done, and she was taking the muffins from the broiler.

"Whatever it is, it smells wonderful," he said.

"Nothing much," Marley said. "It's just late-night food or, as my daddy used to call it, hangover breakfast—minus the tomato juice with a hard dash of Worcestershire. You get your choice of a longneck ale or orange juice."

"Then in honor of your father's recipe, I'll take that beer."

Marley put the plate of food in front of him, then popped the cap off the beer and set it in place.

"Am I going to eat alone?" he asked.

"No, sir. Dig in," she said as she snagged a half of a blueberry muffin and a glass of her favorite soft drink and sat opposite him at the table, while delighting in his obvious enjoyment of her food.

Trey took a bite out of one of the toasted muffin halves and rolled his eyes as he chewed and swallowed.

"Did you make these?"

She nodded.

"Who taught you to cook like this?" Trey asked.

She frowned, thinking back. "I don't really remember who specifically, but I grew up here. It was my grandparents' home before he added the upstairs and the whole front of the lodge, including this massive kitchen, and turned it into a B and B before there was such a thing. My dad also grew up here and took over in later years. I was born here, in the family area at the back of the lodge. January fifteenth I will be twenty-eight. They were snowed in that night, kind of like tonight."

"Wow! You started life off with a bit of drama, didn't you?"

Marley shrugged. "Totally out of my control. I was just along for the ride."

Trey laughed. "Touché."

She nodded and kept on talking. "Mom and Daddy taught me everything about this business, and my college degree was in hotel management, so I was okay in that department. Jack and Wanda Wallis worked for Mom and Dad, and now they work for me. They are all the family I have left. We just finished putting up apple butter before the snow came in. We already made strawberry jam, peach preserves, and blackberry jelly earlier in the year. We have a full basement under the lodge, and all of that is stored down there. We'll serve it all year round, or until we run out. I keep the lodge open year-round and serve lunch to the public six days a week and a Sunday brunch. We're closed now only because the guest rooms were being renovated while I was in Arkansas."

"Why were you in Arkansas? It's a long way from Colorado Springs," Trey said.

"Research trip. I'd made prior contacts with some of the elder ladies in the Ozarks and was there visiting different places and eating food in their homes, learning how they made things. I came home with some wonderful old-time recipes to add to my menu. Ever hear of chocolate gravy?"

He glanced up as he was scooping up another bite. "No. Are you serious? What do you eat that on?"

"I guess anything you'd put syrup on, but my favorite way they made it for me was when they split a hot biscuit, buttered it, and poured the hot chocolate gravy on it. So good," she said. "So, why were you in Arkansas? It's also a long way from Phoenix."

He bought time by chewing and swallowing before he answered. He didn't want to lie, but he didn't talk about being a writer to anyone. But what he did tell her was true.

"Mostly, I was on a sentimental journey. My grandmother and her people were born and raised in the Hot Springs area. I barely remember her, and my mother tries to forget she came from humble beginnings."

Marley frowned. "If I'm not being nosy, why on earth would she want to do that?"

"Because she married up. Ever hear of Austin Enterprises?" Trey asked, and popped the last bite of eggs into his mouth.

"Maybe... Isn't that a Fortune 500 company?"

Trey nodded as he chewed and swallowed. "Yes, and my mother, a pretty young thing from the Ozark hills, married Anders Austin the second…the heir of the man who founded it."

Marley sat looking at him and letting that statement sink in. "Your name…Trey. Does that mean you're the third Anders Austin?"

"Anders Allen Austin, the third, at your service, Cinderella."

Her eyes widened. "Lord. You really are a prince…a prince of commerce, for sure. So, your parents must have been horrified to learn of your near-miss with death."

"They don't know," Trey said. "We're not close." And then he gathered up his dishes and carried them to the sink. "Is the dishwasher empty or…?"

She jumped up and ran to the counter. "Oh…you don't need to do that."

He stopped her with a touch and a smile. "I invited myself here. I am so happy to have found you. I apologize that I've arrived in time to get myself snowed in, but you're not going to wait on me like a guest, okay? I live alone in my house and am fairly competent at taking care of stuff."

She was superaware of his hand on her arm, and trying to be casual about it. "Well, your quest to find me has made me feel a bit special. I can honestly say I have never been the object of a nationwide search before. Yes, the dishwasher is empty. Feel free to rinse and load. I'll clear the table."

"Deal," he said, and then when she wasn't looking watched her flit from one side of the kitchen to the other. She reminded him of a hummingbird. Beautiful, and tiny, and moving too fast to see the wings she must surely have.

A short while later she was standing at the bottom of the stairs, watching him go up for the night, but when he stopped at the landing and looked back down at her, she smiled.

"Sleep well."

"Thank you," Trey said, then started to say something else and changed his mind. She didn't need to know how deeply she'd already dug herself into his thoughts, and he went the rest of the way up and into his room.

Once Marley heard the door shut, she began going through the lodge, making sure everything was locked, and turned out all of the lights except the usual night-lights. She banked the fire, made sure the fire screen was in place, and then took herself to her room and, as always, locked the door to the family quarters before getting ready for bed. It was something she'd seen her father do a thousand times, and it was something he'd imparted to her as important.

"Ladybug, we welcome people into our lodge, and for the time they are here, they are our guests. We cater to their wishes. We enjoy them. But they're not our family, and we don't know them. So, it's not that we're afraid they might hurt us. It's because they are strangers, and you never trust a stranger to be telling the truth until they are no longer strangers. Then you can make the judgement about unlocking the door."

And the moment she turned the lock, she thought of the stranger upstairs. The angels had sent her to help him. She'd held his life in her hands. Granted, he'd been very public about trying to find her, so he wasn't trying to hide anything. But despite everything they'd said tonight, they were still strangers.

She could still hear the wind as she went to her bedroom, but her worry about his safe arrival was over. He was here, and for now, that's what mattered. Being snowed in with Trey Austin was going to be a little bit like making a stew. It all depended on how much they added to their knowledge of each other. Would they form a friendship or a relationship? Would there be more revelations? Or would this just become a charming interlude to talk about in the years to come? She was still thinking about him when she crawled between the covers and turned out the light.

After Trey's hairy drive through the snowstorm, he was reveling in the warmth and comfort of his suite, and so very grateful he was here. He didn't know what Marley Corbett thought about him. She was so friendly and congenial that she was hard to read.

He'd been so adamant about coming to see her, and now that he was here, he didn't want her to feel uneasy about him in any way. For all he knew, she could be fretting about being alone in the lodge and snowed in with a stranger. The deal was, he didn't want to be a stranger. She was delightful and funny and amazing in a thousand ways he couldn't begin to express. He already knew he wanted the whole story of her, and anything else she was willing to share.

He turned out the lights, leaving only a night-light burning in the hall leading to the bathroom, and then moved to the windows and parted the curtains, but there was nothing to see. The snow was but a blur in the darkness. He let the curtains drop and crawled into bed.

As he did, he heard the central heat kick on and closed his eyes.

Heat was a really good thing.

Despite going to bed late last night, Marley was up with the sunrise. Her first thought was the weather. She threw back the covers and raced to the window. It finally stopped snowing, but the world, for as far as she could see, was blanketed in white.

The first rays of sun were sparkling like diamonds on the new-fallen snow. It was awe-inspiring, even majestic, but getting caught out in that wonderland would turn a person's world cold and deadly.

Nobody was going anywhere until the county cleared the main road and Jack cleared her drive, and fortunately, it didn't matter. She had no need to go anywhere, and secretly, she was happy that Trey was snowed in with her. She was curious about the rich man's son and was convinced there was more to him than he let on.

She dressed quickly, clipped her hair up, and went to start her day. She began by unlocking the back doors and stirring the embers in the fireplace before adding kindling to start a new fire. As soon as the kindling caught, she added a log before replacing the screen. It was as routine to her as brushing her teeth before going to bed. Things she did without thinking. She started coffee brewing and thought of Jack, although she didn't expect them to show up today. There was no need and nothing to be done.

Trey woke up to silence.

The wind had laid. The sun was up, and he thought he could smell coffee. That meant his little hummingbird was up, too. He bailed out of bed to shower and shave, and as he was dressing, wondered what this day would hold. Before going downstairs, he got his laptop to check email and saw a message from Meredith.

> Trey, are you still searching for your Cinderella? Also...are you going to be home for the holidays? I want to send you a gift.

He responded:

> M...
>
> No, I won't be home. At the moment, I am snowed in with Cinderella at a mountain lodge in Colorado. Yes, the shoe fit, and she had the mate, still caked in dried mud. No need to worry about my welfare. She knows nothing about Chapel Hill and is about half my size. Tiniest little blond on the face of the earth. How the hell she dragged me out of my car, I'll never know. She owns and runs the lodge. I am here as her guest. Save the gift until further notice. Be on the lookout for your candy.
>
> Happy holidays,
> Trey

As soon as he hit Send, he closed the laptop and pocketed his phone. As he stepped out into the hall, he heard the roar of an engine in the distance and wondered what it was, then guessed he'd find out soon enough.

Chapter 5

Marley had chicken stewing on the stove and would make dumplings later. She had biscuits in the oven for breakfast and was frying sausage when she heard Trey coming down the stairs. At the same time, she began hearing the roar of a snowmobile and rolled her eyes. That would be Jack, coming to make sure she was still alive and kicking with the stranger under the roof. She looked up as Trey walked into the kitchen, ignored the skip in her heartbeat, and smiled.

"Good morning. Did you sleep well?"

"Best night's sleep I've had in years. What smells so good, and what's that noise outside?"

"You smell chicken stewing, biscuits baking, and sausage frying. Eggs coming up, and the noise is likely Jack on his snowmobile, coming to make sure you didn't murder me in my sleep."

Trey blinked, startled by the accusation, and then realized she was grinning.

"You're teasing, right?" he said.

She laughed. "Mostly. He always comes to make sure I'm not in any kind of distress, but he's also nosy enough to want to see what you look like, too."

"That's fair," Trey said, and pointed to the plate of little sausages links already cooked. "May I snitch?"

"Better snitch fast before Jack walks in. No matter what Wanda feeds him at their house, whenever he walks into this kitchen, he has to graze on what's coming out of the oven, too."

"Smart man," Trey said, as he picked up a sausage with his fingers and took a bite. "Good stuff," he said, and moved to the coffee machine and poured himself a cup of coffee. "Is there anything I can do to help?" he asked.

"No, but thank you," she said, and grabbed a potholder to take the biscuits out of the oven. "You had scrambled eggs last night. Wanna try them fried this morning, or maybe poached?"

"Fried is good. Over easy," he said, and then the roar of the snowmobile ended.

"And…Jack has arrived," she said.

Moments later, they heard the back door open, then the stomp of boots in the utility room as Jack kicked off the snow before striding into the kitchen.

Jack eyed the man standing beside the work island with a sausage link in one hand and a cup of coffee in the other, nodded cordially, then eyed Marley.

"Mornin', Bug. Do I smell biscuits?"

"Morning, Jack," she said and pointed to the cooling rack. "I just took them out of the oven."

He eyed the pan of hot biscuits with glee. "I'll be needin' some butter. Got any of that apple butter you put back?"

"Yes, but introductions first. Jack, this is Trey Austin, from Phoenix, Arizona. Trey, this is Jack Wallis. He and his wife, Wanda, work here, but they're also all the family I have."

Trey wiped his fingers and held out his hand. "A pleasure, sir, but what did you call Marley?"

"Bug. Her daddy, Dan, called her Ladybug from the time she could walk. I guess because she was so little. Over the years, it got shortened to Bug. Everybody who grew up with her calls her Bug."

Trey eyed the flush on Marley 's cheeks and nodded. "I think I'll stick with Marley. I can't call the angel who saved my life a bug."

Jack grinned, and Marley burst out laughing, then scooted the butter and jam within Jack's reach.

"Trey, feel free to indulge right along with Jack. I have eggs to fry."

Jack eyed the eggs she was cracking into the skillet. "If you fry one up for me, make it hard. I'll make a sandwich with it out of my next biscuit."

"It's a good thing Wanda isn't here. She'd be fussing at you for eating two breakfasts again. What did she make for you this morning?"

"Bacon and pancakes…but you know how those pancakes are. They don't stay with you long."

Trey grinned. He liked Jack Wallis. And he liked Marley Bug. Even if he wasn't going to call her that.

Marley finally steered the men to the table, put the food in front of them, then ate in delighted silence while they talked and ate. What she noticed most was how intently Trey guided the conversation away from anything personal about himself, while still being open and congenial. Obviously, he didn't want the world to know his connections to the Austin empire, and she secretly admired him for not crowing about it or making himself the topic of conversation.

While they were still eating, Marley's phone rang. She glanced at the caller ID. "Excuse me, but I'm answering this," she said. "Hi, Wanda. Yes, Jack got here just fine. Yes, he's eating breakfast again. Everything is fine. Trey got here well after eleven last night. I think he had a pretty hairy trip, but he made it, for which we are all thankful. Do you want to speak to Jack?"

Jack was shaking his head, waving his hands to indicate a "no," and swallowing his last bite of biscuit.

Marley frowned at him because Wanda was still talking and listening, and then she finally commented. "Don't worry, Wanda. I'll tell him, and I'll let you know when he starts home. Love you, too."

She laid the phone down and frowned. "Jack Wallis. You told her you were going to see how the roads were?"

"Now, Bug… You know I don't lie to Wanda. She just wasn't clear about what I said. I meant these roads right here," he said. "And I'm not getting the tractor with the snowblade out just yet, unless you have a need."

"We do not have a need," Marley said. "But you do. You need to go home. Wanda went out to gather eggs and said something tried to get into the henhouse last night, so you have some patching up to do."

Jack got up from the table, frowning. "Oh lord. Hope they didn't get any of my hens. I'll just check the generator and the perimeter here to make sure everything is okay and carry in some firewood for you. That way you won't have far to go out on the back porch in the snow to get it. Trey, it was nice to meet you. I trust you two will be okay, and if you're not, just call. I never mind an excuse to ride the snowmobile."

"Thank you, Jack. You are the best," Marley said.

Jack hugged her. "You're welcome, sugar." He gave Trey one last look, and then left the same way he'd come in.

It was when the old man hugged Marley that the reality of what Trey was feeling finally hit. He wanted to hug her, too, but he didn't have the right. So, he got up and helped her clear the table instead, while Jack made four trips through the lodge, adding to the stack of firewood on the hearth.

A short while later, they heard the snowmobile fire up, and when Jack rode off, Marley sent Wanda a text to let her know he was on the way home.

After that, they were alone again, and this time, the silence felt awkward. Something was changing between them. A familiarity was growing, but without aim. Neither of them knew what they wanted, or what to expect, but an expectation of more was apparent.

"Marley, if you have things you need to do, please don't feel like

I need to be entertained," Trey said. "If I wasn't here, what would you be doing now?"

She paused, thinking, and then waved her hand. "I like jigsaw puzzles. I usually keep one working for the guests. And I love to read and watch good movies. Want to see the family library? It's something else."

"I'd love to," he said.

"Awesome, follow me," she said, and led him to the great room and then to a wall of bookshelves filled with hundreds of books.

"Some of these editions date back to my great-grandparents' and grandparents' time. Some are Mom and Dad's. And most of the books on the lower two shelves are mine. I'd probably be curled up in a chair by the fire, reading. Or fiddling with the jigsaw puzzle, or watching a movie."

Trey immediately spotted three of his titles, and then the longer he looked, the more he saw. That's when he realized that she had copies of almost all of them.

"I see you're a mystery buff," he said.

"It's my favorite genre…that and romantic suspense. Sharon Sala, who also writes as Dinah McCall, is my absolute favorite writer in that genre, but Chapel Hill writes the best mysteries. Have you read any?"

He nodded. "Yes, I have. I read a lot."

"I think I'll save reading for later. If I get too quiet, I'll get sleepy. I think I'm going to watch some TV. It's game-show time."

"Mind if I watch with you?" Trey asked.

"I would love it. I mostly entertain myself when I'm alone, so company is always welcome. You can guess prices with me. We'll see who comes closest," she said.

"What do I get if I win?" he asked.

She arched an eyebrow. "My undying gratitude for not saying 'I told you so'?"

He laughed and sat down at one end of the sofa as she turned on the TV, found the channel with *The Price Is Right*, and then plopped down at the other end and curled her legs up beneath her.

By the time the show came to an end, they were yelling out prices, high-fiving each other when they got it right, chiding the contestants when they priced it too high or too low, and teasing each other when they were so far off the mark.

Marley had never been so happy, and Trey had never felt this at ease. No one was expecting anything from him. He didn't have anything to prove to Marley Corbett, and yet she liked him. And that was scary. Because what if this was all just lighthearted fun to her? What if she was like this with all her guests?

She'd been special to him from the first sound of her voice, and the one glimpse he'd had of her walking away from him was seared in his memory. He accepted that part of those feelings started out as gratitude. But that was before he met her. Right now, he couldn't put a name to what he was feeling, but it was way beyond gratitude. He knew that wanting more from her was almost selfish when she'd already given him back his life, but it was the truth.

When that game show ended, Marley handed him the remote.

"Help yourself to whatever," she said. "I need to check on the chicken. We're having chicken and dumplings for dinner tonight, and I want it falling-off-the-bone tender before I take it off the stove."

Trey took the remote, but he was thinking about that dish. "I can't remember the last time I had chicken and dumplings."

"Comfort food. If you don't want to watch TV, grab a book or whatever you feel the need to do. I promise I won't bother you. I don't bang too many pans, even when we're up to our necks with hungry guests."

"I will, and thank you. I might grab my laptop and check my email, maybe pay some bills while I'm here."

"You know where everything is now, Trey. Make yourself at home. This place is my business, but it's also my home, and it's huge. I'm rarely here on my own, but when I am, it always makes me feel like the only potato in the bin. It's nice to know there's another human besides me beneath this roof."

He was still smiling when she left the room. *The only potato in the bin.* That phrase would wind up in a book one day.

He went upstairs to get his laptop, brought it back down by the fire, and went through his email, paid the bills that were due, and then without thinking, pulled up his notes on his new mystery. He'd told Meredith he was taking the month off before beginning it, but not writing made him antsy, so he began sorting through the notes.

Marley was down in the basement doing laundry. She had a load in washing and another in the dryer. She'd already washed, dried, and folded a load of kitchen towels and dishcloths, and had just gotten off the elevator and was going to put them up when Trey suddenly appeared at her side.

"I wondered where you'd gotten off to. Should have known you'd be working. Let me carry that," he said, and lifted the laundry basket out of her hands.

"Thanks," Marley said, and led the way to the kitchen. "Just put it down on the work island. I'll put them away."

He did as she asked, stood for a moment watching as she began stacking the clean linens back into a big drawer, then walked to the windows and looked out at the snow.

"How many inches of snow do you think we got last night?" he asked.

"The weatherman said nearly a foot. If it snowed like this in Vail, they would be celebrating. The more snow they get, the better for business," she said.

Trey shoved his hands in his pockets and turned around, trying to picture her flying down the ski slopes.

"Do you ski?"

"Oh sure, but I don't have the time anymore. I'm not even sure where my skis are. Do you?"

He nodded. "It's been a while," he said, without explaining it had mostly been at Saint Moritz in the Swiss Alps.

As soon as she'd put away the towels, she set the basket out in the hall for a return trip down and glanced at the time. It was already after 1:00 p.m.

"I'm going to make sandwiches for lunch. Is that okay with you?" she asked.

"Anything you do is okay with me. Ever since I walked into the lodge, it's made me feel like a kid in a candy store. Everywhere I look, there is something that delights me, and you're the best part of it. I feel a bit like I just invited myself to a party, but I don't have a lick of guilt for doing it," he said.

"Actually, if you remember, you did get an invitation. I'm the one who invited you to stay here, but I sure didn't mean for you to get trapped here."

"This isn't being trapped. This is the best holiday I've allowed myself to have in ages. I'm always alone, Marley, and certainly never with family. The last Christmas I spent with my parents was right before they sent me away to boarding school. I'd written a letter to Santa Claus, asking for a telescope. I like to look at the stars. I watched the nanny give the letter to my mother. She didn't even look at it. Christmas morning, I got a baseball and a mitt. I don't know what they were thinking, but at that point, I'd never played baseball. That same day, my mother told me there was no such thing as Santa Claus, which crushed my ten-year-old soul. So, thank you for this, more than you can know."

There was a poignancy in his voice that she'd hadn't heard before. He'd revealed something very personal about himself, and it hurt her heart to think of going through the world like that. Without saying a word, she threw her arms around his waist and hugged him.

Shock was followed by such a longing to take down her hair, tilt that pretty face up to him, and kiss her senseless. Instead, he wrapped his arms around her and hugged her back.

Marley's heart was pounding with a mixture of fear and anticipation. She had two choices. Act on the impulse, or get her act together. So, she did the responsible thing, dropped her arms, and stepped away. She could chide herself about it later.

"Just for the record, that wasn't the first time I have hugged you, you know. Granted, you were unconscious, but details, details…Right?"

He frowned. "I guess you did, didn't you? I feel a great sense of loss that you have those memories and I do not."

"I understand what you mean. When you arrived last night, you weren't a stranger to me. No, I didn't know your name before I saw the story about your search, or anything about you personally, but I knew your face. I'd felt your heart beat beneath my palm countless times while waiting for help to arrive. I knew what had happened to you. When I found out you were looking for me, I understood your need to tie up loose ends, and I'm glad you're here."

"Thank you. At first, I just wanted to say thank you," he said.

She smiled. "And you have, multiple times."

"I know we've said hello. My problem now is thinking about that goodbye."

"Then don't think about it," she said. "Unless you have other plans, at least stay for Christmas. I know it's a couple of weeks away, but I can't bear to think you'd spend that holiday alone."

It touched him that she was frowning and so serious about his solitary life. "Thank you for the invitation. It would be an honor," he said.

"Good. Now, no more debts of gratitude between us. Let's make lunch. Do you remember where the plates are kept?"

"Yes, ma'am."

"Then would you please get a couple down for us, and glasses, too," she asked, then began pulling out condiments and cold cut, and three kinds of cheese. Then she cut into a large round loaf of sourdough bread and sliced off enough for their sandwiches, then got a jar of pickles, lettuce and tomatoes from the fridge, and a bag of chips from the pantry.

Once she had everything out, she put two long slices of bread on each plate, then looked up. "You tell me what you want. I'll make it happen."

He blinked. *Food. She's talking about food.* And pointed to a jar of prepared horseradish to go with the roast beef. *This visit is going to be harder than I thought.*

After lunch, they wound up at the jigsaw table. Someone must have started a new one during renovations and then left it unfinished when the job was over. The picture on the box was a colorful patchwork quilt. It was a thousand-piece puzzle, and the pieces were about the size of a quarter.

Trey kept picking up pieces and then putting them down, thinking he'd found the right shape and color, only to find it was wrong, while Marley seemed to have an eye for them.

"You're good at this," he said.

She looked up. "Am I? I like jigsaw puzzles. They turn off the static in life."

He frowned. "Static?"

She paused, trying to think how to explain what she meant. "You know how you can start worrying about a thing, and then before you know it, you've added a couple of more things to it?"

"Yes."

"Well, then everything all comes into your head at once, like static on a radio when you can't tune in to a station, and you get so focused on trouble that you forget to listen to the music."

He was so stunned by the analogy that he could only stare. She smiled at him, then went back to scanning the loose pieces on the table. When she picked one up and popped it into place, he picked up a couple of pieces and turned them over, then put them back down.

"What are you doing?" Marley asked.

"Looking to see if the damn things were marked, like a deck of cards."

She started grinning. "Marked?"

He shrugged. "You beat anything I've ever seen. Talks to angels. Smart as a whip. Sees patterns in color and shapes. Damnedest sense of humor ever. And wisdom far beyond your years."

"Is that good, or is that bad?" she asked.

"It's beyond amazing, is what it is," he said.

"So, what you're saying is…I'm all that, and a bag of chips?"

He grinned. "Pretty much."

She suddenly thrust her fingers through her hair and gasped.

"What? What's wrong?" he asked.

"You're giving me the bighead. I can feel it swelling. Stop bragging on me. It leaves me with the feeling that now I have to say something nice about you, and I'm struggling with that, because we've been sitting here almost an hour, and you still haven't found one single puzzle piece that fits."

"Shut it, girl! I will not be maligned by someone named Bug. I have a reputation to protect."

Marley was laughing, in her element. Having someone to talk to—sharp enough for verbal sparring without being insulted—was a gift.

"Now that you've brought it up, exactly what kind of a reputation do you have?"

"Besides being born an Austin?" he asked.

And just like that, the mood shifted. "I did not mean that to sound like I was prying. Sorry. I was just teasing," she said.

"I invest in real estate. I own a few rental properties in Phoenix.

The cleaning ladies who come weekly to my house think I'm a monk. They don't say so, but I hear them talking when they're cleaning. They speak Spanish. They don't know I do, too. And they're very bothered that there's no sign of a woman in my life."

She nodded. "I get that too, sometimes. Marley Corbett! Cute little blond surely too dumb to walk and chew gum at the same time, and no man in her life. But I know who I am. I don't apologize for my choices, and you shouldn't, either. Deal?"

"Deal," he said.

She pointed to a puzzle piece at his elbow. "That one. Put it here," she said, pointing to a spot in one corner.

He did. "It fits!"

"Persistence pays," she said. "I've had enough of this puzzle for a while, and it's nearly dark. Night comes fast to the mountains, especially at this time of year."

She pushed her chair back and stood, then looked down at the table and paused. She leaned over his shoulder, her hair brushing against his neck as she reached out in front of him, picked up one more piece of the puzzle, and slid it into place. Then she patted him on the shoulder.

"I need to tend to the fire," she said, and walked away.

He took a deep breath, and then got up and walked toward the lobby and spent a good fifteen minutes looking at all of the ornaments on the Christmas tree before he could regain his composure. Finally, he looked up and saw the angel on top.

"Wherever she goes, you follow, don't you?" he said.

Trey was kicked back on one of the leather sofas in the great room with his laptop in his lap, and Marley was nose deep in a book when his phone rang. He saw caller ID and paused to answer.

"Hey, Meredith, what's up?"

"I've been approached by a film agent wanting you to consider writing a script about your search for Cinderella. She thinks it will be an easy sell. Are you interested?"

Trey sat up. "Maybe, but only if you can keep all that separate."

"I know what you mean. I don't see the conflict," Meredith said. "Nobody would ever put Prince Charming in Chapel Hill's chair, if you know what I mean."

"I know. Then if they offer enough, I might consider it, but I'm not doing it on spec."

Meredith laughed in his ear. "I already knew that. You aren't your father's son for nothing."

He sighed. "That is not a compliment, but you're forgiven. I love you, anyway."

"I knew that, too," Meredith said. "I'll be in touch."

Trey ended the call, then looked up and realized Marley was gone. Frowning, he got up to go see where she went, and found her in the kitchen, deboning the stewed chicken.

"You didn't have to leave," he said.

Marley shrugged. "I wanted to give you some privacy with your girl, and this has to be done, anyway."

Shit. Now she either believes I have a girlfriend, or I give up some of my anonymity to explain. And in the long run, losing his chance with her mattered more than the secrets he kept to himself.

"Meredith isn't my girlfriend, honey. She's my agent, and she's old enough to be my mother. She's close to me, like you're close to Jack and Wanda."

Marley paused and looked up. "Agent?"

He sighed. "I write stuff now and then, but it's not something I talk about, and no one knows. Well…now you do…but I owe you everything, which includes my truth. And I'm trusting you not to share it."

She blinked. "I'm sure I don't know what you're talking about. I'm just about to make the dough for dumplings. So, unless you want flour all over your pretty self, you might want to make yourself scarce for a bit."

He shook his head. *My pretty self.*

"Making myself scarce now," he said, and left the room, thinking as he went that revealing his long-kept secret could be a welcome relief, even though she didn't know what he wrote. Maybe that would come later. He went back to his laptop, reread his notes one more time, and then took a quick breath, opened a new document, and wrote "There was a scorpion on the wall by Charlotte's foot, but she couldn't scream for the gag in her mouth, and she was tied up too tight to get away."

The first words of the first chapter of a new book. The next best thing to sex.

An hour or so later, Trey reached a point in the story that he needed to think about. He saved it, then set the laptop aside and glanced out the windows.

It was snowing again—but the flakes were the size of goose down and floating as they fell. Mesmerized by the fairy-tale sight, he walked through the lobby and out onto the covered porch that ran the length of the lodge.

The cold air had a bite to it. A reminder that winter beauty had its drawbacks, but he inhaled anyway, drawing the fresh mountain air into his lungs, and then watched the cloud forming from his breath as he exhaled.

He stepped through the thin crust of snow on the porch, extended his arm out beyond the roof, and turned his hand palm up, watching snowflakes falling on his hand and melting in an instant. The mere warmth of his skin ended the flake's journey before it ever reached the ground. He stepped back beneath the roof before his flight of fancy imagined he'd interrupted an important journey. A snowflake's purpose was the same as a raindrop. One was liquid. One was frozen. But they both carried moisture to the earth.

Some days, his life felt like that. Sometimes liquid—everything going smoothly, then sometimes frozen—like he was spinning in place. Not until he'd found the little red shoe had he been jarred out of his routine enough to take this drastic chance. Marley Corbett was his catalyst. The spark he'd needed. And a woman who would be so easy to love. But this was Trey's dream. He didn't even know if she dreamed of him at all.

He heard the door open behind him, and then she was at his side. She leaned against his arm and slid her hand beneath his elbow.

"Isn't this beautiful?"

But he wasn't looking at the vista anymore. He was looking at her.

"Yes…so beautiful," he said.

She glanced up. They locked gazes, and in that moment, she saw her own reflection. It was an eerie feeling—like seeing her own soul within the eyes of another, and she quickly looked away.

In the distance, she could hear heavy equipment moving on the road.

"Sounds like the snowplow is finally on the mountain."

"Do they plow out your driveway?" he asked.

"No, just the main road. Jack has a blade on the tractor. He'll make a road for me. But you don't need it yet. You're staying for Christmas, remember?"

Trey thought he detected a note of anxiety in her voice. Maybe she didn't want him to leave. God knows he didn't want to, either.

"I remember and I wouldn't miss it for anything, but I think we need to go inside. You're shivering."

When he clasped her hand to steady her on the rime of icy snow, she didn't pull back.

Warmth met them at the door.

"It feels good in here," Trey said as he closed the door behind them.

"Chicken and dumplings will make you feel even better, and they're ready to eat if you are."

"I've been thinking about them all day," he said.

"Anticipation always makes everything better," Marley said, but before he could answer, the lodge phone rang. "Shoot, I better get that," she said, and headed for the front desk and picked up the phone. "Corbett Lodge. Yes, we're still closed, but we're reopening January 1st. Yes, thank you for calling. Hope to see you then."

"Customers?" Trey asked.

"Locals, asking about the Sunday brunch and lunches."

"You don't do breakfasts?" he asked.

"Yes, but only for the guests who stay over. Not for the public," she said.

"Do people ever stay over for extended periods of time?"

"Not unless it's a wayward prince, looking for the girl missing a shoe. Let's eat. I'm starving," she said.

He grinned. "Right behind you."

A few minutes later they were seated at the table, eating, and talking as if it was their daily routine.

Trey paused, waving his spoon in the air to punctuate the point. "You know, this time last night I was still on the interstate, following a trucker's taillights because I couldn't see ten feet in front of me. It's amazing what a few hours' difference can make in a life."

"Or a few seconds…like an angel playing crossing guard and sending me to meet my fate," she added.

Trey laid down his spoon. "I've never been someone's fate before."

"I've never saved a life before."

He reached across the table and held out his hand. "There's an old Chinese belief about that. Once you save someone's life, you are responsible for it forever."

Marley laid her hand in his. "We're not Chinese. Does that apply across the board?"

He curled his fingers around her hand. "I think it could, if we wanted it to."

Her heart was pounding. "Do you want it to?"

"I know it took forever to find you, and I was almost at the point of accepting you wanted nothing to do with me when you responded, then I had this overwhelming need to find you before you disappeared again. When you opened the door to me last night, it felt like such a relief to have reached my final destination. It still feels like that, and I don't want to lose that feeling," he said.

Marley stood up, still holding his hand, and swore an oath she might live to regret. "Trey Austin, I solemnly accept the responsibility of your wellbeing for the rest of your life. What we make of that, only time will tell."

Trey stood. "Then I thank you for the sacrifice. Should we seal this vow somehow? Maybe a toast?"

"I'd rather seal it with a kiss."

His pulse kicked. "A stellar suggestion, Cinderella," he said, then let go of her hand and kissed her.

Her mouth was warm, and soft, and yielding. He wanted so much more, but she'd only asked for a kiss. The moment he lifted his head, he felt the loss.

She could still feel his hands on her shoulders and the imprint of his mouth on her lips when she opened her eyes. She felt weightless. And he was waiting, but she didn't know exactly what for.

Whatever you do, do not make a joke.

"I guess now this means I have to buy you a Christmas present."

He blinked, and then threw back his head and laughed, and laughed, and then picked her up and hugged her.

Marley's feet weren't even on the floor, but she was grinning. "You may put me down now."

He set her down easy, but he was still grinning. "Sorry. Didn't mean to overstep, but you took me by surprise. You're beautiful. You're smart. You're brave. And you have the quirkiest sense of humor ever. I love it!"

"And I can cook. Don't forget I can cook." She was laughing with him now. "I hear it's an ancient, but time-honored prerequisite for landing a man, too. A couple of hundred years ago, they would have had me sitting by the fireside doing needlepoint and making candles or something. I choose this life, as hectic as it often is."

Trey just shook his head, delighted by her deprecating humor.

"And now you're bound to me as well. I am one lucky dude. For that, I will happily clear the table and load the dishwasher, if you'll deal with the food."

She started to argue and then realized he offered because he wanted to be needed. "That would be amazing."

Pleased, he set about the task, leaving Marley to admire the sight of him standing there at her sink with his hands in the water. There was no denying she was falling for him.

They flipped a coin about which movie they wanted to watch together.

Trey won. He chose the movie *1917*, based on a true story about a conscientious objector who went to war in WWI.

Chapter 6

An hour into the movie, with bombs dropping and machine guns firing and men falling like flies and dying on the battlefields, Marley fell asleep.

Trey saw her leaning sideways and caught her, then gently pulled her toward him until her head was resting in his lap, and her feet and legs were curled up at the end of the sofa. He covered her with a knit throw, lowered the volume, then laid his hand on her shoulder and allowed himself the freedom to really look at her.

Her hair was soft and so long and thick. Her eyelashes were shades darker than her hair. Her lips were full and slightly parted, and he could feel the steady rise and fall of her breathing. It was the most complete and perfect moment of his life—here, within the bulwark of this beautiful lodge and snowed in with a woman who was stealing his heart. He felt a bit like a knight in a castle, protecting the princess who resided here.

He didn't ever want to move and, as he sat, felt the brutality of the movie had no place in this moment, so he searched for local news, hoping to catch a weather report. He found the station and settled in to wait, only to catch two late-night anchors talking about him and his search, and maybe the magic of Christmas would bring her forward.

That's when it dawned on him that Meredith was the only one who knew she'd been found. He needed to call off the search. He needed to let the world know he'd found her. But he wasn't about to reveal her identity. If he gave up her name, her life would be turned upside down, and he couldn't let that happen. He made a mental note to post an update and then let it run its course.

When she stirred in her sleep, he tugged the throw up over her shoulders, then whispered, "You're okay, Ladybug. I'm here."

He heard her sigh and then felt her whole body relax. Satisfied that she was comfortable, he refocused on the television, waiting for a weather update. Then when it aired, he learned the next few days would be clear. He turned off the TV and then sat within the silence, now knowing the timeline of imminent departure.

Ten more days until Christmas.

Ten more days with Marley, and then—

Then what?

Going back to Phoenix, holing up in his office to write another book, eating takeout and keeping the television on just for the sound of other people's voices?

Finding her had opened up a world he didn't know existed. It had changed him. How could he ever go back to what was, leaving this place and this woman behind?

He glanced up at the massive wooden beams above his head, then down at the wide planked floors beneath his feet. The sitting areas that would be full of people when she reopened the lodge. The walls of books, the art pieces hanging on the walls, the lighting staged for reading or resting. Somehow, the Corbett family had turned a home into a destination, without sacrificing any of the things that mattered.

A log popped in the fireplace, sending sparks flying up into the chimney, and still he sat, with his hand on her shoulder, slowly coming to terms with the looming reality. He lost all sense of time until the grandfather clock in the hallway began to chime.

Marley woke abruptly, startled that she'd not only fallen asleep, but that she was lying on his lap with her mother's knitted throw over her shoulders.

Trey felt her flinch and prepared himself for the launch he knew would be coming. He didn't want to give her up, but it was happening anyway.

She sat up, a little embarrassed and heartily apologetic, and began combing her fingers through her hair, certain it must be all over the place.

"I can't believe I fell asleep in the middle of a war and wound up in your lap. I'm terrible company. So sorry."

"Hush your fussin', hummingbird. Even wings get tired. I felt honored to be your perch."

She sighed. "Sometimes you say the prettiest things with the best words. No wonder you are a writer."

He pushed a curl away from the corner of her eye. "'No wonder' is right." The clock was still chiming. "It's very late. I think we need to call an end to this day. It's been a good one."

She nodded. "You go on up. I have to lock up and stuff."

"Would I be allowed to bring in some wood from the back porch for you?"

She sighed. "Yes, it would be much appreciated, too."

They stood up in unison, then paused, staring intently into each other's faces before they turned and went their separate ways.

As Marley was locking up the front entrance and turning on the porch lights and setting the security, she could hear Trey coming in from outside. By the time she headed back, the fresh logs were neatly stacked, and he was gone.

She banked the fire, secured the fire screen, and then went to make sure everything in the kitchen was shut down and left the night-lights on in all the usual places.

It wasn't until she started toward the family quarters that she realized Trey was sitting on the stairs, waiting for her. He stood up as she approached.

"Oh! I thought you'd already gone to bed."

"I forgot something," he said and, without asking, cupped her face and kissed her like he'd been starved for the touch. It wasn't until he heard her groan that he stopped, then stood with his forehead touching hers—breathing the same air and silently wanting more. Finally, he lifted his head and ran his finger down her cheek. "Sleep well, my little angel," he said softly, then went up the stairs and into his room without looking back.

Marley was still standing where he left her. Mute. Motionless. Telling herself to run. But which way? To her room? Or up the stairs?

It was the ticking of the grandfather clock that finally broke the spell. Time. Time was getting away from them. They barely knew each other. And it scared her to think about life without him in it.

Finally, she lowered her head and walked away.

Trey couldn't sleep and was up before daylight.

He'd deleted all of the final messages from the Cinderella wannabes. Then he composed another message and released it to the media. The message was brief and obviously final.

THE SEARCH IS OVER

My Cinderella mystery is a mystery no more. I found the angel who saved me. She's as brave and as special as I hoped she would be, but for the sake of her privacy, this is the extent of what I will share. I owe a huge debt of gratitude to all of you for sharing my message and aiding in my search. You helped make my Christmas miracle happen. I wish the same blessings and magic for you.

Trey Austin

After that, he pulled up his manuscript and went to work. His life was as confusing as this mystery he was writing, but he knew what to do with the story. He just didn't know what to do with his feelings.

He heard Marley moving around downstairs and knew she was stirring the fire to rebuild it. His heart was pounding as he heard the central heat come on. Eventually, he was going to have to go downstairs and face her, and it was going to kill him if her sunny smile was missing.

When he began to smell coffee and the scent of frying bacon, he hit Save on the file and closed his laptop. It was now or never. He combed his fingers through his hair, picked lint off the front of his sweatshirt, and left his room.

Marley's sleep had been fitful. She'd dreamed of pulling Trey out of the wreck all night—over and over. Every time she got to the point where she got in her car and drove off, the dream would start over at the crossroads with the angels pointing her in the other direction. It wasn't until she woke up that she realized that was a message. That was them, telling her over and over that he was her path to happiness.

But there was a kink in that path. Corbett Lodge was her heritage, her joy, and her purpose. He would have to want into this world for it to work, because she did not belong in his. This was who she was. He was who she was falling in love with. It was the most terrifying, wonderful, uncertain feeling ever to love this hard, this fast, and to find out later that it didn't last.

But lying in bed fretting about it changed nothing. She had things to do. As soon as she was dressed, she stomped off into the lodge with her chin up and fire in her eyes. She'd never quit on a thing in her life and wasn't about to start now. By the time she reached the kitchen to start the coffee, her feet were planted in the present. The future was yet to be, and today was all that mattered.

She got a text from Wanda, telling her they were coming over, and added another egg, more buttermilk and flour to the pancake batter she was making. As soon as it was done, she set it aside to rest and began frying bacon.

Soon afterward, she heard Trey's footsteps on the stairs and took a deep breath.

"Suck it up, Bug. He's just a man, not a god. Even if his kiss curled your toes, it didn't fry your brain," she muttered. But when he entered the kitchen, she had to remind herself… *Just a man. Just a man*, then looked up and smiled. "Good morning. Did you sleep okay? I did not…thanks to that toe-curling kiss. What are you going to do about that, mister?"

All the panic Trey had been feeling turned to joy. There was that smile. There was his girl. He went straight to her and kissed the top of her head.

"Best I can do while that bacon is popping. I don't want to get shot down before I've had whatever it is you're cooking, and no, I didn't sleep any better than you did. I've been up forever, working."

"That's what happens when you throw a match on a bonfire and walk away. We're having pancakes and bacon. I'll make you eggs to go with it if you want."

"Pancakes and bacon sound perfect. So, I threw a match on a bonfire?"

She shrugged and flipped the bacon to the other side.

He slid his hand beneath her hair and gave her neck a slight squeeze.

"I'm sorry. I'll be more careful about starting fires. I also ended the public search for you early this morning. I didn't mention your name or anything about you. Not even where you are from, but I sent out a brief post to social media that my search was over and deleted the thousands of emails I'd received, along with the new ones that came after I'd found you. However, I want to be clear, I did it that way for your privacy's sake, but in no way do I want to hide you. I would shout it to the world, but that's not my decision to make. You are the one who is free to reveal whatever you choose. Okay?"

Marley sighed. "There you go with your pretty talk again. Understood."

Then the roar of the snowmobile shifted their focus. "That's Jack and Wanda. Today is for plowing the snow from my drive, and she'll clean your room and change the sheets on your bed while she's here, and don't fuss. It's part of her job."

"Yes, ma'am. I'll just get out of the way and try to look as pretty as I talk," he drawled.

She laughed out loud, and was still laughing when Jack and Wanda came in the back door.

Wanda looked up at Jack.

"See, I told you she was okay," he said.

"I need to see that man for myself," Wanda said.

"Then come on, honey. I smell something good."

She rolled her eyes. "One of these days your pants are going to be too tight to fasten."

"Naw…I got myself a good metabolism," Jack said, and swatted her backside as she led the way into the kitchen.

Marley looked up and smiled. "Wanda, your cheeks are rosy red. That must have been a cold ride."

"It was a ride, for sure." And then she went straight to Trey and held out her hand. "Mr. Austin, I presume. I'm Wanda."

Trey knew he was being measured, and shook the hand she offered. "Trey, please, and it's a pleasure to get to put a face to a name. I've already learned that you two are Marley's favorite people."

"Bug is the child we never had," Wanda said. "She means the world to us."

"Special people like Marley deserve the best," Trey said. "Can I get you a cup of coffee? You must be cold after that ride."

Wanda's eyes widened. She was the one always serving others. "Oh, I'll get—"

"It's no trouble," Trey said, and quickly poured her a cup and handed it to her. "Wrap your little hands around that and warm them up," he said.

"Thank you," Wanda said, and when Trey pulled out a chair at the table for her, she sat down like a little queen on the throne and cast a glance at Jack, as if to say, *This is how you treat a woman.*

Jack sighed. "Now you've gone and done it, boy! I'll never hear the end of this."

Trey shrugged. "Sorry, dude. This was Manners 101 at boarding school."

Wanda frowned. "Boarding school? Why did you go to boarding school?"

"Because my parents decided I was too old for nannies and not old enough to take care of myself," he said.

"Good grief," she muttered, but stopped with the questions. Something wasn't right in his family, but she didn't have the privilege of knowing his personal business.

Trey winked at her. "It's okay. I'm just the prerequisite heir. After that, I think Mother felt as if she'd done her duty. She'd given birth. The rest of it was up to the hired help."

Wanda's frown deepened. "For pity's sake."

Marley smiled to herself. Trey had just relieved their worries by telling them in his own way that he wasn't after her money or her property, or here for all the wrong reasons.

Wanda glanced at the scar on his forehead and then at Bug, and realized but for her heroism, this man wouldn't be sitting here talking to them. No wonder he wanted to find her. She continued to sip her coffee as Marley plated up pancakes and bacon, while Trey carried them to the table.

"None for me," Wanda said. "I can only hold one breakfast at a time."

Jack snorted as he reached for the butter.

As they sat down to eat, Wanda finished off her coffee. "If it's okay, I'm going to do Trey's room while you're eating. That way I'll be done and out before he needs back in it again."

"That's fine," Marley said.

Wanda set her coffee cup in the sink and slipped out of the room while the others ate.

Jack finished eating, then made an announcement.

"There's more snow predicted, but I'm gonna head on out to the shed to get the tractor. The drifts in the driveway look big enough to ski on, so I need to knock them down before more is added. I'll check the main road and bring in your mail when I come back, okay?"

"Very okay, and be careful," she said.

"Always," he said, then grabbed his sock cap and gloves from the utility room as he went out the back door.

"There's another stack of pancakes in the warmer if you want them," Marley said.

"I'll make room for them," he said.

Marley refilled their coffee, and Trey was already back at the table putting butter and syrup on his second stack when his cell phone rang. He glanced at the caller ID.

"It's my mother," he said, and put it down.

"Aren't you going to answer it?" Marley asked.

He shook his head.

She frowned. "A day will come when you'll want to hear her voice and you can't, because she'll be gone. Trust me. Answer the phone," she said, and then she got up and walked out of the room.

The shock of what she said was enough to make him put down his fork and answer.

"Hello?"

"Trey! OH MY GOD! Are you okay? The daughter of one of our friends was talking about you searching for some girl…that you'd been in a wreck! That you nearly drowned. Your dad is on the phone with me. Why didn't you call us? Why are we the last to know?"

He sighed. "That was weeks ago. I'm fine now."

"But why didn't you call us?"

"You weren't even in the country. I didn't want to bother you," he said.

"But you're our son, and I'm devastated that you didn't think of us."

He sighed. Her feelings were hurt, and he was the one who'd nearly died. Right back to square one.

"Look, Mom. I don't mean to hurt you, but you and Dad taught me at an early age that you were less concerned about my welfare than you were your social calendar." He heard her gasp, but he kept talking. "If you remember, you two were in Bali when I broke my arm. I was eleven. You didn't come home. You and Dad were in Africa on safari when I got pneumonia at the boarding school and was in the hospital for a week. I was thirteen. You didn't come home then. You were in London, dining with some landed gentry when I was mugged on the streets of New York City and wound up with a broken nose and two broken ribs. I was twenty-two. You didn't come home then, either. The day you sent me off to boarding school was the end of the random times we'd even see each other. You are my parents, but you have never shown me that I mattered to you. I'm thirty years old. I don't need either of you, and I didn't think you'd care."

And the first thing he heard was his father's voice, angry and defensive.

"You, by God, sure take the income we furnish to you," Anders said.

The ugliness of the words was nothing but confirmation to Trey of what he'd always known. They were still paying him off to be out of their hair.

Trey took a breath, telling himself not to shout. "If you were half the businessman you claim to be, you'd know I haven't spent a dime of anything you've put in that account since I left college. You don't get to console your conscience by pretending you're supporting me because you're not. I don't need your money. Check your bank later. The money will be back in your account."

Gloria interrupted. "Both of you, stop! Anders. How dare you? And Trey, you do not send anything back. I didn't know you held such a grudge. I'm devastated."

"It's not a grudge, Mother. I have no animosity toward either of you, but at the same time, I am who you two created."

"Where are you? I want to come and talk to you," Gloria said.

"Well, you can't, because I'm not in Phoenix."

"Then where are you?" she asked.

"I'm at Corbett Lodge in Colorado Springs with the woman who saved my life. We're snowed in, and I'm eating her pancakes and bacon, and I'm staying here and spending Christmas with her and her friends, and I'm happy. For the first time in my life, I am happy. So, whatever you want to say, you can say over the phone. I'll always answer if I can. But I made a life for myself years ago, without either of you or your money."

"Then we'll come there and spend Christmas with you," Gloria argued.

"Nope. The lodge is closed until New Year's Day."

"Then why are you two there?" she asked.

"Because the lodge is hers. She owns and runs it. It's been in her family for four generations. And I'm her guest," he said.

"She's just after your money!" Anders shouted. "She knows who you are and she's—"

Trey hung up, then put the phone on Mute. Their words were still ringing in his ears when he felt Marley's arms slide around his neck, and then she laid her cheek against his head.

"I didn't mean to eavesdrop, but I heard what you said to them. You break my heart. I'm so sorry. I'm so, so sorry."

He turned around and pulled her down onto his lap and wrapped his arms around her. He didn't talk. Couldn't talk. He just sat within her love until the despair had passed.

"What can I do?" Marley asked.

He shook his head. "You can't fix them. I learned a long time ago that you can't force something to happen just because you want it."

She hesitated, knowing if she said what was on her heart, she would be opening herself up to rejection, but the sooner she found out where she stood with him, the better off she would be.

"Oh, Trey, I care about you. Maybe too much. I feel so many things for you that I don't even have a name for them. The scariest part is falling for you and knowing whatever passes between us will end when you leave. I belong here. I would never be happy living anywhere else. And that's my cross to bear."

"I envy you this place, and the roots you have here. I don't even know what having roots means. My job is fluid. I can do it anywhere. But nobody knows what I do, and that's because I didn't want any parental interference. I didn't want to hear their opinions of what I chose as my life's work. Nobody has ever known except Meredith…and you. I told you I'm a writer. Most people don't consider it an occupation, and I have had all of the criticism from family I could swallow. I wasn't up to dealing with reviews of my work, as well, and so I kept it to myself. I don't have a plan. But

I've been fortunate to make a good living at my work. Just know that this is who I am, and what I deal with, and tell me again after Christmas that you're not afraid of it. I don't want anything I am, or any aspect of my life to destroy the perfection of yours. Don't say more now. Just think about it," he said.

"It's a deal, but in the meantime, we try out love, okay?"

"Lord, yes, we will love," he said.

At that moment, they heard the tractor start up and Wanda banging cabinet doors upstairs.

"I'm sorry about the pancakes, but I've lost my appetite."

"They don't matter. I always make too many. Come with me. I have something to show you."

She took him by the hand and led him all the way to the family quarters. The moment they entered, his first impression was that it was a miniature version of the main lodge, and he imagined the generations of people who had lived here, and Marley was the last. He understood her need to keep it alive.

"This is the original homeplace," she said. "It's the family side of the property and off-limits to all paying guests. This is my sanctuary."

Trey let her lead him through the rooms without explanation or apology. This was her world. And she was offering it to him as is.

"This is how I separate my life. Work is out there. Home is in here. I make a good living. I want for nothing...except companionship. I go to bed alone. I wake up alone. And despite the love and care Jack and Wanda give me, at the end of the day, they're gone, too. I think you and I are more alike than we are different."

Trey frowned, thinking of all the strangers who sleep under the same roof.

"Are you ever afraid?"

She immediately thought of Jared Bedford, and then let it go. "You mean, of the guests?" she asked.

He nodded.

"I don't let myself go there. If I did, I'd freak out every day wondering 'what if.' We don't have room service or concierge services, so I am not actually at the beck and call of guests night and day."

Trey slid his arm across her shoulders. "I think you're amazing. The lodge is so warm and welcoming…or maybe that is what you give to the place. A sense of home. But in the meantime, if it's okay with you, I'm just going to keep falling in love," he said.

Marley put her arm around his waist and leaned against him. "Permission granted."

When they heard the tractor rolling up outside, they left the family quarters and went up front to the lobby area to watch.

Wanda came down shortly afterward and saw them standing arm in arm near the Christmas tree, watching Jack clear the drive. She smiled. It was early days, but she liked Trey Austin, and seeing Bug so happy made her happy, too.

Anders Austin was still fuming, stomping through the rooms in their hotel suite and swearing a steady stream of invectives, and Gloria was torn between the shock of her son's declaration and irked with Anders for throwing the money card in Trey's face.

"He hung up on me!" Anders yelled.

"You insulted him. He's a grown man and you talked to him as if he was some wayward teenager. What's the matter with you?" she said.

"He doesn't work. He wants no part of this company Dad and I built."

"How do you know he doesn't work?" Gloria said. "Just because he isn't working for you doesn't mean he's idle. He said he hasn't spent a penny of your charity, so he's obviously been productive on his own."

Anders threw up his hands in frustration. "Doing what?"

She shrugged. "I don't know, and that's my fault. When I call, I never ask him what he's doing. I just go on and on about us. What does he say to you?"

Anders's face was still flushed with anger, but now wearing guilt as well. "I don't call him."

Gloria gasped. "At all? You never talk to him?"

"No, that's not what I said. I just meant I don't call him on my own. I always talk to him when you call," he muttered.

Gloria paled and then sank into the nearest chair. "Oh my God! Trey was right. We are terrible parents, and it's far too late to make up for any of it."

Anders didn't like to be wrong. He resented being chastised. And he was as bullheaded as they come.

"Maybe so, but I know that woman, whoever she is, is after him for his money."

Gloria was crying. "She didn't know who he was when she saved his life. She didn't even leave her name when she left the scene after emergency services arrived. She didn't go looking for him. Trey was the one who wanted to find her. And it took weeks before she even responded to his search."

Anders turned, still angry. "So? Would I have been as enticing to you if it hadn't been for the family money?"

Gloria reeled as if he'd just slapped her. Her voice was trembling with hurt and with rage. "That is the most insulting thing you have ever said to me, and I will never forgive you for saying it. I thought you were the most enchanting man I'd ever met. I fell in love with you. The family money was there, but I didn't marry it. I married you. I had no idea you'd turn into this greedy, grasping man. Yes, I know I enjoy the benefits of your money. We travel when we want, and it's nice having the money to buy what I want, but none of it would matter without you! I am ashamed of you. You will, by God, apologize to our son or rue the day."

Anders already regretted what he'd said to her. "I didn't mean it…about you. I was just angry," he muttered.

"So, you didn't mean what you said to Trey, either, but you chose to be mean to him because you were angry? Is that how you run your office? Verbally slashing throats and firing people willy-nilly when something falls through?"

He glared.

She walked out of the room.

"Where are you going?" he shouted.

"Down to the bar. I have a sudden need for a good, stiff drink."

"We have liquor here!" he shouted.

She paused, then turned to face him. "Yes, but I don't want to drink with you. At the moment, I don't even want to hear the sound of your voice. And don't push it, Anders. I need to gather myself to keep from hating you, right now. Just remember…we don't have a prenup, and now that I know what you really think of me…"

She walked out, leaving him speechless and in shock.

It was later that evening before Anders remembered what Trey had said about returning the money and checked his bank account. He just wanted to catch Trey in a lie. Instead, there was a transfer deposit of over ten million dollars from Trey's account to his. Ten years plus of money he'd sent, plus the accrued interest that his son hadn't spent. He was in shock. What the hell had Trey been living on? What was he doing, and why didn't he know about it?

He began going back over the conversation, trying to remember where Trey said he was. He hadn't mentioned the woman's name, but he mentioned the name of the lodge. Corbett Lodge, in Colorado Springs. After running some searches on Google and social media, he easily found information about the lodge that had been there since the early 1940s and, four generations later, was still owned and run by the same family.

Then in one of the advertisements for the lodge he saw a picture of the current owner, Marley Corbett, a curvy blond in blue jeans, boots, and a bright-red sweater, leaning against the sign at the entrance onto the property. The background was trees and a road leading up into the trees, and then a separate picture of the lodge itself.

Anders was taken aback at the elegance and size of the place, but he wasn't changing his mind about what she was after. He kept staring at her, at the open and happy expression on her face. She was a little bit of a thing, but a beauty, and she'd obviously set her hooks in his son.

He put his laptop aside and walked to the windows overlooking the ski slopes. Now he was wishing they were still back in the States, but they already had plans here through Christmas. However, as soon as it was over, they were going home. He intended to fly to Colorado Springs and pay a visit to Corbett Lodge.

Chapter 7

Two hours later, Jack was still moving snow out of the drive and the parking area in front of the lodge. When Marley and Wanda began polishing the woodwork, Trey went up to his room.

They had been at it for almost an hour when they heard Jack heading back to the shed to store the tractor.

Wanda quickly finished dusting the newel posts, then headed for the kitchen. "Bug, I'm going to make some coffee. Jack will be cold."

"Okay, I'm going to finish this room and then join you," Marley said.

A few minutes later they heard Jack on the back porch, stomping snow from his boots.

He entered the room, red-cheeked from the cold. He handed her the mail that had accumulated and took off his gloves, rubbing his hands together to try and warm them.

"Lord, it's cold out there. The drive is passable now, and the main road is, too. Looks like they graded it down after the last snow. If you need to go into town, do it before the sun goes down. There's more snow predicted tomorrow, and it'll get icy after that."

"I don't need anything, but I better run upstairs and see if Trey does," Marley said, and left the room.

"She's stuck on him, isn't she?" Jack said as he took the cup of coffee his wife handed him.

"They're stuck on each other, which is how it's supposed to be," Wanda said. "Now, drink your coffee. I'm ready to go home."

"Yes, ma'am," Jack said, and winked. "Can't wait to get me all to yourself, can you?"

Wanda laughed. "Wishful thinking will get you nowhere. I have things to do and presents to wrap."

Marley heard their laughter and smiled to herself as she knocked on Trey's door, then heard him call out, "Come in."

She opened the door and stepped over the threshold. "Jack has everything cleared, and he said the main road out has been cleared as well. If you need to go into town for anything, you should go before it gets dark, because everything will get icy again."

He shut his laptop and stood. "Since I'm going to be here for Christmas, I would like to pick up a couple of things."

"Good reminder," she said. "I'll take you. I'm used to driving in snow, and I need a few things, too."

"Yay me. Another excuse to spend time with you," he said.

"You don't need an excuse. I'm a willing accomplice to whatever you have in mind. Come down when you're ready. I'm going to get my snow boots. I don't want to lose another shoe in the snow."

He wrapped his arms around her, pulling her close, then cupped her cheek. "Get your boots, but this time, I won't lose you."

She leaned into his touch. "No, you aren't going to lose me. I promise. See you in the lobby."

She was halfway out the door when he called her name.

"Marley."

She paused and turned around, but he hadn't moved. "Yes?"

"Are you really serious about there being an us?"

She heard the uncertainty in his voice and went back to where he was standing. "Look at me, Trey. I can only guess at the disappointment you grew up with. I understand why you are slow to trust and that we're still mostly strangers to each other. But I have never experienced such an instant attraction to anyone as I have to you. From where I'm standing, it's kind of scary. If I'm willing to take a chance on getting my heart broken, then the answer to your question is, yes. I want there to be an us. So, if you don't paint me in a corner then walk off and leave me, we're good."

His eyes darkened. "I suck at painting, and I can't imagine life without you in it."

Before Marley could respond, Wanda shouted from downstairs. "Bug! Jack is going to take me home. Call if you need us."

Marley turned and ran to the landing, then looked down and waved.

"Okay! Trey and I are going shopping. See you tomorrow."

"Yes. I'll lock up in the front. You can lock up the back when you leave."

Marley waved her thanks, then turned around and walked straight back into Trey's arms. "Where were we?"

He smiled. "Right about here," he said, eyeing her pretty mouth and those slightly parted lips, waiting for him to do something about it, so he did.

The moment they connected, her heart skipped a beat. He not only knew all the pretty words, but the fire he lit with one slow, sensual kiss was engulfing. There were too many clothes between them. When he finally lifted his head, the gleam in his eyes was impossible to ignore.

He wanted her.

And she wanted him.

"Savin' this for later…when the sun goes down and the roads ice up," he said.

Marley just nodded, still too rattled to focus. "There was something I needed to do," she mumbled.

"Shoes. You were going to change your shoes," Trey said.

She blinked. "Right. Snow boots. Downstairs. I'll…uh, I'll…"

He grinned. "You'll meet me in the lobby."

She groaned. "You make me crazy."

"I'll take that as a compliment," he said. "Shoes. Downstairs. Now, or we're shifting major gears right here."

The thump of her heart was so hard, it felt as if it had slammed against her rib cage.

She pivoted out of his arms and flew down the stairs, muttering something about his pretty words, and losing her mind, and best holiday ever.

If levitation was a thing, Trey could have floated all the way to the ceiling from the feelings she evoked. He'd found his woman. She was one small package of dynamite, and he'd just lit the fuse.

Marley negotiated the snowy drive from the lodge to the main road, and then headed down the mountain, pointing out places of interest like a tour guide, trying to make a good impression. She knew he was expressing interest in all the right places, but he'd ruffled her feathers and was gentleman enough now to give her space to regain her composure.

"It's a winter wonderland up here," Trey said.

Marley glanced at him as he spoke. "It is, isn't it?" Then all of a sudden, she heard a voice shout *STOP!*

When she slammed on the brakes, Trey instinctively braced for some kind of impact, even though there was nothing to be seen.

Then, within a heartbeat, a huge elk leaped out of the trees, landing right in front of them in the middle of the road before bounding off into the trees on the other side.

Trey's thoughts were in free fall. He kept looking at Marley, and then into the woods where the elk had gone, and back again. "How on earth did you know to stop? Did you see it beforehand?"

Marley shook her head. "No, I was looking at you, remember? I just heard them shout STOP and hit the brakes."

"Them?"

"My angels," she said.

A shiver went through him. "You actually 'heard' the word 'stop'?"

"Obviously, or I wouldn't have hit the brakes," she said as she took her foot off the brake and accelerated slowly.

He leaned back in the seat and took a deep breath. He'd just witnessed something he didn't understand, but he was beginning to realize there was far more to Marley Corbett than brains and beauty.

"Is that going to be the deal-breaker?" Marley asked.

Trey jerked, saw tears in her eyes, and reached for her shoulder. "Absolutely not! What just happened is a lot to digest. I am in actual awe right now."

Relief flooded her. "Okay then," she muttered, and kept driving.

As they entered the city, Trey leaned forward. "I only saw this at night when it was snowing. This place is beautiful," he said.

"It's a well-kept part of Colorado history, founded in 1871. There is a lot to see around here, but we're going to Old Town. We call it OCC, but technically, it's Old Colorado City, which is a neighborhood now within Colorado Springs. Lots of gift shops, boutiques, and great places to eat. I think you'll find what you're looking for there," Marley said.

"I really appreciate that you took the time to come with me. I would have driven all over the place without knowing where I was going."

"I usually do everything on my own. I love having someone to do things with," she said as she stopped for a red light.

"And, I can't remember the last time I went shopping with anyone, so this is a pleasure. Today is a day for making new memories. I feel greedy, wanting to know everything about you… the big stuff and the little stuff. You mentioned the other day about being born at the lodge in January. What day did you say was your birthday?"

"The fifteenth of January. When is yours?"

"The fourth of June," he said.

"Ahh, a Gemini. That fits."

He grinned. She had no idea how right she was. He was living life as two people, but he'd never thought of it like that before. Trey Austin and Chapel Hill were one and the same.

When the light changed, she drove through it heading west, and drove straight to a designated parking lot, found an empty space, and parked.

"We walk from here," she said. "Zip up your coat. The sun is shining, but the air is cold."

As soon as they started walking, Trey reached for her hand. "Just in case you hit an icy spot."

"Just in case," she said as his fingers curled around her hand, dwarfing it, just as he dwarfed her.

The streets were filled with people, and as they walked, people would call out to Marley to say hello. Some even called her Bug, which told him they knew her well, and all of them asked about the lodge.

Clark and Heidi Rogers, regular lunch customers at the lodge, stopped them just as Trey and Marley were about to go into a shop on Tejon Street.

Heidi eyed Trey curiously, then shifted focus. "Bug! Great to see you. Have you reopened yet?"

"No. New Year's Day is opening day," Marley said.

Heidi glanced back at Trey again, as if waiting for an introduction, but Marley said nothing.

"But you're still doing your New Year's Eve bash, right?" Heidi asked.

"Yes, of course. Can't mess with tradition," Marley said.

Heidi frowned as she looked back at Trey. "I'm sorry for staring, but you look very familiar. Have we met?"

Trey took the issue out of Marley's hands by introducing himself to both of them. "No, ma'am, I don't believe we have. I'm Trey Austin."

"Heidi Rogers, and this is my husband, Clark. I swear you look so—" And then she gasped. "Trey Austin! Yes! I knew I knew your face. You're the man who is looking for Cinderella!"

"Busted," Trey said, and laughed. "Nice to meet you both, but it's cold out here, and Marley is shivering. Merry Christmas," he said, slipped his hand on Marley's back and ushered her inside.

Marley was grinning. "That was slick. I didn't know how to handle that, because I didn't know if you wanted to stay incognito, so to speak."

"Well, since I plastered my face all over the nation, I have only myself to blame. But it was worth it just to find you, darlin'." Then he took a deep breath, inhaling the scents within the shop. "This smells like a great place to linger."

Marley held the *darlin'* part close to her heart. She'd always wanted to be somebody's darling.

"Candles, candy, books, and gifts. You can find the best gifts ever in Poor Richard's. So how about we separate to shop, and text when we finish," she suggested.

"Yes," Trey said, then kissed her cheek before wandering off into the store.

Out of courtesy, Marley went in the other direction. The only other gift she wanted to get was something for Trey. Her problem was that she hadn't known him long enough to know if he had hobbies, or what he liked. The only thing she knew he didn't like was matcha tea, and the only thing she knew he did like was her. She could work around that.

Marley was still standing in the same spot when she heard a familiar sound. There must be a Santa Claus nearby! She could hear children's voices and every so often, a hearty *ho, ho, ho*, and followed the laughter to a corner of the store and found Santa, resplendent in all the proper gear, with the most glorious white beard she'd ever seen.

There were a couple of children in his lap and a few more waiting to have pictures taken with Santa, and all of a sudden, she knew one thing she was going to give Trey.

Glancing over her shoulder to make sure he wasn't anywhere in sight, she quickly got in line, shivering with excitement. She recognized the photographer, and as he stood waiting for the next child to get in Santa's lap, she tapped him on the shoulder.

"Benny!"

He turned around. "Bug! What are you doing here?"

"I have a huge favor to ask," she said.

"Name it."

She whispered in his ear.

He grinned and nodded. "Yeah, and I'll have someone bring it to the lodge in a few days, okay?"

"Thank you, Benny. You're the best. I owe you. I'm reopening the lodge on New Year's Day. First time you and Darla get a chance, come up to the lodge for lunch. It will be on me."

He gave her a thumbs-up. An elf with a clipboard took her name, address, and an email link. She paid the twenty-dollar fee and then got in line.

A couple of minutes later, her coat was lying on the floor nearby, and she was sitting on Santa's lap.

"Well, hello, little lady," Santa said. "And what's your name?"

Marley smiled. "Just call me Cinderella, and I hope there's no age limit for this."

"Ho! Ho! Ho!" Santa said. "Okay, Cinderella, what do you want for Christmas?"

"Prince Charming. I want Prince Charming for Christmas."

Santa laughed, only this time it was a real, booming belly laugh. "I'll put in a good word when I see him," he said, and then they turned to the camera.

Santa's arm was around her shoulder. Her black snow boots with white fur trim around the tops were barely touching the floor, and she was congratulating herself for wearing red-and-black plaid pants and a white Christmas sweater. Benny handed her a big piece of poster board.

"Hold this up against your stomach," he said.

"What's going on?" Santa asked.

"Just a little Christmas magic," Marley said.

Benny snapped the photos, then gave them a thumbs-up.

She laid the poster board aside as she got up. An elf gave her a little candy-filled stocking, and she was finished.

She grabbed her coat and purse and quickly headed for the toy section. Because as she'd been standing in line, she had remembered Trey's story about writing to Santa for a telescope and getting a baseball and a mitt instead. And that's when she knew what she was going to get.

Trey headed straight toward the book section of Poor Richard's and was scanning the shelves when a clerk approached.

"Are you just browsing, or are you looking for a specific title?" he asked.

"Do you have the latest Chapel Hill mystery? It's a new release," Trey asked.

"We do. The mystery section is this way. Follow me." They moved a few feet down and then took a left into a narrow alcove of shelves. "This is the mystery section. I believe our Chapel Hill titles are just here." He looked a bit, and then reached toward a shelf and pulled down a book. "Here you go. *The Shallcross Legend*. It's a good one. I've already read it," the clerk said.

Trey smiled. "Good to know, and thank you for the help."

"Of course. Look all you want. When you're ready to check out, there are registers all over," he said.

"Thanks," Trey said, as he dropped the book into the shopping basket he was carrying and continued browsing the shelves. When he saw a cookbook that was a compilation of old-time recipes, he added it to the basket.

As he was walking back through the store, he came upon a stunning display of handmade crockery and stopped. The glazed coffee mugs caught his eye, and he thought of Jack and Wanda, always pouring themselves coffee throughout the day, and thought that would be a gift they might like. After a little debate with himself about color, he chose two that had been glazed with marbled shades of blue and turquoise green.

Then, as he was passing a jewelry display, he saw a necklace with a tiny red-and-black ladybug dangling from a gold chain and pointed it out to the clerk.

A short while later, the necklace had been boxed. The coffee mugs were in their individual packing boxes, and the books were safely tucked at the bottom of the tote bag he'd bought to carry his gifts.

At that point, he sent Marley a text.

> I'm finished. I smell pizza.

Marley already had what she'd come for, and as soon as she got the text, she sent one back.

> So am I. Pizza is at the far end of this wonderful shop. Meet you there.

Trey looked for Marley but didn't see her, so he started walking, following his nose, and then suddenly she slipped up beside him.

He looked down. Her eyes were twinkling with mischief.

"You have secrets, don't you?" he asked.

She nodded.

"So do I. So many secrets," he said, and winked.

Then they entered the bistro area.

"No anchovies on mine," she said.

"Me neither. Match made in heaven."

They were seated at their table waiting for their order to arrive when a woman at a nearby table recognized Trey and pointed. And then word began to spread throughout the restaurant that the man who'd been searching for Cinderella was in the house.

"I think we've been made," Trey said.

Marley blinked. "What do you mean?"

"Look around us. Everybody is staring. They recognized me. Most of them may have already read my post about finding Cinderella. Now they're all discussing the possibility of it being you."

Marley's cheeks turned pink. "Is this bad or what?"

"Not from where I'm sitting. You're my heroine. I owe you my life, remember? But they are considering your tiny self and trying to decide if it could possibly be you, or if you're far too fragile to have turned into Wonder Woman and dragged my sorry ass out of that ditch."

Marley laughed, and when she did, the sound carried over the buzz of voices in the room. And now everyone was looking at her, including Trey. Her unabashed joy for life was what he'd been missing, and there he sat, falling deeper in love—waiting on a pizza.

"I'm not going to announce it," she said. "But if they ask, I won't deny it. That would be the same thing as belittling you. We met by a twist of fate. Your desire to find me is admirable. Wanting to personally thank someone for saving your life is the most human part of us, but what is happening between us now is none of their business."

He leaned over and whispered in her ear, "Thank you, love," then kissed the side of her cheek.

Before Marley could react, their food arrived, ending the

moment between them, but it didn't end the diners' curiosity. They were in the middle of eating when Marley glanced up.

"Oh no," she muttered.

"What?" Trey asked.

"Brace yourself. Incoming rude," she whispered, just as a local couple reached their table.

"Hello, Bug. We couldn't help but notice your lunch partner."

Marley sighed. "It would have been weird if you hadn't. He *is* pretty amazing, but he has yet to figure out how to make himself invisible."

Trey almost choked on his bite, and quickly chewed and swallowed. It was obvious Marley didn't like this woman, and he hid a grin as she introduced them.

"Trey, this is Rilla and Edwin Charles. Rilla and Edwin, this is my friend, Trey Austin."

"It's a pleasure," Trey said.

"So, are you here on holiday, or visiting family?" Edwin asked.

The whole dining room had suddenly gone silent. Everyone was waiting for the answer.

Trey glanced at Marley. She rolled her eyes and nodded slightly, as if to say, *Go for it.*

"Not exactly. Apparently, you recognized me from my post about searching for Cinderella. So, I finally found her and came to thank her for saving my life."

Rilla blinked. "Surely you're not expecting us to believe that Bug Corbett pulled you from a wreck all by herself?"

Marley bristled. "Surely you are not calling him a liar?"

Rilla blinked. "Well, of course not, but I just don't see how—"

"That would be because you weren't there," Marley said.

Trey frowned. Now he didn't like Rilla, either. "I can assure you that I didn't get myself out, and yes, that's exactly what Marley did, and I have eyewitness accounts from the deputy sheriff who showed up at the wreck site with the ambulance. If you read the post, then you know what she suffered in the process and what superhuman strength it took for her to do it. Happy holidays," he said, then reached for another piece of pizza and put it on his plate. "Marley, honey...would you please pass the red pepper flakes?"

"Sure," Marley said. She handed him the shaker, then took a bite of her pizza and started chewing to keep herself from saying more.

Rilla glared at being dismissed. Obviously, Bug Corbett still held a grudge because of a simple comment she'd made to Wanda Wallis at the lodge a few years ago that wound up getting them banned. They hadn't seen each other until today. Now, she'd clearly said something that Trey Austin fellow didn't like, either. She glared at the couple, but they weren't paying her any attention, and Edwin was muttering beneath his breath.

"Rilla, we're leaving," he snapped, then took his wife by the elbow and escorted her out, while diners began sneaking pictures of the couple.

Marley sighed. "We're going to be all over social media now, aren't we?"

He nodded. "Quite likely, so be prepared to be inundated with phone calls and requests for interviews. You can either play along until they find something new to talk about, or refuse them all. It's your call, but I'll back you all the way, whatever you choose to do."

She shrugged. "I just won't worry about it," she said. "Oh, I have extra wrapping paper and bows if you want to wrap anything when we get home, but right now, I'm going to finish off this piece of pizza."

Trey eyed the pizza still on the pan. "We're going to need a to-go box."

"Awesome. I love leftover pizza, and I love that you put that woman in her place," she said.

"I could tell you didn't like her, and then she popped off about you, and that doesn't fly with me. Now we both don't like her," he said, and winked.

"She's rude to everyone. We always just ignored her until Rilla said something appalling to Wanda one day during lunch service, and I gave her an ultimatum. Either go and apologize to Wanda, or get out, and don't come back. This is the first time I've seen them since. Time didn't change her for the better. Thanks for having my back."

"Always," he said, and signaled their waiter. "We need a to-go box and the check."

"Right away, sir," the man said, and hurried off through the dining area.

A few minutes later, they were back in their coats and walking out the door carrying the pizza and their shopping bags.

Wind hit them in the face as they started across the street. "Brrr. It sure didn't get any warmer while we were inside," Marley said.

"If my arms weren't full, I'd wrap them around you," Trey said as he paused to help her up the curb.

Marley cut her eyes at him. "There you go, talking pretty again."

"I can't help it. You enchant me. It feels like I've known you forever."

"Maybe we knew each other in another life," Marley said.

"If we did, and we were in love, I want that back." Then he added, "Just saying," to lighten the moment, and it worked.

Marley laughed. "I consider myself properly put on alert."

They hurried to the car to get out of the cold and went back to the lodge, unaware that Jared Bedford had witnessed their little interlude, with a measure of shock and then growing rage. He would become even more incensed later when he learned the man with Bug was the Cinderella man and she was the missing heroine he'd been looking for.

The drive back to the lodge was uneventful. No near misses from elks in the road, and no early warning signs from Marley's angels. But her running commentary of different Christmas dinners at the lodge as she was growing up were revealing to Trey, and even more validation of how entrenched she was in her home and the idea of family, and how sparse his own experiences had been. He might never have known how much he'd missed if he'd never met her.

"So, what was your favorite part of family Christmas?" Trey asked.

Her face lit up. "My favorite part was Christmas morning. The excitement of opening gifts and then eating breakfast in our pajamas. Mom would always make Dutch baby pancakes with spiced apple fillings, and Dad would float little marshmallows in my hot chocolate. I don't remember the incident, but there's this story about me getting a mini marshmallow stuck up my nose one Christmas when I was little and crying about it."

Trey laughed. "You put a marshmallow up your nose?"

"Apparently. Dad pulled it out with a pair of tweezers. I was an adventurous little twerp. What about you?" she asked.

He frowned slightly, trying to remember. "There aren't any cute stories like yours, but I do remember flashes of things. The resident nanny brought me down to the tree when I was young. I remember that. I don't remember special foods. I rarely ate with my parents. They didn't like the messes kids made and didn't want them at the table. I was always in the kitchen with the nanny and the staff. They were good to me, but looking back, I think they felt sorry for me. I distinctly remember hearing one of them call me a 'poor little rich boy,' and I didn't understand how you could be rich and poor at the same time. My parents always bought me presents, but rarely watched me open them."

Marley gave him a quick glance. "I think I was the one who grew up rich...with love and family. You grew up with rich parents who were stingy with the things that matter to a child."

"True, but from a child's standpoint, they only have one reference of how life is, and for me, everything that happened—or didn't happen—was my normal. It wasn't until I was sent away that I felt adrift."

"But you came home at holidays, right?" Marley asked.

"Sometimes, but they were never there. After a while, I just chose to stay at the boarding school. There were others like me. We sort of hung out together."

Marley shook her head. "I can't bear the thought of that happening to the little you. When I have children, I will treasure them and enjoy every moment of the days we are together."

Trey opened the thought of being married to her and raising a family together, and then pulled back, almost afraid to hope for such a joy that might be taken away.

"I don't feel deprived. I was ignored, but instead of feeling sorry for myself, I gained a lot of self-confidence, okay? And I'm very happy with what I'm doing in life," he said.

"You mean writing?" Marley asked as she took the turn off the road into the driveway.

"Yes. I mean writing…and finding you."

She smiled and then focused her attention on their arrival as she drove around back and into the garage. They got out, grabbed their packages, and went inside.

"I'll bring the wrapping paper stuff to the kitchen. You can wrap yours on the island, okay?" Marley said.

"Okay," he said, then slid his hand beneath her hair and cupped the back of her neck as he kissed her.

Every time he did that, Marley felt it all the way to her toes. By the time he pulled back, she was at the point of *don't stop*, and aching for more. She opened her eyes, saw him watching her, and sighed.

"Yes, you turned on all the switches, if that's what you want to know. I am at the point of shameless."

He ran a finger down the curve of her cheek. "I'm always testing the waters, where you're concerned. I had this Wonder Woman mindset the whole time I was looking for you and, without realizing it, fell in little bit in love with a woman I didn't even know. So, meeting you didn't seem like seeing a stranger. You were just someone I'd lost that I needed to get back. I didn't have a thought past that...until I saw you, and every day since, I'm falling more and more in love with the woman you are."

"I never dreamed I would see you again, but when you arrived here, I did not see a stranger. I saw a man I'd once held in my arms who'd come looking for me, and I let myself believe we already had a kind of bond, but I was open for more. It didn't take two days for me to know I was falling in love. I have been honest with you about everything. The rest is completely up to you. I heard your father shouting that I was after your money. You and I both know that's not true, and they are never going to approve of me, but I don't need their permission to love you."

His eyes darkened. "Hell, Marley. They don't even approve of me. Why would I care what they thought of us?" He hugged her again. "We're wrapping presents now and being happy, and whatever evolves, we follow... Okay?"

She knew he meant making love, and she wanted that, too. "Okay, now this is me, being happy and going to get the wrapping stuff," she said, and left the room carrying her packages.

Trey hung his coat on the newel post at the foot of the stairs, stirred the logs in the fireplace, and added another one before replacing the screen, then wandered back into the kitchen, put the pizza in one of the refrigerators, and waited for the sound of her footsteps, knowing that his life had changed and that it would never be complete again without her.

Chapter 8

HOURS LATER, THE PRESENTS THEY'D WRAPPED WERE under the tree along with the others already there, and then they danced around the obvious the rest of the evening. It was foreplay at its most intense.

A look.

Shoulders touching, and then moving away.

Sharing bites of the snacks they chose instead of an actual dinner.

Country music soft and slow, playing in the background.

As night fell, security lights came on.

Marley locked up the lodge and set the alarm.

The lights were turned off.

The fire burned itself into ashes.

But a different kind of fire had been laid. The kindling was already smoking, just waiting for the spark that set everything ablaze.

And down in the family quarters, the last lock was turned.

Trey picked her up in his arms, kissed the spot below her ear, then asked the question that had been haunting him all day.

"Now?"

Marley sighed. The magic word she'd been waiting for. She turned her head slowly, letting his lips brush against her cheek and then her mouth, and when she felt his breath against her face, she whispered, "Now."

Her bedroom was in shadows. The king-size four-poster bed was turned back, waiting to receive the weary. But there would be no sleeping tonight.

It was a night for passion, promises, and discovery. It wasn't the how of it that was at question. It was a test of the intensity that had been building between them.

They stripped in front of each other, one garment at a time, hearts pounding in frantic unison as the image of what clothes had hidden was being revealed.

Perfectly pillowed breasts and a slender, but firmly toned body—final proof of the strength she'd used to save him.

For a moment, Trey forgot to breathe, and then inhaled slowly. "You are so beautiful."

Marley was speechless at the sight of that much man.

The width of his shoulders. The flat abs and long muscles in even longer legs. A dusting of chest hair as black as his winged brows. And no doubt of his desire.

She shivered where she stood, wanting him—inside her. "I ache, Trey."

He swept her into his arms, laid her on the bed, then stretched out beside her. "I can fix that," he whispered, and slid his hand between her legs.

Her eyelids fluttered and then closed. She'd meant to watch his face, wanted to see him seeing her, but all conscious thought left her mind as he began what amounted to a sensual onslaught.

His mouth was on her lips, and then in the hollow of her neck, and then her breasts, and then her belly, while the coil of need within her grew and tightened.

In the hall, the grandfather clock struck once. It was already tomorrow, but time no longer mattered and was being measured by rapid heartbeats and the intermittent shock waves rolling through her.

She never knew when he moved over her until she felt him inside her. Solid muscle within a silken sheath, adding motion to the madness and the ensuing race to catch fire. And then he began to move, and all she could do was hold on.

Over and over. Harder and faster. Minutes that felt impossible to bear. Needing the release, and when it hit, it hit her like a tidal wave, washing her under. She was still trying to catch her breath when she realized it wasn't over. He was still there. Still inside.

She locked her legs around his waist and pulled him deeper.

The first time she came, it took everything Trey had to pause long enough to let her ride it out, but when she locked her legs around his waist, he lowered his forehead onto the pillow beside her shoulder and resurrected the ride until he lost control. When the climax hit him, it was like flying and drowning, and still being able to breathe.

He came to himself slowly. First conscious of her arms around his neck and her hands fisted in his hair. He could feel the thunder of her heartbeat against his chest, and the rapid pace of her breath against his shoulder.

"Have mercy," she whispered, as she loosened her hold. "I never felt… I didn't know…"

He raised up on both elbows and looked deep into her eyes. There were tears shimmering, a slight flush upon her cheeks, and a look of wonder on her face that he would never forget. His voice was raspy with emotion as he cupped the side of her face, then gently brushed his thumb across her lower lip.

"It's just me loving you, and God, how I love you. You fill every empty piece of me."

Then he rolled her up in his arms, pulled the covers up over the both of them, and held her, letting the thunder of their heartbeats settle into normal rhythm, and thought about what it would be like to live here with her in their own private part of the lodge, making love in this bed, making a family, and growing old together here.

Marley was so still, and so quiet, he thought she'd drifted off to sleep until she said his name.

"Trey?"

"Yes?"

"Would you want to move your clothes and stuff down here with me?"

He rested his chin on the top of her head and smiled. "Yes, very much so."

She sighed. "I know it's selfish, but I want all the time I can get with you before you leave."

"I don't want to leave you at all," he said. "I'll be back if you'll allow me. I'd stay if you'd have me."

Marley shuffled around beneath the covers, then raised up on her elbow.

"Would you stay forever?" she whispered.

"Yes, and if you would marry me, I'd stay forever and a day," he said as he pushed a curl away from her eye.

Overwhelmed by the request and the vow, her eyes welled. "It was that offer of another day that did it. I never could pass up a bargain."

He threw back the covers as she rolled over onto her back.

Marley shivered as she felt the rock-hard jut of his erection against her leg. After that, all conversation ceased.

Marley woke to the weight of an arm across her waist and the warmth of a huge body spooned against her backside and remembered.

Trey.

She'd never slept with a man before.

Sex, yes. Spent the night, no.

It was new, and she was unsure as to what the proper etiquette was, so she lay there, savoring all there was about having a man in her bed. It was early, and yet there was so much to do. And getting out of bed before Jack and Wanda arrived was a necessary goal. But before she had time to worry, she felt the warmth of Trey's breath against the back of her neck, and then his lips as he kissed it.

His voice was raspy from sleep, but after all the lovemaking from last night, his touch was familiar.

"Good morning, little hummingbird. Before you fly out of my arms for the day, I need a good-morning kiss."

Marley rolled over within his arms and gave herself up to the blood rush of his touch. He got the kiss, and so much more, before she could bring herself to abandon him and the bed.

Still reeling from a rather mind-blowing climax, she headed for the bathroom on shaky legs, leaving Trey flat on his back with a smile on his face.

He watched her disappear into the bathroom before rolling out of bed. Then he grabbed his clothes and made a mad dash upstairs to his room where he showered and shaved and dressed for the day before he packed up his stuff and carried it all downstairs.

Marley was putting on her shoes when he returned with his things. She was wearing blue jeans, running shoes, and a white Christmas sweatshirt with a sequined red cardinal on the front. She had pulled her hair up on the top of her head and fastened it with a hair clip decorated with a little red ribbon and a sprig of mistletoe.

He immediately recognized the mistletoe and smiled.

"Now, that's a handy little piece of Christmas you're wearing in your hair."

She smiled.

"Does that mean I have free rein to steal a kiss whenever I want?" he asked.

"You don't have to steal anything. I'm all yours, my beautiful man. Oh...the top drawer of my dresser is empty. I never use it. It's too tall for my comfort. There is room for you to hang your clothes in the walk-in closet, and you can put your toiletries in the bathroom. I'm not starting a fire this morning until after Jack cleans out the ashes, but I am going to start breakfast. Come when you're ready."

Then she jumped up, blew him a kiss, and flitted away.

Trey carried his things into the bedroom to settle in, then quickly checked his messages.

He had an email from his mother. It was full of drama and excuses and apologies. Nothing new. Just more of the same. She wanted peace between Trey and his father, but in Trey's mind, there wasn't even a war. The problems were nothing but his father's opinions and wishes not being met. What else was new?

He had an email from his agent, Meredith, that set him back on his heels. She'd turned down the low-ball offer from the film company wanting a script about Finding Cinderella, and had received a far more interesting offer that had to do with Chapel Hill and his mysteries.

A major motion picture group wanted to option the film rights to the entire library of Chapel Hill novels. All twelve of them. He was stunned. The option offer was five million for ten years. If they began production on any one of them, there would be additional money per book, plus a small percentage of the net profits in all formats.

The hitch was...they wanted to promote the author as well as the stories. The fact that the identity of Chapel Hill was unknown would make the revelation of his identity part of the selling point. He would then be part of the promotional advertising.

Meredith ended the email with a question.

> Do tell me your thoughts? Oh...and FYI...I'll wring your gorgeous neck if you don't accept this. It's time, Trey. No more hiding.

He didn't know what to think, but he knew he needed to talk

to Marley. The last secret between them was about to be revealed. He knew she loved his writing, but she didn't know it was him. Was she ready to be in the middle of whatever this would unleash if he finally revealed he was Chapel Hill when she had her own business to run? There was only one way to find out.

He sent a quick message to Meredith, telling her he'd get back to her before the day was over, and then headed for the kitchen.

Marley had bacon already cooked and biscuits in the oven. She was making gravy when Trey walked in.

"Hey, honey, I smell chocolate. What are you making?" he asked.

"Chocolate gravy. It's one of the recipes I brought back with me from Arkansas."

"Oh yes! I remember you talking about it."

"Good. We're having it this morning, and I'll make you eggs afterward if you don't care for it."

"What's not to like about biscuits and chocolate? I'm gonna love being married to you. Think of all the foods I get to taste test first!"

She laughed, and kept stirring. As soon as the food was ready, they sat down to eat. Trey's first bite was tentative, and then he rolled his eyes.

"Oh man, this is good! And the salty bacon just adds to the whole bite! I give it two thumbs up."

She beamed. "Good deal."

He finished his plate, then set it aside and reached across the table and clasped her hand.

"I had a message from Meredith. There's a really big opportunity ahead for me, but it's a bit complicated, and I want to talk to you about it first before I respond. It has to do with my work."

"Your writing?"

He nodded. "You've very politely never grilled me about what I write and just accepted the fact that I did. But Meredith has been approached by a major film production company about optioning all of my work to date for possible films."

Marley gasped. "Oh my gosh! Trey! How wonderful for you! Congratulations!"

He nodded. "I'll be honest. It's been a dream of mine ever since I began writing. But there's a hitch. Part of the company's request is that the writer will be part of the pitch they make to fund the first film."

"So, you'll travel some, right?" she said.

"Likely, yes, but that's not the hitch." He took a deep breath. "Meredith's been at me for years to come out of hiding, so to speak, but I do not write under my name."

"I don't understand the problem, Trey. Lots of writers use pseudonyms."

"Yes, but people still know who they are."

She was watching his face when a thought occurred. "What genre do you write in?"

"Mystery."

"Oh my God, Trey. Are you Chapel Hill?" The look on his face said it all. "You are, aren't you?"

He nodded. "You think being the guy looking for Cinderella was crazy. You have no idea how this is going to blow up in the publishing world, never mind the thousands of fans who hold yearly contests trying to guess the identity of Chapel Hill. What if it gets so crazy that it interferes with your business and your guests?"

She circled the table and sat down in his lap.

"It will more likely cause an influx of reservations with fans wanting to sleep under the same roof as their beloved writer. This is wonderful news for you, and I'm so proud of you. You were born into money. You had all the money in the world to grow old doing nothing but living a life of ease, and instead you followed your heart and created your own path. You absolutely do not hesitate because of me. Understand? We do life together, not apart. My job will be to make sure you have all the peace and privacy you need to continue to write your wonderful stories. We'll even set up a tiny corner of the front desk with a display of autographed copies for sale. You'll be the star of the lodge, whether you like it or not."

"Marley, you have no idea how important your acceptance of who I am and what I do really is."

She frowned. "I know a day will come when I come face-to-face with your parents, but you need to know I will be your strongest advocate. One derogatory word about you and they'll get an earful."

He grinned. "The image of that is quite delightful. Like siccing a Chihuahua onto a pit bull."

"So, I'll be the ankle biter," she said.

He burst out laughing as he hugged her. "God, woman, how I love you."

"You better. I ruined a good pair of shoes pulling you out of that car...but you were definitely worth it."

His dark eyes narrowed. "And I spent weeks of my life looking for your pretty little ass...and you turned out to be the woman I've been looking for all my life. So, I let Meredith know I accept?"

"Absolutely! You can't turn down opportunities like this."

"A five-million-dollar opportunity, as it turns out, with a ten-year option for all twelve books, with more money to follow if they begin production."

She gasped. "Five million?"

He nodded. "I do okay in the writing department, but this will change everything."

"So, go give her your answer! Do what you have to do." Then she looked up and out the window. "Oh wow! Look! It's snowing! The roads are going to be impossible again."

He shrugged. "Being snowed in with you sounds like heaven, and I have no need to go anywhere except to bed with you every night."

Marley wrapped her arms around his neck and leaned in for the kiss she saw coming. It might be snowing outside, but as she closed her eyes, all she saw were stars.

"Message received. Hold that thought. I'm going to let Meredith know it's a go," he said.

She watched him leave, shivering at the thought of making love to him again. He was her Rochester—a dark, brooding man of mystery. Only she was a far cry from Jane Eyre. She was too opinionated and nowhere near poor.

Trey wasted no time in calling Meredith. The phone rang a couple of times, and then she answered.

"Hello, and give me some good news," she said.

He smiled. "I bring tidings of great joy. It's time to unmask Chapel Hill. Have the paperwork reflect we're optioning the titles to date, and no more. I'll agree to doing whatever promo they want to publicize my identity, and I'm changing residence shortly, so no Phoenix address on the paperwork. I'll text you the new address, and I can e-sign the paperwork as usual."

"Wonderful, but where are you going?"

"I'm already here with Marley. I'll go back to Phoenix long enough to get my house set up to lease, and then I'll be calling Colorado Springs home for the rest of my life."

Meredith squealed. "I don't believe it! The perennial bachelor has caved! So, your little Cinderella stole your heart! It's so romantic I can't stand it! You better invite me to the wedding!"

He laughed. "First name on the list. Count on it," he said.

"First billing above the parental units? Marvelous!"

"You earned your place in my heart," Trey said. "I treasure your friendship." There was a moment of silence, then he heard her sniff. "Are you crying?"

"Of course I'm not! Don't be absurd," she muttered. "Now, I'm off to do agenting things. Just don't get sidetracked from the delivery date for your next book."

"Yes, ma'am. No, ma'am. I wouldn't dream of it," he said, and then smiled as she hung up in his ear.

After that, Trey began making a list of things he needed to do when he went back to Phoenix, while Marley was clearing away the breakfast dishes.

After she was finished, she walked past the Christmas tree in the lobby and stood at the front entrance, watching it snow. Even when it sometimes caused issues later, she never got tired of the sight, remembering the days when she was young, and the snowball fights with her dad, and the hot chocolate her mother had waiting when they finally came inside, fingers numb, noses running, and the rosy spots on their cheeks so windburned they were just shy of frostbite.

Good times.

Times long gone.

But she could resurrect those times again when she had babies. Raising them beneath this roof and hoping a fifth generation would live on to keep the dream alive, but at the same time accepting they might all choose other paths—like their father had with his own family.

She smiled at herself. *Me and my long-range plans, right? One night in bed with the man and I am already seeing us as the elder generation. I know. I know. Slow down, Bug. Slow down.*

She turned around, remembered the fire needed tending, and went to take care of business.

Marley had mostly forgotten about Jared Bedford, but he had not forgotten about her. What Marley didn't know was that while she was gone, Jared had been spending his days off at the lodge with the reno crew, ripping up carpet for the men to lay new flooring, spackling and patching Sheetrock to ready for painting. He knew the layout of the entire place, except for the family quarters, which had been locked. He had plans for Bug Corbett, but today he had bigger problems. He was a little short on money.

When the boss wasn't watching, he slipped a twenty out of the till and then went back to the flat he was changing. The boss's wife was always coming down to the garage and getting money before she went shopping. He was confident it would never be missed, and when he got off work, he was going to drive up the mountain and do a little reconnoitering.

He couldn't just drive up in the dark because of the motion lights and security cameras. But he knew the camera's blind spots and knew he could come in from the woods on foot.

He finished fixing the flat and was getting ready to put the next car up on the lift when he saw it was snowing again, and coming down heavy. There would be no mountain drives tonight or stomping through the woods. From the looks of it, he'd be lucky to get home tonight.

His visit to Marley Corbett would have to wait.

Anders and Gloria weren't speaking.

They weren't even sleeping in the same bed.

This was the biggest crack their marriage had ever suffered, and Anders was afraid it wouldn't heal.

He'd apologized to her again and again, and her only answer was, "You don't mean it," and she'd walk away.

He had nightmares of a divorce court and losing half his holdings. Of million-dollar alimony checks and trying to hold his head up at board meetings. It never occurred to him that his biggest fears had nothing to do with what her absence in his life would mean. Only what it would cost him to set her free.

One day came and went, and then another, and then another,

until it was less than a week before Christmas, and he hadn't even bought her a present.

That day, he left the ski lodge and took an Uber into Lucerne. His first stop was a jewelry store, but the longer he looked at the most expensive pieces, the more certain he became that these would only make things worse. To her, it would appear that he was hoping to buy his way back into her good graces, and she'd already accused him of being interested only in how much money he could make.

So, he left the jewelry stores and began walking the streets. Up one and down another. He even stopped at a coffee shop for a sweet roll and a coffee and sat at a table by the window, watching couples walking past arm in arm.

He felt lost. Like he'd walked into the wrong room and couldn't find his way out. It was the most frightened he'd been since his childhood.

After a while, he paid and left, then resumed the search for the perfect gift. He was passing by a little shop tucked in between two very large ones when he saw the window display and stopped.

He read the sign on the building:

LOETSCHER'S

The name rang a bell, and without hesitation, he turned around and went inside.

The first sound he heard was ticking all over the store. There were cuckoo clocks all over the walls, in the most unique chalet designs. He walked the length of one wall, and then down the other, eyeing the detailed work, and listening to the sound the little cuckoos made on the half hour and the hour.

But it wasn't until he saw one called Heidi's Farmhouse that it felt like he'd come to the right place. He was immediately taken back to the first time he'd seen Gloria at her parents' home and knew this was the one. Little hand-carved pigs. Little chickens, flowers, pots, garden tools, and a two-story chalet in vivid primary colors.

A clerk appeared at his elbow. "Have you finally made your choice, sir?"

Anders nodded. "Yes. That one," he said, pointing.

The clerk wrote down the price on a piece of paper and handed it to Anders.

"This is the cost, sir."

Anders barely glanced at the number. $3,499.00. At this point, the price was no object.

"That's fine," he said. "Could you wrap it as a Christmas gift?"

The clerk nodded. "Certainly. Follow me, sir."

A half hour later, Anders walked out of the shop with his present in a gift bag and, for the first time in years, felt like he'd done something for all the right reasons.

He called for an Uber back to the ski lodge and sat back with the bag in his lap as he rode.

Gloria had awakened to a note on her pillow.

Back later. Save a seat for me at lunch. I really, really, really, really love you.

She clutched the note against her breasts and cried, and then glanced at the time and flew out of bed. She needed to get dressed and run down to the apparel shop in the lodge to pick up the present she'd bought for Anders.

It was a Capranea ski jacket—the finest Switzerland had to offer, but the style she'd wanted was a Badus, in the color red, and they didn't have one in stock. However, they had promised it would be in their shop today, and if it suited, they would gift wrap it for free, for the trouble they'd caused her.

Gloria had money, but she'd grown up without luxuries, and she'd never gotten over the joy of a deal. Scoring free gift wrap made her happy, and she couldn't skip giving him a gift. She was heartbroken by what he'd said, but she still loved him.

She dressed in haste, then headed for the lobby. To her delight, the ski jacket was exactly what she wanted, in the right size and color.

"Yes, I'll take it," she said, and paid for it as another clerk took it away to wrap. She thought nothing of the $1,400 she'd just spent, and it never occurred to her to spend a dime on Trey. Someone else had always done the shopping for him when he was growing up, and since he'd been out of their lives for so long, Gloria was an out-of-sight, out-of-mind kind of woman.

She brought the gift back to their suite and put it under the Christmas tree near the window—a perk of the hotel—then ran to get dressed for lunch.

Anders came back to their room while Gloria was dressing, saw his present under the tree, and thought, *There may be hope for me, yet.* Then he slipped his present toward the back of the tree and went down the hall.

"Gloria! I'm back. I made reservations for half past twelve."

Another four inches of snow fell during the next two days before it quit, but during that time, Trey and Marley had adapted something of a rhythm to their days. Marley told Jack and Wanda that they were fine, and to stay home and enjoy a few days off.

Trey worked on his manuscript by the fire and became the keeper of the flame since he was sitting right beside it.

Every time Marley walked past the jigsaw puzzle, she added a piece here or a piece there. And if she wasn't dusting or mopping, or answering phones, she was nose deep in a book or in the kitchen making something for them to eat.

Chapter 9

On the third day before Christmas, Jack and Wanda showed up to clear the parking area and the driveway again, and Marley was baking desserts for Christmas dinner.

As soon as she had her workspace cleared, she pulled out her largest mixer and began measuring out flour and sugar to get sugar cookie dough made and in the refrigerator to chill, then make some pie fillings before starting on crusts.

She was breaking eggs into creamed sugar and butter when she heard the snowmobile. A few moments later, the back door banged, and Jack and Wanda appeared.

"Morning, Bug, am I too late for breakfast?" Jack asked.

"Yep. I'm already starting cookie dough. Sorry."

"Jack, for heaven's sake. You not only ate breakfast at home, but you had a cinnamon roll on the way over. If you were a dog, I'd have you at the vet getting checked for tapeworms," Wanda mumbled.

Marley laughed and kept measuring ingredients.

Jack grumbled something at Wanda beneath his breath, then looked up at Marley.

"This is the day to clean the ashes out of the fireplace. Did you let the fire go out last night?" he asked.

"Yes, sir, I did, so clean away, and thank you," she said.

Jack winked at Marley, swatted Wanda on the butt, and sauntered out of the room.

"That man," Wanda said. "I'll go on up and start on Trey's room and then come down and help."

"He isn't sleeping in his bed. He's sleeping in mine," Marley said. "He's moved his stuff to my place days ago, so go ahead and get the room ready for guests again."

Wanda stood, her hands on her hips, waiting.

Marley looked up, saw the look, and frowned. "What? Did you forget I'll be twenty-eight years old next month? We're serious about this relationship, and as they say, if the good Lord's willing and the creek don't rise, we'll be married before summer. There is nothing to discuss."

"Did the angels approve?" Wanda muttered.

Marley waved a spatula in the air to make her point. "They're the ones who told me he would matter before I ever pulled him out of that car. At the time, I just didn't know they meant forever. That message came later, right before I contacted him about the lost shoe, and you will keep that to yourself."

"All right, then. Going up to ready the room, then I'll be back down to help. Are we making pies today?" she asked.

"Yes, we are," Marley said.

"We'll need at least three pecan pies. They always go first," Wanda said. "Do we have a firm number of who's coming?"

Marley nodded. "Fifteen counting Trey," she said, then turned on the mixer to finish the dough, put it in the refrigerator to chill, and began making dough for pie crusts.

She could hear Jack banging about at the fireplace and Wanda's footsteps as she walked around upstairs. It was business as usual at Corbett Lodge, except for the big, sexy man who'd entered her life.

Thank the lord for Trey Austin and tender mercies. His presence was about to color her world in ways she could only have imagined.

Jack had finally finished cleaning the fireplace. He'd laid a new fire and just lit the kindling when he heard a vehicle drive up. He watched the fire catch, then removed his gloves and was starting toward the lobby when he saw the news van parked out front, and a quartet of people coming up the front steps, one of whom was a cameraman.

"Marley. You have company!" he yelled.

Trey was just coming out of the family quarters when he heard Jack shout, and hastened his steps. He arrived just as Marley came out of the kitchen.

Marley was still keeping the lodge locked up, which left the news crew on the porch, reduced to ringing the doorbell. She was headed toward the front door when Trey appeared at her elbow.

"This is the cost of that pizza at Poor Richard's," he said, and reached for her hand.

"It would have happened sooner but for the snow," Marley said, but she was clutching him tightly as they neared the door.

"The sooner we say our little piece, the quicker they'll be gone," Trey said.

Moments later, she unlocked the door and opened it. "I'm sorry, but the lodge is closed until New Year's Day."

The only woman in the quartet barely acknowledged Marley's presence as she flashed a big smile at Trey and showed them her identification.

"I'm Farrah Welty from the NBC affiliate in Colorado Springs. You're Trey Austin, right? The man who was searching for Cinderella?"

"Yes, that's me," Trey said.

Farrah beamed, then finally turned to Marley. "Marley Corbett, owner of Corbett Lodge, am I correct?"

"Amazing bit of research considering my family has been here for four generations," Marley said. "I'm up to my elbows in pie crusts and fillings. You have arrived without prior notice at an inconvenient time, so let's cut the chat and get down to business. I don't have all day. What do you want?"

Trey blinked. Something told him he wouldn't be having problems with overzealous fans once the news broke about his identity. This was Marley's lodge, and she handled business.

Farrah Welty wasn't used to being denied, and most people wanted to be on TV. Apparently, Marley Corbett wasn't most people.

"I do apologize. We should have called to make an appointment, but we didn't want to be scooped. Trey, is Marley your Cinderella?"

"Yes, she is."

"We'd like to get some footage of the two of you together, and hear about what happened."

Marley sighed. "You get fifteen minutes, and I need to go tell Wanda what's happening. I'll be right back," she said, and walked away.

"Come in," Trey said. "We'll sit here in front of the bookshelves, but know that neither of us is interested in fame from this. I owe my life to this woman, and she's amazing in her own right, so cut her some slack. She didn't ask for all this, and my public inquiry has caused it. Please make nice comments about her lodge in your piece, while you're at it."

"Of course," Farrah said as she followed him to the furniture grouping, then instructed the crew on what she wanted from them.

Moments later, Marley returned, without the baker's apron and without the mistletoe hair clip.

Trey stood to make room for her, then sat down beside her.

Farrah noticed the look between them and leaned forward. "This is off the record, but have you two developed a relationship? We heard rumors that—"

Marley's eyebrows rose, and Trey jumped in before she could let loose.

"I'm sorry, but rumors hardly seem like something a respectable media source would choose to spread. We'll stick to the incident and nothing more, or it ends here," he said.

This was not going how Farrah Welty expected it to go, but she wanted the scoop of getting the first interview bad enough to play along, and Marley Corbett had already looked at her watch, so she laughed it off.

"Of course, but I had to ask, right?" Then she cleared her throat and began with questions directed at Trey about how the wreck occurred.

Marley sat without comment, listening to him charm Farrah Welty up one side and down the other, and thought about how good he was going to be with notoriety, and wondered why he'd chosen anonymity to begin with, then glanced at her watch again.

Farrah noticed Marley looking at her watch again and smiled at Trey.

"You have quite the story to tell your grandchildren one day," she said, "and our own little Marley Corbett has become the Cinderella in your story who saved Prince Charming. Marley, we'd love to hear your part in this heart-stopping drama. How did you come to be on that road in Arkansas?"

Marley frowned. "The little Marley Corbett comment is a bit misplaced. I left childhood behind years ago. As for why I was in Arkansas, we'd shut the lodge down for renovations and updates in the guest suites. I took some time for myself and was on a quest to visit a few elders I'd come to know online who live in the Ozarks. We'd been corresponding off and on for almost a year about food and recipes, and at their invitation, I went to make the rounds and visit. I was hoping to get some unique recipes for the lunch menu here at the lodge. I'd been there a couple of weeks and was finally heading home when I drove into heavy rain, which quickly turned into a storm. I happened to take the same road Trey had been on and drove up on the wreck in the middle of nowhere. As he explained, the car was missing a driver's side door and a windshield, and upside down in a ditch, and the seat belt was all that was keeping the driver from falling headfirst into the flooding ditch and drowning."

"How frightening," Farrah said. "But you are a very petite woman. How on earth did you manage?"

Marley shrugged. "I didn't think about what I couldn't do. I just focused on what had to be done to keep him from drowning and made the rest of it work." Then she explained in detail what it took to get him out, from the Swiss Army knife to using body weight and momentum to get him out of the car and up onto the road. She told how long she knelt beside him with the umbrella, waiting for the ambulance, and how she'd been so cold that she didn't even realize she'd walked out of her shoe until miles later when she stopped to refuel. She said she'd still been in some sort of shock through it all, and that she finally fell apart after she'd stopped for the night.

"I didn't know his name, and after help arrived for Trey, no one asked me my name. I stood for a moment watching them working on getting Trey stabilized, but I was so cold I couldn't think and just headed for shelter, which happened to be my car. I was no longer needed, and so I drove away. I finally broke down and cried for hours after I reached the motel. I think it was shock. And even after I came home, I didn't know anything about him searching for me. It was only by accident that I saw it at all."

"I don't know how you missed it. It was in all the papers, on social media, and on television for weeks," Farrah said.

Farrah's smile looked more like a smirk, and Marley resented the comment even more.

Marley smiled sweetly. "I guess that shows you how little time I give to the news. Also, you have to remember that we'd been closed for renovations, so when I returned, we were busy unpacking everything we'd stored and putting the bedroom suites back together, and getting ready for Christmas. My family has always hosted

Christmas dinner at the lodge for our friends here on the mountain who don't have family to share it with. And then there's the big New Year's Eve party we host annually. It's been happening for generations. It's reservation only, so lots of preparation goes into that as well. Basically, I didn't know what was going on outside these walls because we were busy. We officially reopen on New Year's Day, and after that, it will be business as usual here."

"So, Trey is spending Christmas with you?" Farrah said.

"Yes, of course. He arrived in the middle of that blizzard, and after he got snowed in, I invited him to stay as my guest. When I found out he had no plans for Christmas, I immediately invited him to stay over for that. And then it snowed again. No one should spend Christmas alone. We had plenty of empty rooms, and we've had plenty of time to visit, and I've learned what a really great man Trey is. He's smart and funny, and my weird sense of humor does not offend him. He also likes my cooking, which I should be doing right now. Today is baking day for Christmas desserts."

Farrah knew this was her signal to end the interview.

"This is such an inspiring story, and we at the station want to thank you for allowing us to interrupt your day and your work for this interview. It will air on the evening news."

"It will be interesting to see it. I hope this satisfies everyone's curiosity," Trey said.

"And, cut," Farrah said.

They all began gathering their things and putting on their coats.

"I'll see you out," Trey said.

"I'm heading back to my pies," Marley said, and left the great room.

"She's an interesting little thing, isn't she?" Farrah said.

Trey frowned. "Interesting little thing? Don't mistake her size for her value. She's worth ten of most people I know."

Farrah blinked. She'd stepped on more toes, this time his, and changed the subject as they were walking through the lobby.

"I did my research on you. You're Anders Austin's son, aren't you?"

"Yes," he said, and kept walking.

"But you don't work for your father."

"No," he said, and opened the front door and stepped aside. "Drive safe."

"What exactly do you do?" Farrah asked.

He sighed. "Lady, this interview is over. I'm pretty sure there's a bowl to lick or a cookie to taste back there, and I don't want to miss out on any of it."

He shut the door behind them, and before they were even off the porch, he turned the lock. There'd be no more uninvited people wandering in until Marley was ready for business.

Marley looked up from rolling pie crusts as Trey walked in. "Are they gone?" she asked.

He kissed her cheek. "Yes, ma'am. I locked the front entrance again, and I want to commend you for not nailing her to the floor on camera."

She smiled sweetly. "It was the least I could do for you."

Wanda looked up. "Did Bug get snippy?"

Trey shrugged. "Let's just say she wasted no time telling Farrah Welty what she thought about being sideswiped by the media. But she was very polite. And very succinct, and that was all before the cameras were on."

"That's my girl," Wanda said.

"Now that's settled, is there anything I can do to help?" Trey asked. "Any taste testing needed? I am virtually worthless when it comes to helping Jack unless he needs a strong back. That, I have."

"We're going to have to make room in the dining area for the long tables we set up for the Christmas dinner. Jack would definitely appreciate help moving those," Marley said.

"I'm on it. Save me a cookie," he said, and left.

Wanda glanced at Marley. The expression on her face was unreadable.

"So, tell me what you really think," she said.

Marley rolled her eyes. "If that Welty woman doesn't refer to my size in a passive-aggressive tone on the piece that airs, I'll be surprised."

Wanda hid a smile. "Was she fawning all over Trey?"

Marley nodded.

"Did it make you jealous?" Wanda asked.

"More like territorial," Marley muttered, "but he handled her like a pro. I was proud of him…and for the time being, it's over."

Wanda frowned. "What do you mean, for the time being?"

Marley shrugged. "It's not my news to share, but it's all good. No worries, Wanda. He's got my back, and I have his." Then she looked up. "How many bowls of pecan pie filling did you make?"

"I have three done, waiting to go in the crusts you have chilling."

"The crusts should be chilled enough. Pour them up and let's get them in the oven. I'm going to roll out more crusts to chill, then get some apples peeled for apple crumb pies. I'll bake the cherry cobbler in one of the big steam trays, and an old-fashioned raisin pie for Mr. Doolittle. He loves them."

"What about pumpkin rolls?" Wanda asked.

"That's your specialty. Go for it," Marley said. "And we'll have the big tray of sugar cookies. Tradition, right?"

Wanda knew what Marley was thinking. The sugar cookies had always been what Marley's mother contributed to the desserts, and she was missing her parents. Wanda put down the carton of eggs she was holding and gave Marley a hug.

"Jack and I love you so much. We can't replace your mom and dad, but we're here for you."

Marley was blinking back tears. "I know, and I am so grateful. You know I love you, and I'm not usually this weepy, but it's been an emotional day. I just want to get pies in the ovens so we can do cookies later."

"Then that's what we're going to do," Wanda said, and began pulling crusts out of the refrigerator.

All the time they were working, they could hear the rumble of Jack and Trey's voices in the dining area, along with occasional bouts of laughter. It made Marley happy. Jack was a hard man to please, and he'd already taken to Trey, which was good, because Trey was about to become a permanent resident.

Unaware of Trey's ongoing drama, Meredith Bernstein was back in New York City working her magic, arguing the fine points of the option contract with Morris LeHigh, the head of the production company.

"Yes, Chapel Hill is agreeable to an identity reveal, but only after the contract has been signed and the money is in the bank. After that, Chapel Hill will be available to you as the need arises."

"Is it a man or a woman?" Morris asked.

Meredith chuckled. "This is not a scavenger hunt, Mr. LeHigh. We're not obligated to give you clues."

His laugh rumbled in Meredith's ear. "It never hurts to ask," he said. "So, we're a go with all twelve titles?"

"Yes, all the titles to date with a ten-year film option for five million. This does not cover any ensuing releases. And the other points are agreeable in that if a book goes into production, there will be an actual contract and more language to add, right?" Meredith asked.

"Not if, but when. I already have interested investors, and yes, all the language will be in the option," Cohen said.

"Can we expect the contract before the first of the year? That way we can start the new year off with a very nice check on signing. Not three months afterward. Understood?"

LeHigh sighed. "Understood. You drive a hard bargain, lady."

"What can I say? I take care of my clients," Meredith said. "I'll notify my client of this conversation, and we'll be ready to e-sign when the contract is submitted."

"Excellent! This will be the scoop of the publishing world, and I don't mind being known as the one who did the unveiling," he said. "You'll be hearing from me soon."

"Excellent," Meredith said, and disconnected.

Trey already knew this was in the works, so there was nothing further Meredith needed to call him about until the actual option contract arrived for him to sign.

Satisfied that she'd covered all the bases, she poured herself a cup of tea and then carried it to the window overlooking the city she called home and silently celebrated for them both.

Gloria Austin was getting dressed for a gala event at their ski lodge. The event began at 8:00 p.m., and she had less than fifteen minutes to get the rest of her makeup on. She'd spent most of the day in a spa and then finished up at a salon getting her hair and nails done. The silver fabric of her gown sparkled under the lights as if it were made of diamond dust. The neckline accentuated her most recent breast lift, and the last round of Botox she'd had left her fiftysomething face looking as close to twentysomething smooth as possible.

She was looking forward to the dinner and the dancing afterward, but not with Anders. She was never going to forgive him for insinuating that she'd married him for his money and did not grieve the parting shot she'd given him about not having a prenup. Her very words had ended the tirade and turned her husband a whiter shade of pale.

She'd always known he could be an ass, but his sudden concern for Trey's private life had nothing to do with their son's welfare and everything to do with his concern for his own money. A royal ass.

Gloria had already gotten over the shock of Trey's comments about their parenting. There was no ignoring the truth. It bothered her conscience a little, but she'd never been good at motherly love. She just regretted that he'd suffered because of it.

Anders was still eating crow because of the careless comment about why Gloria had married him. He couldn't deny he'd said it, even though he hadn't really meant it, and now he didn't know how to take her. She'd been livid about his fighting with Trey and shocked that he'd never taken it upon himself to call his son on his own. But Anders had convinced himself years ago that his son would automatically follow in his footsteps—and held it against him when he would not.

Then Trey sent back every penny Anders had been sending him, and now he didn't know what to make of his son, either. What was he doing to support himself? What if it was something illegal? If it was, it would look bad for Anders.

The fact that he even believed that could happen was the painful proof of how little he knew of his son, and he didn't like being in the dark about anything.

As soon as Christmas was over, they were flying home, and then he was going to Colorado, with or without Gloria. He wanted to see that Corbett woman face-to-face, whether Trey was still there or not.

Moments later, Gloria entered the living room.

Anders stood. "You look beautiful, my dear."

"I know," Gloria said, and waited for him at the door.

He sighed. She was still angry. What a miserable trip this had turned out to be.

Jack and Trey had finished setting up the tables and seating. The holiday tablecloths were in place and the candlesticks had been pulled out of storage, dusted and polished, and were sitting at one end of the table.

"What next?" Trey asked.

Jack shook his head. "Nothing here. The rest is up to the women. I tried helping set the table once and got in trouble for putting all of the cutlery in the wrong places."

Trey grinned. "Picky about that, are they?"

Jack nodded, then winked at Trey. "Just a tip. What you don't know just means you don't have to do it."

Trey threw back his head and laughed. He was still laughing when Marley came bouncing out of the kitchen with a handful of undecorated sugar cookies. She handed three to Trey and three to Jack.

"They're still warm from the oven. We're decorating the rest after they cool, and I do not want to know what outrageous thing Jack Wallis just told you that made you laugh like that," she said.

Trey leaned over and kissed her cheek. "Thank you for the cookies, love. As for Jack, his secrets are safe with me."

Jack grinned. "Thanks, Bug. You know the way to my heart."

"Yes, food," she said, and then waited to see their reactions as they took their first bites.

"Delicious," Trey said.

Jack nodded. "Good stuff, Bug."

"Thank you," Marley said. "I'm going back to work."

But before she could make good on her word, they heard another vehicle pulling up at the front of the lodge. When Marley saw it was yet another news van from the other local TV station, she frowned.

"I've got this," she said. "Lunch will be ready in about an hour. Both of you should take a break."

"I'll take a break when you do," Trey said. "And I'm not leaving the lobby until I know you haven't started a fight."

The doorbell rang.

She took a breath and strode through the lobby like she was going to war.

"She's a pistol, isn't she?" Jack said as he took another bite of his cookie.

"She's amazing," Trey said. "One of these days I'm going to be the innkeeper's husband, and I cannot wait to see her in her element."

Jack grinned. "You're about to see a hint of it right about now."

They watched her open the door and then listened as the voices carried all the way back to where they were standing.

Marley stood in the opening without giving way to the entrance they wanted.

"I'm sorry, gentlemen, but the lodge is closed until New Year's Day."

"Miss Corbett, we're from—"

Marley smiled. "I can see where you're from. It's written all over your van."

The reporter nodded. "Yes, of course. We want to ask you and Trey Austin some questions about—"

Marley waved her hand like a little fairy queen dismissing her subjects.

"Oh, I'm sorry, but we already gave our interview to the NBC affiliate. You can watch the interview tonight on the evening news. We'll open again on New Year's Day. You must stop in for lunch. It's served from 11:00 a.m. to 2:00 p.m. We'll be serving black-eyed peas for luck, and all kinds of good foods."

The reporter looked stricken, and when Marley stepped back and started to close the door, he shoved his foot in the door.

The hair rose up on the back of her neck.

"Please move your foot," she said.

"I just want—"

The tone of Marley's voice went from calm to critical mass.

"Little boys write to Santa Claus for what they want. Are you seriously about to force your way in? I'm not in the habit of being harassed on my own property, so are you going to move your foot, or would you prefer to unwrap presents this year with your foot in a cast?"

He yanked his foot back so fast he staggered.

Marley shut the door in his face, locked it, then turned her back on all of them and headed back to where Trey and Jack were standing.

Trey looked at her and grinned. "Write to Santa Claus," he said, and then picked her up in his arms and carried her back to the kitchen, laughing all the way.

Wanda heard the laughter, then when Trey came carrying Marley back into the kitchen, she frowned.

"Bug, what have you done now?" Wanda asked.

"She told a reporter to write to Santa Claus for information and shut the door in their faces."

Wanda giggled. "That's a good one. Where's Jack?"

"I told him and Trey to take a break," Marley said as Trey set her on her feet.

"Then he's probably stretched out in front of the fire. I think I'll take him something to drink," Wanda said, and grabbed a pop from the refrigerator and left.

"She and Jack take care of each other. They still act like teenagers together. I always loved that about them."

"I can't wait to be that man for you," Trey said, and pulled her into his arms.

"You already are," Marley said. "Love you forever," she whispered, and melted beneath his kiss.

Jack went back to the fireplace, stirred the fire, added another log, and then sat down with his feet up and closed his eyes, thinking how fine it was going to be to have another man in the house again. He was thinking about those cookies he'd just eaten when he felt a hand along the side of his cheek.

Wanda.

He opened his eyes.

"I brought you something to drink," she said.

He pulled her down on his lap and then took the bottle of pop. "You're my best girl," he said. "Can you sneak me another cookie?"

"No. You already had three, and lunch is in about an hour. You'll survive."

He sighed. "It's a good thing I love you, even if you're trying to starve me to death."

Chapter 10

By evening, the Christmas baking was over, and pies were stored away. Tomorrow was Christmas Eve. Marley was curled up on the sofa next to Trey, with her head on his shoulder. The television was on, and the local evening news was up next. They had just seen the lead-in to their story during a commercial break, showing a clip of them sitting together on the sofa.

"Just look at how innocent and adorable you look sitting there beside me," Trey said. "No one would have a clue as to how deadly you can be."

She poked him. "I am not deadly. Just determined."

He hugged her. "I'm just teasing you, darlin'. You're perfect in my eyes. I wouldn't want you any other way. You are nobody's fool, and that is something I truly admire. Your beauty is just icing on the woman within. I will always see you first as the woman who cared enough to save a stranger. Allow me the privilege of making sure you are safe and treasured for the rest of your life, okay?"

Marley's eyes welled with sudden tears, and Trey groaned. "Don't cry. I didn't mean to make you cry. I just keep feeling this need to reaffirm how much you mean to me. And maybe that's my insecurity, not yours, okay?"

"Happy tears, that's all. Blame it on your pretty words," she said.

"Okay," he said, and handed her a tissue and upped the volume. Apparently, the lead from the commentator was to reference their scoop as being the only station in the nation with the first interview of Trey Austin's search for Cinderella. They went on with how proud they were here in Colorado Springs to learn that the woman he'd been searching for was none other than Marley Corbett, a native to the area, and the owner of Corbett Lodge, a favorite B and B and local lunch spot in the area.

"Good promo for the lodge," Trey said.

"She thinks you're hot," Marley muttered.

"I only worry if you think I'm hot," he said.

She blew him a kiss. "Then you have nothing to worry about."

"Oh, here it goes," Trey said. "Let's see if they got my best side."

"You would have had to strip for that," she said.

He laughed out loud. "God, I love every sassy bone in your body. Behave. I don't trust the media, and we need to see what she did to us."

They sat through it in silence, and when it was over, Marley reached for his hand. "It was good. They didn't turn it into some fluff piece, which was about what I expected. They dwelled on the wreck, and the rescue, the shoe left behind, and your quest to find me. It will, for sure, impact the people who rooted for you during your search. The search I didn't know was even happening. I just kept having dreams about it the first week I was home. In the dream, I kept trying to keep your head out of the water, but you just got heavier and heavier. And then I'd wake up just as the water washed over both of us."

"Lord, honey…What a nightmare!"

"I knew the moment I woke up that it was just a reflection of all the fears I'd had trying to get you out of the car before it was too late. And I finally came to terms with the fact that you were still breathing when they took you away. I told myself the angels would never have sent me if you hadn't meant to live through it, so I just imagined you alive in the world and let it go."

He leaned forward and kissed her. Already the feel and the scent of her was so ingrained within his psyche that he could have found her in the dark.

"It was all I could do not to react when you told Farrah Welty that you—what was the phrase?—came undone after you stopped for the night. That you finally allowed yourself to feel the fear and panic you went through when you began crying after you got into your motel room. That was a testament to your emotional strength...that you held it all together until the danger was over. It's how people become heroes. They focus on what has to be done, instead of themselves. You are one of those people."

Marley sighed. "I know I am one tired woman tonight. I feel a soak in the bathtub is on my agenda."

"We've already locked up and banked the fire out in the lodge. You go get your bath ready. Would you like a glass of wine to keep you company?"

"Sounds like heaven," Marley said. "I'll even share the tub if you don't mind smelling like lavender bath salts."

"I'd be a fool to turn down an invitation like that," Trey said, and pulled her to her feet. "I just have to respond to an email from my mother. What's odd is that they think I've suddenly gone to war against them, when the truth is they're just shocked by the picture I painted of my life and the part they didn't play in any of it."

"I'm sorry, sweetheart. Just know that you have me now, and I will feed you, and worry about you, and check on you, and make every day of your life special for the rest of your life and hope it makes up for some of the sadness you carry with you," Marley said.

"I don't think I feel sad," Trey said.

"And yet you are. I hear it in your voice when you talk about your childhood, and it breaks my heart. Now, go get the wine. I'll be soaking in the bubbles, waiting for you to come shatter my sanity."

His eyes darkened. "I do that to you?"

"In ways for which I have no words," she said, and left him standing.

"Damn," he whispered, then looked around, trying to remember what he'd been going to do, then remembered the wine.

They drank the wine and soaked in the Jacuzzi until the bubbles were gone and the water was no longer hot before they got out. Trey dried Marley off in slow, sensuous strokes, then wrapped her in a bath towel and sent her off to bed.

"I'm going to shave before I join you," he said.

Marley dropped the towel as she was walking away, leaving him with a perfect view of her bare self.

If she'd turned around at that moment, the look on his face would have taken her breath. He'd never wanted to be with a woman as much as he did with her, so he dropped his towel and followed.

"I thought you were going to shave," Marley said when he walked up behind her and slid his hands beneath her breasts.

"You changed my mind," he whispered, and pulled her off her feet and into his arms.

But the moment they both hit the bed, Marley pushed him flat on his back and then eased herself down on his erection.

"Tonight's for you, love. All for you."

Trey groaned as she began to move and gave himself up to the sensual pleasure of her body. His last conscious sight of her before she blew his mind was of her body arched, her eyes closed, riding the climax between them.

Jared Bedford was in his apartment, eating cold pizza and drinking his last beer when the evening news aired. He heard the promo for the upcoming interview and downed his last two bites of the slice he was eating and upped the volume. Marley Corbett and her Cinderella man were going to be on TV. This he had to see.

When it began, he barely heard what they were asking Trey Austin. He was waiting for the random shots they showed of Marley's face while he was talking, and he could tell by the way she was looking at him that they were together.

It pissed him off in a way he couldn't explain. He had no words for how it made him feel to see her and know she despised him. He didn't get that he'd caused it. That his every action from the time she grew boobs to his recent grope in the supermarket was the reason for her feelings. The guys he hung out with now and then called him crazy and then laughed, and he'd laugh with them, but in the back of his mind, he knew they considered him a source of amusement.

He didn't have the guts to make them mad. But Marley was an easy target for his rage. After the interview was over, he just sat there with the near-empty can of beer in his hands and the cold pizza sitting heavy in his belly until he snapped.

He threw the beer can across the room, showering a chair and his dinette table before the remaining contents splattered against the wall. Within minutes he had his winter gear on and was headed out the door. The streets were fairly clear but icy in spots, and he knew they'd already plowed the blacktop leading up the mountain. It wasn't the worst idea he'd ever had, but it ranked a possible disaster, regardless.

It was nearing 11:00 p.m. when he drove past the Corbett Lodge sign out on the road, but he kept driving, and then pulled off into the lay-by about a hundred yards past the sign and parked.

Jared pulled his sock cap down over his ears, zipped his coat all the way up beneath his chin, grabbed his flashlight and gloves, and got out. He locked the truck, dropped the keys in his pocket, and then zipped it shut, making sure not to lose the keys anywhere in the snowy dark, then turned on the flashlight and started walking through the trees and angling down toward the lodge as he went.

Security lights were blazing outside the lodge like spotlights on a stage, giving him an easy target to follow. He came out of the trees at the back of the lodge and paused, looking for lights inside the family quarters.

Even though shades and curtains were drawn, he guessed everyone was asleep. He wanted to see her asleep in her bed with Trey Austin, but there was nothing to see. Frustrated, he peed in the snow right beneath her window and then made his way back to his truck and drove home.

Marley woke up the next morning with her nose buried against Trey's back and her arm slung across his waist. The steady rise and fall of his chest was like a metronome setting the rhythm for the rest of her life. He had been in her life such a short time, but he didn't feel like a stranger.

She didn't want to move, but there was so much to be done today. It was Christmas Eve. Everything that hadn't been prepped for tomorrow had to be done today. She was excited to introduce Trey to the people who knew her best and longest. The people who remembered her grandparents and her parents and had watched her grow up—like kinfolk at a family reunion that you don't see every day, but who know and love you anyway.

She gently kissed his back, and then slipped out of his arms and out of bed, and hurried to the bathroom to wash up and get dressed.

Trey was dreaming.

Marley was walking away in the rain, and he had no voice to call her back. He thought he was shouting, but nothing was coming out of his mouth, and the terror of never seeing her again was overwhelming.

In the dream, someone threw a blanket over his body, then pulled it over his face as if he'd died, and he was shouting, "I'm alive, I'm alive!" but they couldn't hear him. Just as they shoved him into a hearse and closed the door, he woke up with a jerk, gasping for air and reaching for Marley.

Then he heard water running in the bathroom and bolted from the bed.

The door was ajar, and when he pushed it open, she was putting up her toothbrush. She turned to him with a smile on her face, and seconds later she was in his arms.

"Good morning to you, too," she said, but he kept hugging her. "Hey, what's wrong?"

He shuddered. "Bad dream. Just needed to feel the real you."

"My sweet man… I'm so sorry," Marley said. "Get dressed and come to the kitchen with me. It's Christmas Eve, and I don't allow bad dreams to have a place here. I'm going to stir the fire and then make breakfast. You don't want to eat behind Jack. He doesn't leave leftovers."

Trey shook off the last remnants of the dream with a last hug. "I won't be long, but now this morning I really have to shave, or I'll look like Blackbeard before nightfall."

Marley narrowed her eyes, as if trying to see him in a different light. "I don't know about that. I think those coal-black whiskers are a little sexy, even if they do turn your pretty self into a rather intimidating man."

He grinned. "Now who's talking pretty? I'll hurry. I don't want to eat Jack's leftovers, either."

Marley was laughing as she left.

Trey heard the door to the family quarters open, then close, and reached for his electric razor. As soon as he was dressed, he headed to the kitchen.

She had scrambled eggs and bacon on the plate and cinnamon muffins coming out of the oven. He poured their coffee, grabbed the cutlery, and they sat down to breakfast.

"What's the usual protocol for conversation over breakfast after great sex the night before?" Trey asked.

She shrugged. "Well, we can't talk about the chickens slacking on the egg laying, because we don't have chickens. And we can't talk about the kids because we don't have any of those, either. I don't know any local gossip. And I don't really want to talk about that interview or Farrah Welty again."

"She called you an 'interesting little thing,'" Trey said.

Marley looked up. "I hope you called her down for that."

"Yes, that I did. She also wanted to talk about my father. I shut that down as well."

"It never goes away, does it?" she said.

"Not really, but it's to be expected. I'm sure people still talk about your parents in reference to the lodge, but they were good people and you loved them, so it gives you pleasure to belong to them, right?"

She nodded.

"So, it's the same principle for me. I am my father's son, and he's a big deal. But I'm the unknown in our equation, and people are curious. I can't fault them, but I also am not required to satisfy their curiosity."

She was quiet for a few moments, absorbing the wisdom in that comment. "You have learned to be a very remarkable man without anyone's help. I promise I will never let you down."

"Thank you, love. I love you more, and the trust between us is not in question. Okay?"

She nodded.

They finished eating, and then Trey carried their plates to the sink. "I noticed you put the last two logs on the fire this morning. I'm going to replenish the stack."

"There are several pairs of gloves on the dryer. Find a pair that fits."

"Yes, ma'am," he said, then winked before he left.

Once he was in the utility room, he put on an old coat hanging on a hook, grabbed a pair of gloves, and put them on as he went out the back door.

The fresh air was wonderful, full of pine scents and the smoke from the fireplace, but it was so cold it burned the inside of his nostrils. He wasted no time getting his first armful and went back inside and stacked it near the hearth.

"I'm going to get tablecloths," Marley said, and took off down a back hallway as Trey went outside for a second round.

He had his arms full when Jack and Wanda rode up on the snowmobile and followed him inside.

"Hey, Trey, I was going to do that," Jack said.

"Just helping you out," Trey said. "Marley left cinnamon muffins on the counter. She's gone to get tablecloths, wherever that is."

"Oh, I'll go help," Wanda said, and took off down the back hall.

Jack went into the great room with a bag of Christmas presents to put under the tree and then went straight to the kitchen for muffins.

He ate two and had a third one in his hands as Trey came back into the kitchen with the last load of wood.

"That's plenty for now," Jack said. "I need to run into town to get some feed for the critters. I'll be back in an hour or so. Tell Bug for me, will you?"

"Sure," Trey said. "Hey, Jack, since you and Wanda are Marley's only family, I feel like I should give you a heads-up about us. I'm leaving within a couple of days after Christmas is over, but I'm coming back as soon as I can get my house listed with a leasing agent and pack up my office equipment."

"Coming back for how long this time?" Jack asked.

"For good. And whenever she can squeeze me and a wedding into her schedule, we'll make it legal. But there isn't a ring or a piece of paper that will make her more mine than she already is right now.

The wreck that nearly killed me was the luckiest thing that ever happened to me. I cannot imagine my life without her."

Jack wrapped Trey up in a bear hug and thumped him on the back. "Welcome to the family, son! I couldn't be happier for the both of you."

"Thanks," Trey said.

"Have you told your parents yet?" Jack asked.

Trey's eyes narrowed. "They know where I am. They don't like it. We don't have much to do with each other, so it's no big deal to me what they think. Anyway, just didn't want you and Wanda thinking I was not going to treat Marley right."

"Oh, we have all the faith in the world in Bug's choices. She's as true blue as a woman can be, but she's also nobody's fool. If she says you're okay, then that's high marks. And if she loves you, then I know you're the real deal. However, I appreciate the thought you gave to telling us."

Trey grinned. "I'm one lucky son of a gun, aren't I?"

Jack laughed. "Yes, you are, and my name is gonna be mud if I don't get myself into town and back."

Trey watched Jack leave the lodge, then followed the sounds of voices until he found Marley and Wanda sitting on the floor in a hallway with a stack of old photo albums in their laps. The tablecloths they'd gone to look for had already been set aside to take into the great room, and they were head-to-head, wiping tears or laughing as they turned the pages.

They looked up when they saw him coming.

"Trey, look what Wanda found. They were behind a stack of tablecloths in the linen closet. Four albums of family photos. Some of the photos are from before I was even born, and then another album is of me growing up. They should be in the family quarters. Will you take them there for me?"

"What a find," he said. "Sure thing, and we can look at them together tonight, okay? I'll get to see pictures of your parents and you when you were little."

Marley handed him the albums, then she and Wanda picked up the tablecloths and matching cloth napkins, with Trey and the albums following along behind. When they went left into the great room, he turned right and went down the hall to the family quarters.

The urge to peek was strong, but he wanted her commentary on all of them, so he left them on the coffee table and went back to help.

The simple chatter between the two women as they covered the tables was a novelty to Trey. He'd never been a part of prepping tables or making food. His parents hired people for all that.

To his knowledge, his mother had never washed a dish in her life after she'd married his dad, and he didn't even know if she could cook. It stood to reason that she once had when she was just a girl from Arkansas. But whatever the little mountain girl had been was long since lost in glitz and glamour.

Watching Marley and Wanda talking about every piece they pulled out of a cabinet was a story in itself.

Wanda pulled out two gravy boats and set them on the table.

"Hey Bug, remember the first time Craig came to Christmas dinner and Jack passed him the gravy boat?"

"Yes. He asked what he was supposed to do with it. Jack told him it was gravy, and to pour it on whatever he wanted to have gravy, and he poured it all over everything," Marley said.

"Even the peas. They were floating in his plate," Wanda said.

"Didn't faze Craig a bit, though. As I remember, he used a spoon on most of the food."

Wanda nodded. "But what could you expect, right? That boy pretty much raised himself, and he's the most reliable woodcutter on the mountain. He has a client list a foot long. He was so young then and still lacking a few social graces. He's all about using the right fork now."

"We love Craig. He's one of us," Marley said as she began laying plates around the table. "Remember the year Alvin brought his sweet potato casserole? We didn't know until he removed the foil that he'd forgotten to bake it first."

Wanda nodded. "Yes, and you went running with it to the convection oven and dinner was delayed thirty minutes."

"And there was the year when Doolittle fell coming up the steps. We thought he'd killed himself, and he just got up cussing, brushed off the snow and said, 'It's a good thing Alvin's carrying my casserole.'"

Trey was sitting and watching them, listening to their old stories and realizing he had none. At least nothing to remember fondly.

Marley paused. "I'm not assigning seating, but if you can, get Jack seated beside Mr. Doolittle. I saw him in the store a while back, and his fingers were so crippled with arthritis that he couldn't sort the change in his pocket when he was trying to pay. So, I know cutting meat is hard for him now."

"Marley, honey, what a thoughtful thing to think of," Trey said.

She shrugged. "Every year we still have with him is a gift. He is nearly ninety."

"Does he still drive?" Trey asked.

"No. His neighbor, Alvin Smith, is his taxi service, but they don't tolerate each other for long, so they always sit as far away from each other as they can get," Marley said.

Trey was curious. "They don't get along, but Alvin is willing to drive him where he needs to go, and Mr. Doolittle is willing to spend time with him to get his business taken care of. How did all that come about?"

"I don't know. I never thought about it," Marley said. "It's just how they've always been."

"Jack said when they were young, they both fell for the same girl. She played them along, and then dumped both of them for another guy. Alvin is a widower, and Doolittle never married. Now they kind of depend on each other," Wanda said.

Trey nodded. "I get that. Life isn't easy. Who else is coming that I should know about?"

"Gert and Mabel Jukes. They're sisters who still live in their home place and never married. Arnie Fitzsimmons, who's retired from the army. Patsy and Charlie Barrett are retirees who moved here from Michigan some years ago. Keith Murphy is the youngest. He's about thirty-five or so. He works from home and writes code for some tech company. Shirley Lowrey is a retired waitress, and Lawrence Atwood is a widower. They always come together. And that's the list, except for the four of us."

"What an eclectic group. I can't wait to meet them," Trey said. "How are they with strangers?"

Wanda smiled. "You have nothing to worry about. Once they find out you're Marley's sweetheart, you're in."

Trey winked at her. "So, you're my pass to this amazing feast."

"I guess I am," she said. "And speaking of feast, everyone who comes brings a covered dish to the table. They're all good cooks, except Craig. He doesn't cook much, so we have a deal. He always brings me a big bag of kindling to keep the fire going during dinner. Don't expect dinner from the Ritz-Carlton, but do expect to have the best time of your life," Marley said.

"Oh, I've had dinner at the Ritz-Carlton. I ate alone. I would choose your way every time," Trey said, and then the conversation ended when the doorbell rang.

Marley glanced toward the front entrance and recognized Benny from the Santa photo shoot. "It's a delivery for me. I'll be right back," she said, and bolted. She barely got the door open before Benny handed her a package and began apologizing.

"I'm sorry I didn't get this done sooner. One of my kids got sick and I clean forgot. I hope it's not too late?"

"It's perfect timing, Benny, and I appreciate it. I hope it was nothing serious with your little one. Christmas is a horrible time for anyone to be sick, but especially for children."

"Ear infection. She's getting better, and thanks for asking. I'd better go. Merry Christmas, Marley."

"Merry Christmas, Benny. My best to your family, too," and then she closed the door and slipped the package beneath the tree on her way back.

"Now, where were we?" she said, and then remembered what she'd been going to say. "Oh…Trey, Jack will be back later to help, but why don't you go back to the family area and choose whichever extra bedroom you want to use as your office. Then you and Jack can take the bed down and move it to the attic and any other furniture that's in there that will be in your way, like dressers or tables, okay?"

"Really?" Trey said.

She smiled. "Yes, really. You have to have your own place to work, and I'd advise choosing either of the two that are at the far end of the hall because they will also be the farthest away from the noise of guests at the lodge."

"Good point," he said, and hurried away.

Wanda glanced at Marley. "You're one smart lady," she said.

"Why do you say that?" Marley asked.

"You changed the concept of choosing for him to giving him power to make his own choices. Every man likes to feel needed, and they need to feel wanted. You don't need him for you to be able to do your job, but he needed that freedom to choose the place to do his job."

"Oh. Well, I didn't think about anything except wanting him to know he belongs."

Wanda nodded. "I'm not much on reading, but what, exactly, does he write?"

"I think it could fall under contemporary fiction," Marley said.

"I'm going to get the flatware," she added and made a quick trip to the butler's pantry to get it so they could finish setting the table.

Per Marley's advice, Trey looked at both of the bedrooms she'd suggested and then chose the one with a window overlooking the forest. At first, all he saw was snow and snow-covered trees, but as he stood, he realized he was also seeing a line of tracks within the trees coming toward the house and then out of his line of sight.

He frowned, wondering who might have made them, then shrugged it off. He was a newcomer to mountain life. It could have been a hunter taking a shortcut to somewhere else, or even Jack, doing whatever it was he did for Marley. It was, after all, a place where people came and went, even though it was momentarily closed, and he turned back to the room in question.

The full-size bed looked small and would be easy to take down. The dresser was more like an armoire, and when he opened it and saw the shelves and the inner drawers below, he decided to leave it. It would be a great storage cabinet for supplies.

The walls were a rich burgundy color, while the floor-length curtains over the single window were a soft, pearl gray with burgundy cords as tiebacks, and the floors were made of ancient, wide-plank pine. It felt good just being in this room. It was elegant and manly and welcoming.

Every day spent at the lodge was beginning to feel like less of a visit and more like home, and every night he spent with Marley solidified everything he'd ever wanted in his life.

When Jack returned, they moved the bed and mattress to the attic, along with the braided rug that had been beside the bed. The armoire was empty. The closet was empty. And the overstuffed chair by the window was too inviting to take away. Even better, the room was wired for TV and Wi-Fi, which meant he was fixed for the technology he used as well.

"What do you think?" Jack asked as they gave the room one last look.

"I think it's perfect," Trey said. "Thank you for helping."

Jack patted Trey's shoulder. "It's what I do. Let's go see what else is on the agenda."

They left the family area and went back into the guest section of the lodge. The dinner table was all set up for tomorrow, right down to candles waiting to be lit. All they needed now were the people and the food to make Christmas Day complete.

"Are we going down for dinner?" Gloria asked.

Anders shook his head. "No, I ordered room service. I wanted to spend Christmas Eve with you, not a room full of people. And I have a gift for you."

"I have a gift for you, too," Gloria said. "Should we wait until after we eat, or open them now?"

"Now," Anders said.

Gloria jumped up, clapping her hands. "You first," she said, and handed him her gift.

He could tell by the light in her eyes that she was waiting for his reaction, and when he opened it and saw the ski jacket, and then the color and the style, he knew she'd picked out something special.

"Oh wow! Darling! It's beautiful. Thank you so much. You know how much I love this style. It's perfect, just like you," he said, and leaned over and kissed her. "Now you," he said as he set his box aside and retrieved her gift from behind the tree and put it in her lap. "Don't shake it," he cautioned, knowing she always shook a gift before she opened it.

She nodded, then carefully removed the bow, and then as she tore off the wrapping paper and saw the box itself, she gasped.

"Is this what's inside?"

He nodded.

She started to cry. "Oh my God, Anders. Oh my God. Help me get it out, okay?"

He knelt down on the floor in front of her and began carefully removing all the packing, because he was going to have to repack it for the flight when they left.

And when he finally had it free and put it back in her lap, she was stunned. "All the animals, and all the flowers, and the two-story chalet. It reminds me of home!"

"The clock is a Loetscher. They're the finest makers of cuckoo clocks in all of Switzerland. The clock is called Heidi's Farmhouse. I bought it because it reminded me of you and where you first took me home to meet your parents."

Now she was sobbing.

Anders sighed. "Don't cry, honey. There are so many sins I will never be able to forgive myself for, but the worst one of all was what I said to you in anger. We may be lousy parents, but I always strived to be the best husband I knew how to be. When we get home, I'll hang it wherever you want it, okay?"

She nodded, but she couldn't quit looking at it—at all the tiny details in nearly hidden places.

"It's perfect. It's the best gift I've ever been given. Thank you."

Later, when their food came, they turned it into a picnic and ate with a view to the snowy alps.

As they were finishing up, the light snow that had been falling started coming down harder, and by the time they'd gone to bed, it had turned into a little blizzard, and Anders couldn't sleep.

Bringing more snow would certainly close the ski slopes and raise the imminent danger of the possibility of avalanches from the surrounding peaks.

He was secretly wishing they'd left the lodge yesterday. If they stayed another day, it could be too late to get out. The roads might be closed.

It was too late for a lot of things, but maybe not too late to escape.

Finally, he sat up in bed and turned on the light.

Gloria rolled over. "What's wrong? Are you all right?"

Anders scrubbed his hands across his face.

"I'm fine. I'm just worried about the weather. We might not be able to leave tomorrow, and I don't want to get trapped here."

"There could be worse things," she said.

"Yes, I know. But I'm still thinking about Trey. What are we going to do with our son?"

She frowned. "Absolutely nothing, and don't pretend this is you worrying about him. We both know that's a lie."

"Trey sent back all the money I'd sent him over the years, plus the accrued interest. He didn't lie. He hadn't spent a penny," Anders muttered.

She sighed. "So?"

"What's he doing? How is he supporting himself? What if it's something illegal?"

She rolled her eyes. "You're an idiot for even thinking that. In all his years growing up, he never so much as got a speeding ticket. He wasn't a confrontational kid. He wasn't a troublemaker."

"Then how do you see him?" Anders asked.

"A man who figured everything out without us, and we've lost the right to care or judge," Gloria said.

"That woman wants his money," Anders muttered.

"Then it will be his money, not yours. He gave yours back. You have no horse in this race. And how dare you belittle his feelings? Your father wasn't impressed with me. Did he tell you I was after your money?"

Anders frowned. "That's different. I knew my own mind."

Gloria snorted. "You were younger than Trey is now when we married, and Trey has managed to stay single all the way past his thirtieth birthday, so I hardly think he's some novice at the mercy of the female sex. He's drop-dead gorgeous and single. And now he's in love."

Anders frowned. "He's just grateful to her, that's all."

"I'm not talking about this with you again. You're wrong. I'm right. Leave them alone."

"When we get back to the States, I'm going to talk to Trey."

"And you'll just make things worse because that's what you do. I'm not going with you. I don't want to be any part of this. We didn't care about his welfare before. I'm not going to show up like the cavalry and watch you make an ass of yourself."

She pushed out of his arms and got up.

"Where are you going?" Anders asked.

"To the bathroom to contemplate my toes while I pee," she muttered, and slammed the door shut behind her.

He hadn't heard anything like that come out of her mouth since they first married. That was his little Ozark girl talking, not the high-society woman she'd turned into.

But now that she was up, he got up as well and headed for the minibar in their living area. As he passed the windows, he saw snow drifting down onto the terrace, then picked up his laptop from the coffee table, pulled up info for international flights out of Lucerne, and checked flight status and weather. So far, so good. Then he pulled up their flight plan to see if he could switch it to an earlier flight.

To his relief, there was a plane leaving Lucerne just before 10:00 a.m. tomorrow. He switched their reservations for that flight, and as soon as he got confirmation, he breathed a sigh of relief and went back to tell Gloria.

Chapter 11

When morning came, Gloria and Anders were already checking out at the front desk, with a car waiting for them outside. Once they were on the way into the city, Anders began to breathe easy. But it wasn't until they reached the airport, got themselves and Gloria's cuckoo clock through security, and then to their gate, that he finally relaxed.

"I'm sorry we're traveling on Christmas Day," Anders said.

Gloria shrugged. "I'd rather be going home."

Anders nodded, but he was hearing something more in her voice than the words expressed. Resigned. She was resigned to her life. Not excited about it. Not anymore, and it bothered him.

"Gloria, when I'm gone from the house all day, what do you like to do? And I don't mean what do you do. I am sincerely asking, what would you like to do?"

She looked up. "I don't know. I just have lunch with friends, shop for stuff I don't need, and wait for you."

His eyes suddenly welled, but they were in broad sight of everyone coming and going, so he blinked away tears and just reached for her hand instead.

"What's wrong?" she whispered. "Are you ill? Is there something you're not telling me?"

He shook his head. "I've been blind to everything that mattered. I wanted you for a wife and then set you on a pedestal like a pretty thing to just look at when I wanted to. I wanted a son, and you gave me one, and I ignored him. I don't know him. And I almost lost you with hateful words I didn't mean. So, I guess, in a way, I am sick. Money sick. Greed sick. And I don't like how it feels. The worst part of it all is the reality of how our son felt all his life. Like he said, we were never there for him when he needed us, but I can't just let this ride. I have to face him. I have to find out what he became...who he is as a man today."

Gloria sighed. "Then, if that's your mindset, I will go with you, but I won't belittle what we did to him with a simple apology. It's a trip to admit our guilt and nothing more. You don't threaten him or his girl. You don't. Understand?"

Anders nodded, and then a few minutes later, they began boarding their flight.

It was still Christmas Eve in Colorado Springs.

The lodge was decorated. The dining table was set. Food was prepped for tomorrow, and all the desserts and rolls were already made. The giant ham was already baked and ready to reheat tomorrow, and the dinner rolls were covered up and waiting to be warmed, and presents under the tree.

They'd spent part of the afternoon looking at the pictures in the old albums, and seeing Marley as a toddler was the sweetest thing.

"No wonder your dad called you Ladybug. You weren't much bigger than one," Trey said, and turned a few more pages before Marley stopped him, and pointed to a very old black-and-white rectangular photo that had been taken with an old Kodak Brownie camera.

"That's my grandma Katie and my grandpa Vester, short for Sylvester. Sylvester's daddy built the original log house. Grandpa added the lodge. Dad took it over after they retired, but they all still lived together under the same roof. She's the reason for my lack of height."

Trey lightly touched the face of the woman in the picture. "Something tells me that you got more than that from her. She looks pretty determined here."

Marley nodded. "When the Korean War broke out, Great Grandpa and Great Grandma Corbett had already passed, and Grandpa and Grandma hadn't been married quite a year when he enlisted. He told Grandma to hold the fort, that he'd be back. They didn't have children then, and that's when she took in boarders here in this place to make ends meet. He was so impressed with what she'd done to stay afloat that when he came back, he built the lodge around their house. Dad always said his mom was the smart one and his dad was the strong one, and together, they were invincible. I like to think that is also the beginning of us."

"I like that, too," he said.

A short while later, Marley put her grandparents' pictures on a shelf in the living room area. "Keeping them close. I don't intend to lose them again."

Hours later they were back in the great room, with Marley curled up in Trey's arms before the fireplace, listening to the excitement in his voice about moving here and silently thanking the angels for sending him her way, when she heard what sounded like a tinkle of laughter, and then a voice.

You are blessed because you heed.

Marley sighed.

Trey heard the sigh and hugged her closer. "Are you okay, darlin'? Is this a little bit of a sad time for you?"

"Not sad, just reflecting. And not on what was lost, just what I've gained, and that includes your presence in my life. I would never have seen this coming, but I feel so blessed."

He kissed the top of her head. "Let's open our presents to each other now."

"Yes, let's!" Marley said, and jumped up with a bounce and headed for the tree.

Trey was right behind her, thinking that this was the first of many Christmases they would share.

She was down on her knees digging through the packages for the ones she'd put under the tree for him, and Trey pulled hers out, then eyed the armload she had.

"Need help?" he asked.

"Nope. I've got it!" she said, trying to balance the long package with his telescope and the flat package of her picture with Santa Claus.

"They've almost got you," Trey said, eyeing the load up under her chin.

Marley carried them back to the sofa without a hitch, then put them on one end of the coffee table, leaving the other end free for him.

"We always take turns," she said. "You first," and handed him the package Bennie had dropped off for her yesterday, hoping it was what she'd asked for.

Trey paused, holding the package in his lap as if the gift alone was already enough, but Marley was waiting. He tore off the paper and saw the back side of a picture frame. Then he turned it over.

It was Marley, sitting in Santa's lap holding a sign that read: ALL I WANT FOR CHRISTMAS IS YOU!

"Oh my God! Marley, this is epic," he said, and hugged her. "This is going in my office, and every time I look up from my laptop, I'll see you, reminding me what a lucky man I am. Thank you."

She clapped her hands. "Yay!"

"Now I pick one out for you to open?" he asked.

She nodded.

He picked up the two books he'd bought her and put them in her lap.

"This one first," he said.

Marley clutched it to her breasts. "My first ever present from you!" she said, and then tore off the bow, then the paper. The moment she saw the books, she squealed.

"Ooooh! The new Chapel Hill! I'm so excited. And this cookbook! I can't wait to read the recipes! Thank you!" Then she opened the cover and noticed it had been signed on the flyleaf. "You signed it!"

He nodded. "You own the only book Chapel Hill ever signed. Of course, that will change now, but you're the first!"

"And you signed it to 'My Marley'! I will treasure this forever. Thank you for loving me!"

He shook his head. "Oh, honey, loving you is the easiest thing I've ever done in my life." Then he handed her the other present he'd gotten for her. "I know it's my turn to open next, but we're on a roll here. Open this next," he said.

She was squirming with delight as she began to remove the bow and paper from the little box. It was long and slim and nearly flat. Jewelry, she thought, and opened the lid.

It *was* jewelry, but nothing she would have expected, and it moved her so deeply she was struggling not to cry.

"Trey…oh, sweetheart! A ladybug. This is the most exquisite thing I've ever seen, and the personal meaning is everything to me."

She threw her arms around his neck and kissed him. "I love it so much. I'm wearing this tomorrow! This is beautiful."

"Not as beautiful as you are," he said.

She touched the little ladybug one last time and then closed the lid and picked up the last present.

"Now you!" she said, and handed it to him.

He knew she was excited about it, but he couldn't imagine what it might be and began tearing into the wrapping paper to the box beneath.

The moment he saw the outside of the box, his heart skipped a beat. His eyes widened.

"Are you serious?" he whispered.

Suddenly his fingers were all fumbles, and his heart was pounding as he opened the box lengthwise. The tripod was on top. He pulled it out, and then removed the Styrofoam packing it had been in and saw the telescope beneath. When he looked up, there were tears in his eyes.

"In this moment, I am a child again, with all the hope and expectations of my little self just being fulfilled. I have no words to express how deeply this touches me, or how much I will enjoy this in the years to come. A thank-you is too simple for the love with which this was given."

"I am so happy you're happy," she said. "You know, tonight the sky is littered with stars, and heaven always looks closer from here. I think you should set it up and take it out to the front porch to see what you can see."

"Will you come with me?" he asked.

She hesitated, then gave his hand a quick squeeze. "I will, later. But this first time, I think it should just be you, making peace with a broken part of your past."

She got up and started to walk away.

"Where are you going?" Trey asked.

"To get your coat. You can't go outside without it. It's too cold."

He took a slow, shuddery breath and then pulled the instructions out of the box, read them over, then extended the tripod legs to their full length and fastened the telescope into the bracket on top just as Marley came back with his coat.

"Hold out your arms," she said, and helped him into it, then turned him around. "Button up, love. I don't want my best guy getting sick."

"You might be spoiling me," he said.

"Somebody needs to," she said. "You grab the telescope. I'll open the door for you."

"Leave the porch lights off. It will make the view clearer. I'll have enough light from the lobby," he said, so she did.

The moment he stepped out onto the porch, she quietly closed the door behind him, then watched from within as he set up at the edge of the porch and aimed the scope toward the stars. He was motionless, fixated on what he was seeing.

Mission accomplished, she thought, and walked away.

Trey never heard her leave. His heart was pounding as he tilted the telescope heavenward and began searching the sky.

"Where are you?" he said, as he adjusted the focus, then looked again. He knew where it was in the sky. He knew what it looked like. He just couldn't—and then it came into focus. "Ah, my God! There you are! From one Gemini to another, long time, no see."

Marley didn't know what was going through Trey's head, but whatever he was thinking, it was a healing thing. He was living something he'd been denied. He could have bought this for himself years ago, but it wouldn't have been the same. It wouldn't have come with love attached—until now.

Trey had lost track of time, but he was cold enough now that he couldn't feel his fingers. It was time to go back inside. With one last backward glance at heaven, he picked up the tripod and went inside, locking the door behind him. Marley was nowhere in sight, but he knew she hadn't gone far. She hadn't just given him a Christmas gift. She'd given him back a measure of faith he thought he'd lost.

He picked up the tripod and was heading to the family quarters when she came out of the kitchen with a cup of hot chocolate.

"Right behind you," she said, and followed him inside. As soon as he put the tripod away in a closet, she handed him the mug. "I know your hands have to be freezing, and I'm going to need them a whole lot warmer than they are before you put them on me."

He laughed as he took the mug. "Thank you, baby, and yes,

you're right. They're cold as hell, but I have been fulfilled. I'll warm up, but I'll never get over this night…or you."

"Drink up, love. I'm going to set the security alarm and put the lodge on lockdown. I won't be long."

Trey had downed the warm chocolate and was stripped down and getting ready to get in the shower when Marley walked up behind him and wrapped her arms around his waist.

"Do you want company?" she asked.

He turned around, admiring the beauty of her naked body. "You know I do. I would have to be a fool to ignore the offer."

"After you," she said, and when he stepped in beneath the flow of warm water, she was right behind him.

Never had a bar of soap been more erotic, and never had she let a man have his way with her in such a manner. And when she came, she lost her hold on his soap-slick body and rode out the climax on her knees.

When they finally made it to bed, Marley fell into his arms, exhausted.

"You fly through my dreams at night, and you die in my arms when we love. My heart. My love. My life."

"You set me on fire, my sweet-talking man." Then she snuggled up against him and closed her eyes.

Marley had set an early alarm, but woke up before daylight and turned it off so it wouldn't wake Trey, then sat on the side of the bed watching him sleep. His head was resting on a pillow she used to hug against her when she slept, and he was taking up half of the bed with his big body and long legs.

Awake, he changed the energy of the room with his booming laugh and long, sure strides. Sleeping, he gave her his trust, and from what she knew of his past, it was the most valuable thing he could share. He'd promised her forever and a day, and she was holding him to it.

Finally, she made herself abandon the bed for the day ahead. There were still little things to do, and she didn't want to be rushed. Just before she slipped out, she laid a Hershey Kiss on her pillow for him to wake up to. She was on her way to the kitchen in pajamas and slippers. She'd dress for company later. Soon, she had diced apples with raisins, sugar, and cinnamon cooking down on the stovetop and was making batter for Dutch baby pancakes. Tradition was alive and well at Corbett Lodge.

Trey woke up alone, rolled over onto his back and stretched and, as he did, saw the Hershey Kiss on Marley's pillow. He grinned, peeled it, and popped it in his mouth.

"Sweet, but not as sweet as her," he said as he got up to shower and shave.

A short while later, he left the family quarters for the front of the lodge and headed for the kitchen. When he walked in and saw Marley at the work island, wearing pj's and slippers, his heart skipped. This was how his world was going to be for the rest of his life. What a gift. He walked up behind her and wrapped his arms around her waist.

"Merry Christmas, my love. Thank you for the chocolate kiss. May I have a real one now?"

She turned within his embrace. "I thought you would never ask," she said, and let herself melt in his arms.

"Something smells so good," Trey said.

"I made a Dutch baby pancake with an apple-raisin filling. Are you hungry yet?"

"I'm always hungry for you…and for what you make," he said. "What can I do to help?"

"Coffee for both of us. I'll plate the food. It's just us this morning. Jack and Wanda won't be here until closer to dinner."

Trey filled two mugs and carried them to the kitchen table

while she brought servings of the Dutch baby pancake to their places.

"Your mother's special Christmas breakfast, right?" he said.

She nodded. "I'm all about tradition."

Even though she was smiling, he caught a glimmer of tears. "They would be so proud of you," he said.

"I know. I wish you'd had a chance to know them," she said.

"At least I got to see photos, and in doing so, I see pieces of them in you. You have your father's blue eyes and your mother's blond hair."

"And my grandmother's height," Marley said.

Trey took his first bite of the food and rolled his eyes as he chewed and swallowed. "Oh, my lord, darlin'. This is delicious. Gorgeous, sexy, smart, and you make magic in the kitchen! You're my Christmas every day."

Marley resisted the urge to giggle. It was too "high school" for how she was really feeling.

"Merry Christmas to us," she said, and forked another bite.

Hours later, Marley was dressed for guests in her red slacks and a white long-sleeved blouse with a deep vee at the neckline—the perfect frame for her ladybug necklace. Her hair was down, and her black shoes with the tiny heels made little tapping noises as she walked, making it easy for Trey to keep track of her, even when he couldn't see her in the crowd.

All of the guests had arrived with their covered dishes and immediately put them on the dining table. They knew the routine. After shedding their coats and their snow boots, they began milling about, visiting with each other, sampling the little crudités Marley had put out, and catching up on the local news, while making no secret of their curiosity about the stranger in their midst.

They knew his name, because Marley had introduced him as they arrived, and all of them recognized him from the piece Farrah

Welty had done on him and Marley for TV. But they weren't sure about his place in Marley's life, and they didn't want to consider the fact that Trey Austin might take their Marley away.

Finally, Jack came out of the kitchen with serving platters full of slices of the baked ham on a rolling cart, and Wanda was right behind him with baskets of dinner rolls. They set them down in intervals through the middle of the table to make everyone serving themselves easier.

The arrival of the ham was the signal for everyone to gather.

As always, Marley sat at the head of the table, but this year, Trey sat at her right, and Jack and Wanda on her left. The other guests chose where they wanted to sit, except for Mr. Doolittle, who was already seated beside Jack.

As soon as everyone was seated, Marley stood.

"Before we give the blessing, Trey has something he wants to say to all of you. Trey, my love, the floor is yours."

Trey stood, a handsome sight in dark slacks and a soft, grey sweater.

"Thank you for such a warm welcome. I've been looking forward to meeting you, and I feel like I have a head start, because Marley has told me about all of you, and I love that she has you as family. We wanted you to know that I'm joining the "We Love Marley Bug" fan club in a permanent position. I have fallen in love with the woman who saved my life. Who knew? Right?"

There was a titter of laughter that rolled around the table, but they were still nervous about what else he had to say.

"And, I have also fallen in love with this place because it's part of who Marley is. So, while we're about to spend the rest of our lives together, we're doing it here, at Corbett Lodge. I'll be moving here permanently in the days to come, and you're gonna be stuck with me, because I'm not leaving her."

A huge cheer went up around the table, along with some sighs of relief.

"Welcome to the family," Jack said.

"Hear, hear!" the diners shouted.

Trey was beaming as he sat. This being welcomed into a family was a damn-good feeling.

Marley lifted her hand, and everyone immediately hushed.

"Thank you for that. Your acceptance was very important to Trey, and to me. Now…whose turn is it to give the blessing?"

Charlie Barrett pointed at Arnie Fitzsimmons. "It's Fitz's turn, right?"

Arnie nodded. "Please bow your heads," he said, and gave the blessing. When it ended, everyone looked up, put their napkins in their laps, and began passing bowls and dishes all around the table, laughing and talking as they went.

It was a meal like no other Trey had ever experienced. The food was often something he'd never had before, and the informality and the chatter around the table was delightful. And watching Marley keeping the conversation light and happy—while making sure everyone's drinks stayed topped off, and her continuing reminder of the array of desserts on the sideboard across the room—made him think of a general in charge of his troops.

The meal lasted two full hours, counting dessert, before they finally retired to the sitting area closest to the Christmas tree. It was time to open the presents.

Trey played Santa and picked up the presents from beneath the tree, then handed them to Marley, who delivered them to the proper recipients. Everyone had brought little things for each other, and once all of the presents had been distributed, the mass opening began. It was everyone tearing into them all at once, and exclaiming over what they'd received, and shouting out a thank-you to the gift giver.

The Jukes sisters, Gert and Mabel, had knitted scarves for everyone.

Craig, the woodcutter, gave miniature hand-carved animals to everyone.

Alvin Smith's gift was a half pint of honey from his bees.

Mr. Doolittle's gift to each of them was a little box of lemon drops.

Arnie Fitzsimmons's gift was a small bag of chestnuts apiece.

Charlie and Patsy Barrett's gift was a small box of homemade fudge apiece.

Keith Murphy, the young man who wrote code for a tech company, gave each of them a bag of peppermint candies.

Shirley Lowrey and Lawrence Atwood's gift to each were small birdhouses that Lawrence had made and Shirley had painted.

Marley's gifts were specific. A new pocketknife for Jack. A bottle of Wanda's favorite perfume. Heavy-duty gloves for Craig, the woodcutter. A turtle figurine for Alvin Smith. A packet of beef jerky each for three of the men. An old-fashioned cookbook for Shirley Lowrey. Pink ice scrapers for Patsy and Charlie Barrett, and a special book of crossword puzzles for Doolittle.

Jack and Wanda gave Trey a book about the history of Corbett Lodge. When he opened it, he held it up for Marley to see.

"Look! How cool is this?" he said.

"If you're gonna live here, you need to know all the deep, dark secrets," Jack said.

Wanda swatted Jack on the arm. "There are no deep, dark secrets to be told. You are such a mess."

Jack grinned.

Trey laughed. "I don't care. I am really looking forward to reading this! Thank you."

"And thank you for these beautiful coffee mugs," Wanda said.

In the end, it was the elder guests who were the first to leave, gathering up their gifts, their empty casserole dishes and empty bowls, and taking home their share of the leftover ham. It triggered the others to begin gathering up their things and thanking Marley for a wonderful Christmas Day, and shaking Trey's hand a dozen times with reminders to take good care of Bug.

Jack and Wanda stayed behind and helped clear the table and get the dirty dishes into the kitchen to the commercial-size dishwasher. Then Jack and Trey took down the tables and returned them to the basement, while Marley and Wanda gathered up the tablecloths and napkins and put them in to wash.

By the time everyone was gone, the great room was back in place, the wrapping paper from the gifts was in the trash, and Trey and Marley were sitting by the fire with their feet up, talking about the day.

"I had the best time," Trey said. "You have amazing friends."

She snuggled in closer. "I do, and they all fell for you."

A burning log suddenly broke in two and fell down among the embers, sending sparks flying up the chimney.

Trey glanced out the window, then pointed. "Look, honey! It's snowing."

Marley barely gave it a glance. "It does that a lot up here this time of year, but they'll keep the roads plowed. You'll still be able to get down the mountain tomorrow. It's going to be awfully quiet here after you leave."

"It won't be for long, and it won't take me as long to get back and forth because I'm driving down to the airport tomorrow and flying home. Dealing with my leasing agent is easy. I've already told him to have the paperwork ready. I have several other properties already listed with them."

"Oh yes, your rental property," she said.

"Yes. I have investments in real estate, unlike my father, who's all about the stock market, mergers, and buying up small companies and spitting out the old employees like gnawed-up bones. I've also already been in contact with movers, so as soon as I show up, they'll be ready to load up on my call. Then, as soon as they've loaded, they'll start to Colorado the next day, but I'm immediately flying back. With everything I've already set up, I should be back on the third day, and you'll be back in my arms before my stuff even arrives."

Marley sighed. "I think I can handle that long without you."

"I've never had anyone to come home to before. You're giving me roots I didn't know I was missing, but I'm so happy you did. I had no idea how wonderful it would feel to belong somewhere with someone," he said.

"Just remember you are loved," Marley said, then glanced up at his profile. He was clenching his jaw. "You're thinking about your parents, aren't you?"

He jerked, then turned his head and stared. "How did you know that?"

She ran a finger down the side of his jaw. "You looked like you were about ready to step into the ring and go ten rounds with someone."

He sighed.

"Have you spoken to them at all since the angry call?"

"No."

"Then let it go. It's up to them to make the first move, and if it's not an apology, you don't have to hear them out when they call again, unless you want to. From this day forward, we're in this together. I'll be their friend if you need me to be, or I'll be their worst enemy if they disrespect you again. Just sayin'."

"Your friends were nice to me. My parents weren't kind speaking about you, and they haven't even met you. Hell, they're not even kind to me, but I'm used to it. I just don't want you to be hurt. I won't have it," he said, holding her closer.

That night, there was a hint of desperation in the lovemaking, and when they finally rolled over into each other's arms, Trey whispered in her ear.

"Two nights apart. Back here on the third day. I promise you."

Trey left the lodge at sunup with the taste of Marley's kisses on his lips, and a little something he'd snuck out of her jewelry box. He glanced up once in the rearview mirror just before he drove out of sight of the lodge and saw her standing on the porch, watching him leave. And then, as if she knew he'd looked up, he saw her blow him a kiss. Then he drove around the curve and couldn't see her anymore.

It was a wrench to the gut. Like he'd left a piece of himself behind.

"Three days for a lifetime. Best deal ever," he muttered as he reached the main road and headed down the mountain.

While back up at the lodge, Marley was already inside, stirring the embers in the fireplace and adding a log to the fire, then turning up the thermostat. As she went about the day, everything fell back into place. The only thing missing was the man who held her heart.

But he'd be back. He promised.

Jared Bedford was sitting at a stoplight the same morning that Trey Austin drove through it, destination unknown. But Jared took it upon himself to follow him, just to see where he was going.

When he figured out the man was going to the airport, he grinned. He watched Austin park his car, then enter the terminal. He didn't know how long the man would be gone, but for the time being, Marley Corbett would be alone again. The people who worked for her at the lodge were still off work. This was the opportunity he'd been waiting for.

He went straight up to the mountain, and just as he was nearing the turnoff, he saw a pickup truck coming toward him and taking the turn into the drive.

Jared recognized Jack Wallis and cursed his luck, then turned around and went back down the mountain. So, Marley wasn't alone after all. Jack Wallis was still on the job.

Chapter 12

Unaware he was being followed, Trey reached the airport without incident and boarded on time with an empty suitcase. He was taking it so he could bring it home packed with more of his clothing and sending the rest back with the movers.

Less than two hours later, he landed at Sky Harbor International Airport in Phoenix. The sky was clear. The temperature high was sixty-three degrees.

The ride home in his cab was uneventful, but for the first time, Trey was looking at the city as if he'd never been there before and realized he missed the mountains and the trees. He was not going to be sad to leave this behind.

Once inside his house, he adjusted the thermostat, dumped his things, then sat down at the table with his laptop and phone.

The first person he contacted was Rudy Allen, his leasing agent. The phone rang twice, and then Rudy answered.

"Trey! Hello. What can I do for you?" he asked.

"I'm home. Bring the paperwork. Like all the others, yearly lease and so on, only this house will be furnished."

"Interesting. I don't have even one furnished listing. We'll see how that goes."

"If it's a deterrent, then let me know and I'll have the furniture removed and donated to Habitat for Humanity," Trey said.

"Sure. I'll need to take some pictures, get the square footage. When would be convenient for you?"

"Today. I'm only here for a couple of days, so it all has to be done before I leave," Trey said.

"Then Billie and I will be along shortly. She takes the good pictures we upload to the website," he said.

"Thank you. I'll see you soon," Trey said, and disconnected. Then he called the movers, set up a time for tomorrow morning for them to come pack his things, and then sent Marley a text.

> I'm at my house in Phoenix. The leasing agent is on the way. Movers are coming tomorrow to pack up my office. I already miss you. No little hummingbird flitting around this house. I love you. So much.

Trey hadn't even been gone for more than a few hours, and Marley was already missing him. When Jack drove up, she was pleased to hear him banging andirons and stirring embers and hauling in wood.

When he wandered into the kitchen later looking for coffee and the possibility of something to snack on, she knew he was mostly there for her company.

"Missing him, aren't you, Bug?"

Marley sighed. "Terribly. But he'll be back soon. It's just that he made such a big shift in my life that I forgot how to be alone. I'm fine. I just miss him."

Jack hugged her. "I know, sugar. If you feel the need to get out of the lodge for a bit, just say the word and I'll take you for a ride on my snowmobile."

She laughed. "So, you're offering to replace my lonesomeness for a chance to break my neck?"

He frowned. "I don't go that fast."

Marley shook her head. "That's not what Wanda says."

"Dang woman. It's not that bad," he muttered.

Marley slid a cookie across the island and blew him a kiss. "I love you anyway. I'm fine. If you're finished for the day, go home and bother Wanda."

"I'll need two cookies, for sure," he said.

She pushed the cookie bin across the island, laughing. "Help yourself, Jack Wallis."

He grinned. "Don't mind if I do," and left with a handful. "Call if you need me."

"I will," she said, then followed him to the back door and locked it after him.

As soon as he was gone, she took a cold drink and a cookie to the great room, sat down in her favorite chair, and reached for her new Chapel Hill mystery. She was beginning Chapter Two and already hooked on the mystery, trying to figure out "whodunit" when her phone dinged an incoming text. She grabbed it, saw it was Trey and read the message, then quickly replied.

> It quit snowing. Jack has come and gone with a half-dozen cookies. Wanda didn't come with him. I'm reading my new Chapel Hill book. It's riveting. You are amazing. I love you more.

Trey was smiling from ear to ear as he read her text, then opened his laptop and began contacting people in Phoenix who needed to know he was leaving, basically tying up loose ends. The sooner he got this done, the sooner he could get back to Marley. This was the first day back. As soon as Rudy left, he had an errand to run, then home to do some packing. The movers were on for tomorrow, and then Trey would be on a plane back to Colorado Springs.

He had skipped eating at the lodge before he left Colorado, so he went to see if the milk was still good in the refrigerator, and it was. He started coffee, made himself a bowl of cereal, and ate it standing up while he glanced around at the place he called home for the past eight years.

Oddly, he could already feel the separation between what had been and what was waiting. The house didn't feel like home anymore. Nothing was home without Marley.

About an hour later, the doorbell rang.

It was Rudy Allen on the doorstep with his bag of tricks, which was what he called the briefcase he carried with all the necessary paperwork, and his photographer, Billie, was packing her camera.

"Come in," Trey said. "Thanks for doing this on such short notice."

Billie smirked. "You fell for your Cinderella, didn't you? You're going back to Colorado Springs to be with her."

Trey grinned. "Just go take your pictures, sassy face. And I may have left an empty suitcase on the bedroom floor. Toss it out of the way and do your thing."

She winked. "I already got the shots I needed of the front of the house. You two go stand in the foyer for a minute and let me get some here, and then I'll be out of your way while you do business."

They complied, and as soon as she'd moved into a different area of the house, Rudy pulled out a chair at the dining table and sat, then opened his briefcase.

"So, what do you think about leaving this furnished?" Trey asked.

Rudy had already eyed the furnishings as they came in. "You have very high-end stuff here. I think this might really appeal to the right people. Some up-and-coming young professionals with little to no furniture of their own, who still want to present an impressive front when the need arises. Let's begin with leaving it furnished, and I'll let you know if we need to revise the decision. Now to add another property to your listing with us."

It didn't take long for them to get the photos taken and the paperwork signed. Rudy had been instructed to check with TLC Cleaning services to make sure they'd cleaned one more time after he cleared out his things, and then the property would be listed.

But now they were gone. Trey was here without a vehicle, and he needed to go downtown, so he called an Uber, checked to make sure he still had Marley's ring in his pocket, then began scrolling through his phone, checking out jewelry stores while he waited.

By the time the Uber arrived, he had a list of jewelry stores he wanted to visit and a specific ring design he had in mind. What he needed was to find one that fit without having to have it resized, because when he left Phoenix, he wasn't coming back.

The driver let him out. Trey approached buying jewelry the same way he bought a car. Looks. Fit. Availability. And when he walked into the first store, he went straight to a saleswoman and told her exactly what he wanted, then pulled out the ring he'd brought with him.

"I won't waste your time. If you don't have the style in this size, then we can't do business. I'm leaving town within the next day or so and don't have time to wait on it being resized."

"Understood," she said. "If you'll follow me, I'll show you what we have in oval cut, and then we'll discuss the rest."

"Rest being?" he asked as she slipped behind a counter and began pulling out trays of rings.

She smiled. "Like, what's your budget? How many carats?"

"Money is no object, but don't show me anything cheap." He pulled out Marley's ring.

She sized it.

He put it back in his pocket, and the search began.

To the saleslady's dismay, they didn't have a ring in stock that size.

"I'm so sorry. That's a very small ring size," she said. "We just don't keep many in stock."

"No problem," Trey said. "Thank you for your help," and out the door he went.

Her boss sidled up beside her. "No sale, huh?"

"We didn't have the right size. He's in a rush. And he looks familiar. Like I should have known who he was."

"I recognized him the moment he came in," her boss said. "He's Trey Austin. The man who was looking for Cinderella."

She groaned. "Oh wow… I heard he found her. I wonder if the ring is for her?"

Unaware he was the topic of a conversation, Trey went three blocks down and turned south. The next store on his list was in the middle of the block, and when he entered, he gave them the same speech.

The salesclerk this time was a man and, like Trey, wasted no time chitchatting. He pulled out trays of engagement rings with oval cuts, sized the ring Trey brought, then sorted through the stock. There were two. The first was an oval cut, one-carat diamond. The other was the same cut in a three-carat diamond.

"That one," Trey said, pointing to the three-carat.

The clerk showed him the price. Trey nodded. The clerk nodded, put all of the trays back into the display case. A short while later, Trey was out the door with the engagement ring in its box and safely in his pocket.

He paused on the street long enough to call an Uber, then waited in the coffee shop next door for it to arrive.

By nightfall, Trey was ready for the movers. He had everything unhooked and unplugged in his office, and all of his files and research books in stacks waiting to be boxed up. His clothes were all in one place in his walk-in closet, ready for the movers, and he'd packed a suitcase full to take back with him.

The movers were due here by 8:00 a.m. tomorrow, and with what little he was taking with him, it was unlikely it would take more than two or three hours to pack and load everything. He'd already asked TLC to clean out his refrigerator and pantry on their last trip to the house and realized he would just be killing time for no reason staying over another night.

Curious about later flights tomorrow, he got online and checked. When he realized there was a flight leaving at 1:45 tomorrow afternoon, he switched his ticket to an earlier flight and breathed a sigh of relief.

For some reason, he kept feeling uneasy about Marley, and the thought of her being alone at night in the lodge was unnerving.

Marley made it through the day without incident, and when night came, she set the security alarm, locked up everything, and left the Christmas lights still twinkling. The tree would stay up until after Boxing Day, which meant the little treetop angel was still on guard.

It was a fanciful thought that gave her comfort as she went back to the family area and locked herself in. She showered, then dressed in pink flannel pajamas and slippers, and meandered through the little kitchen for snacks while she watched TV.

She opted for popcorn, and while it was popping, sent Trey a text.

> I'm locked in for the night. You have spoiled me for sleeping alone again. However, I have pink flannel pj's to keep me warm instead of being wrapped in your arms, so I will survive.
> Love you,
> Me

Then she took her popcorn to the sofa, turned on the TV, and settled in to watch a movie from the 1940s called *It's a Wonderful Life*. Another holiday tradition she didn't want to let pass.

"'Every time a bell rings, an angel gets his wings,'" Marley said, and snuggled down to watch.

Trey found the text after he got out of the shower. He read it with a mixture of humor and regret. He would so love to replace those pink pj's.

> I will happily remove those pj's for you when I get back. Things are moving faster than I expected, so as soon as the movers leave tomorrow morning, I'll be on a flight back to you. It takes off at 1:45 p.m. You'll be in my arms tomorrow night. I promise.
> Love you so much.
> T.

Marley was right in the middle of a sad part of the movie when she got a text back. She beamed when she read it, and quickly replied.

> The best news ever! Safe travels.

She was getting ready to hit Send when she heard a voice.

Tell him not to linger. It will matter.

A shiver ran up the back of her neck as she read it. What did that mean? But she knew better than to ignore it, and added it to the text.

> Also, my angels just told me to tell you, "Don't linger. It will matter." I have no idea what that means, but it's your message, not mine. Love you forever. See you soon.

Then she finished her movie, put the popcorn bowl in the sink, and went to bed, thinking of his homecoming.

When Trey read her response, he got goose bumps. Maybe this had to do with his uneasiness about her being there alone? Or... Then he stopped himself. *Don't create trouble when there's none to be had.*

Jared Bedford had just slipped a couple of twenties out of the till while his boss was locking up. But when he went to clock out, his boss gave him a pink slip instead.

"What the hell?" Jared asked.

"I've got you on video with your hand in the till. Hand over the forty bucks you took, or I'm calling the cops."

Jared's heart skipped. He pulled out the two twenties without an ounce of guilt, just angry at being caught.

"Damn it, boss. You kept telling me you were gonna give me a raise. A man's got a right to live."

"I never said you were getting a raise. You just kept asking for one, and I've been coming up short in that till for months. You come in late for work at least once a week. You are undependable, and you are a thief. Get out, and don't show your face here again."

Jared hunched his shoulders and strode out of the garage, but instead of going home, he went straight to a bar and got drunk. It was just after two in the morning when he finally staggered back to his car.

He slid into the driver's seat, leaned over the steering wheel until his head stopped spinning, then started the engine and drove out of the parking lot. He wanted payback. He wanted retribution. But he was afraid of his boss.

The only person he could think of who was too little to fight back was Marley Corbett.

He made a U-turn at a street corner, drove out of the city and up the mountain. When he got to the turnoff for the lodge, he slowed down to a crawl to keep it quiet. But he was drunk enough that he forgot about the security cameras and motion detectors until he drove into the parking area and was blinded by the lights.

"Damn it," Jared mumbled, then made another U-turn and drove back out the same way he'd come in. He paused at her mailbox and got out to pee, but he didn't go back to the city. Instead, he drove up to the lay-by again, then parked and fell asleep.

He woke just before daylight needing to pee, and with the hangover from hell. He got out to relieve himself and then thought of Marley Corbett again and took off walking into the woods, using the trees to hide his presence. He didn't have a plan. He was just trolling for trouble to see what he could see.

He knew the general direction of the lodge, but he didn't have a flashlight and kept walking into tree limbs and brush. Again, it was the security lights that led him to her property, but when he saw the lodge looming in the distance, short of breaking in a door and alerting the police when the security alarm went off, he didn't know how he was going to get in.

It was so damn cold, and he was freezing. He huddled down next to the side of the lodge out of the wind and waited for daylight—and dozed off.

Trey's sleep was restless. He woke up before his alarm. Then, when the movers arrived early, it felt like a sign that he must not miss that flight.

They came inside the house carrying box flats and quickly taped up the bottoms and started packing in his office, filling the boxes with research books and then carefully packing more fragile things. They had heavy boxes for computers and the printer and the television. They wrapped his office chair and file cabinets and, as soon as they'd finished with the office, headed to his bedroom.

"The furniture is staying," Trey said. "But everything inside every drawer needs to be packed, and all of the clothes in my closet and the things in the drawers in my bathroom."

"Any other personal effects going? Pictures on the wall? Any art in the house you want to take?" one of them asked.

"No," Trey said.

"The cookware and dishes stay, too?" the mover asked.

"Yes. The house will be leased as furnished property."

"All right, then. We'll finish up here in a bit."

"Awesome," Trey said.

They'd come early and were working quicker than he'd expected. He was going to have all kinds of time to make that flight.

Marley slept without dreaming and woke just before 7:00 a.m., excited that Trey was coming home today. It dawned on her as she was dressing that neither she nor Jack had checked the mailbox yesterday, so she started the coffee, traded her shoes for snow boots, then grabbed her coat and gloves and headed out the front door.

It was bitterly cold, but the sky was clear, the sun was up, and the snow was crunching beneath her boots as she started down the driveway to the mailbox at the main road.

Jared Bedford had been awake for a while, certain he was on the verge of frostbite, when he heard a door slam.

He scrambled to his feet just as Marley Corbett walked out the front entrance. As soon as she walked out of sight, he celebrated his stroke of good luck by making a mad dash for the front door, taking care not to get caught on camera.

But the moment he started to walk inside, he realized he was covered in snow. And she'd know the moment she came back and saw all the drips and tracks on the floor, that someone had come inside.

He needed the element of surprise to make sure she didn't have time to go for that shotgun she said she had. So, he took off his shoes, stripped down to his underwear on the porch, and the moment he got inside, made a run for the attic door at the end of the long hallway.

The door was unlocked, so he flipped the light switch on and took off up the stairs on the run, exiting into the attic. The warmth from the chimney that ran up the east wall was a godsend. He dumped his clothes, made another mad dash down to the kitchen, and grabbed a loaf of bread, a package of cold cuts, and two cans of pop from the fridge, and ran back to the attic.

He shook the snow from his clothes and got dressed. He was leaning against the warm bricks and eating his second sandwich when he heard a door slam.

She was back!

But he knew better than to jump the gun. He had a good hiding place, and Jack Wallis was likely to show up unannounced again, so he would bide his time until he knew for certain Marley was alone. In the meantime, he indulged his own fantasies, imagining what they would do, and how she would succumb to his charms after he showed her what a real man was all about.

Marley felt good to be out and was taking in the scenery and the tiny footprints of animals left behind in the snow as she went. She could hear a few cars coming down the mountain—likely people who worked in the city already on their way to work, but by the time she reached the road, it was clear both ways. She gathered the mail from the box and started back up the driveway, but the sun was behind her now, and she was seeing other tracks in the snow that she hadn't seen before. Human tracks with treads from running shoes, not the boot tracks Jack would have left.

It put her on alert, and then she told herself to calm down. It could be anything from a driver having car trouble to someone stopping to change a flat tire. It didn't have to mean anything, although now that she was a bit wary, she hastened her steps as she headed back to the lodge. She didn't rest easy until she was safely inside, but the moment she locked the door behind her, she realized it had been unlocked the entire time she'd been gone.

She turned around to face the lobby, looking past the Christmas tree to the great room, and then stared down at the floors, looking for wet footprints, but there were none. She sighed, chiding herself for being silly, and carried the mail into the kitchen and sorted it as she was having coffee and cereal.

Unaware of the danger that had invaded her home, Marley laid aside the bills to pay and trashed the junk mail. She wanted to make something special for Trey's homecoming and decided on cinnamon apple hand pies.

She headed for the basement to get a couple of quarts of canned apples and, as she did, thought she heard a floor creak from somewhere up above, but then Jack came in the back, and she chalked it up to him and his noise and forgot about it.

"Bug! I'm here. Where are you?" he shouted.

"Just about to go down to the basement," she said.

He came down the hall at a trot. "What do you need? I'll get it."

"Two quarts of canned apples."

"On it," he said, and gave her a quick hug before heading to the elevator.

Grateful for the help, she returned to the kitchen, finished the pie crust, and put it in the refrigerator to be rolled out later.

Jack came back and set the jars of apples on the counter. "What are we making?"

The interest in his voice was a sign he was hoping for a sample.

"Cinnamon apple hand pies. Trey is coming home a day early. He's catching an early afternoon flight today."

"Good news! Might there be a hand pie done before I leave?" he asked.

She laughed. "There might be, if you drag out your jobs and I hurry with mine."

"I think we can make that happen. Oh...Wanda will be along later. She's in town right now, but said she would stop by before heading home. I'm going to do the fireplace first, then carry in more wood. It's also time to change the filters in the central heating system, so I'll be banging around a bit in the basement again." Then he stood long enough to watch her emptying the apples into a pan and adding cinnamon, cloves, and sugar before he left her on her own.

An hour passed before Marley had the filling cool enough to use and got the crust out and began rolling it out. She was cutting out circles of crust when she heard the lodge phone ringing and grabbed a towel to wipe her hands, then answered the extension on the kitchen wall.

"Corbett Lodge."

"This is Quinn Jones. I'm a journalist with *USA Today*. May I speak to Marley Corbett?"

"This is Marley."

"Miss Corbett, it is a pleasure to speak with you. The reason I'm calling is that we would like to do a story about your role in saving the heir to Austin Enterprises. We can do the interview over the phone or via Zoom. And we'd like—"

"I'm sorry, but we've given out the only interview we are going to give on the subject. Thank you for calling," she said, and hung up, even as he was still trying to convince her. "Lord...what a way to denigrate an existence! Just skin it all down to the importance of social standing, instead of a life. Saved the heir, my ass. Wait until Trey hears that," she mumbled, and went back to the pie crust.

It was just before eleven when Marley finally got all of the hand pies in the oven, and Jack was still moving wood from the big woodpile to the back porch. The tractor had been stubborn about starting, mostly because of the cold, and he'd had to jump the battery before he could use it, so he was already behind his work schedule.

A short while later, Wanda arrived, drove around to the back of the lodge, and went inside to wait for Jack.

"He's just now hauling wood," Wanda said as she entered the kitchen.

Marley was cleaning up after the baking as Wanda hung her coat on the back of a kitchen chair. "Tractor wouldn't start. He said it was because of the cold."

"Then I'll get the dust mop after that flour on the floor. What yummy thing did you just make?" Wanda asked.

"I made apple hand pies. Trey is coming back this afternoon, and Jack is dithering, hoping they get done before he leaves."

"Of course he is," Wanda said, and went to get the cleaning equipment.

A short while later, everything had been swept up, cleaned up, and put away. Wanda and Marley were sitting at the table, going over canapé recipes to make for the New Year's Eve party, when Jack came into the kitchen. He headed straight for Wanda and gave her a hug and a kiss.

"Did you miss me?" he asked.

"Always," she said. "What's next on your list? I can help."

"Changing the filters in the HVAC system. It's cold in the basement. You don't need to be down there."

"I don't mind. The sooner you get done, the sooner we can go home."

He sputtered. "I was hoping to get a hand pie before I leave."

Wanda giggled. "I know. I was just teasing you. You go do your thing. I'm going to go home. The pies won't be done for a while, and Marley doesn't need me to watch them bake."

Jared Bedford was leaning against the brick chimney and finishing off the last of the lunch meat he'd filched, curiously eyeing the items stored all around him while listening to the little he could hear of what was going on downstairs.

He knew Jack Wallis was still on the premises because he'd heard the tractor making trips back and forth to the lodge. And when he heard another car arriving, he cursed.

"Freaking family reunion," he muttered. He lay back down on a mattress that had been leaning up against a wall, rolled up in the quilt that had been covering it, and fell asleep. It was a long time until dark. Plenty of time to get a little rest before the party he had planned for her.

He was sound asleep when Marley's pies came out of the oven and when Jack Wallis finally left the premises.

And Marley was downstairs by the fire, back to reading her book with one eye on the clock. When she heard the clock in the hall strike twice, she knew Trey was already in the air and headed her way.

She was getting sleepy, but didn't want to fall asleep, so she went to the office and worked on the books for a while. The next time she looked up, it was a quarter to four. Her heart skipped. Trey should have landed by now! Maybe he was already on his way to the lodge.

She got up, made a quick trip to wash up and brush her hair, then left the family area. As she did, she glanced down the hall and noticed the light switch by the attic door was in the on position. Jack and Trey must have left it on when they moved the bedroom stuff up before he left.

She jogged down to flip it off, and the moment she did, she heard a curse and then a resounding number of thumps, bumps, and curses—like someone had fallen down the stairs.

Horrified that Jack must have come back and she didn't know it, she quickly flipped the switch on, opened the door, and saw a man crumped at the foot of the stairs.

But it wasn't Jack. It was Jared Bedford! And he was already crawling to his feet and spewing filth about what he was going to do to her.

She slammed the door in his face, turned the lock and flipped the light back off, and turned and ran—back up the hall, past the great room, through the lobby, and out into the cold.

Jared was still cursing the ground she walked on when he finally found the doorknob in the dark, only to realize she'd locked the door and there was no way to unlock it from inside. He kicked the door with all the force in him, screaming from the pain as he did. The door swung open and he burst out into the light, just in time to see Marley going out the front door on the run.

He took off after her, in so much pain he could hardly breathe. He was pretty sure his nose was broken. It was bleeding, and so was his lip. His ankle was throbbing, and his left shoulder felt like it was out of place, but he couldn't let her get away.

Chapter 13

Trey's plane landed at a quarter to four, and the moment they began to disembark, he remembered the message he'd been given. *Don't linger. It will matter.*

He had his suitcase in his hand as he headed for the parking lot to retrieve his car. He hit the remote to unlock it, then opened the back to stow his luggage. Then without thinking, he picked up the crowbar lying near the wheel well and took it with him as he got in. He put it in the front seat and buckled up.

It wasn't until he started the engine that he saw the crowbar in the seat beside him and realized what he'd done, and wondered why.

Don't linger. Don't linger.

He drove out of the airport parking lot, through the city, and then headed up the mountain. He hadn't stopped to even let Marley know that he'd landed, or to check and see if there was anything she needed from the city.

Don't linger. Don't linger.

The closer he got to the turnoff, the more tense he became. It was like watching a storm gathering, waiting to see what trouble it might create. And then he saw the sign to the lodge and gripped the steering wheel even tighter as he took the turn without slowing down.

His car fishtailed a little on the icy surface before it straightened out. All he needed was to see her smiling face and know all this nonsense he'd created in his mind was nothing more than another scene from a story he had yet to write.

He came around the curve, saw the lodge straight ahead, and then his heart stopped. Marley was coming down the steps, her mouth open in a scream he had yet to hear.

He slammed on the brakes to keep from hitting her, and when he saw a man come running out of the lodge behind her, obviously enraged and dripping blood, he grabbed the crowbar and got out just as Marley ran into his arms.

"Get in the car and lock the doors," he said, and then bounded toward the man in long, angry strides and stopped in front of him, giving Marley time to get inside.

Jared was beyond rational thought, and when he saw her man getting out of the car, he roared and came at him with his hands fisted.

Trey didn't back up. He didn't duck. He didn't flinch. He just swung the crowbar as hard as he could at the man's knees.

The crack as bones crumbled under the impact was not unlike the sound of a piece of firewood being split apart.

One second Jared Bedford was all rage and payback, and the next he was writhing on the ground, flat on his back in the snow.

"You killed me! You killed me!" he screamed.

"Not yet, I haven't," Trey said. "But that possibility still exists. Shut the hell up, and don't move."

He looked back at his car. Marley was sitting in the driver's seat on his phone. He knew she was calling the police.

"They'll need an ambulance, too," he shouted.

Marley nodded and kept talking, while Trey watched blood seeping into the snow beneath where the man was lying.

Trey needed to know what happened. He needed to hear Marley's words, telling him she hadn't been hurt. But all he had to hold on to at this moment was the angel message that had saved Marley's life.

Don't linger. It will matter.

Within a few minutes, he began hearing sirens, and then police cars came flying up the drive with an ambulance behind them. They got out of their cruisers with their hands on their weapons.

"Intruder is down," Trey said, and handed them his crowbar. "I'm gonna need that back when you're done with it."

"What happened here?" an officer asked.

"I'm not real sure. I drove up just as Marley came running out of the lodge, screaming for her life. This man was right behind her, bloody and screaming at her in a rage. I stopped him. Whatever happened between them, you'll have to ask her," he said, and then opened the door to his car.

Marley climbed out shaking and crying.

"I've got you, baby. I've got you," Trey said as he picked her up in his arms and carried her inside the lodge, then sat down with her.

An officer followed them. "Miss Corbett…Marley… I'm Officer Dewitt. What happened here? Where did this man come from, and do you know him?"

After that, Marley began to explain everything, beginning with Jared Bedford approaching her in the supermarket and putting his hands all over her, and when she'd objected loudly, he'd laughed and said he knew her daddy was dead and she was all alone.

She explained about him stalking her when she was in town, and then her walking to the mailbox this morning and guessing he slipped into the lodge while she was gone. Then she explained how she discovered he was hiding in the lodge.

"I thought someone had just accidentally left the light on in the attic, and without thinking, I flipped it off. Seconds later, I hear a huge amount of thumping and bumping and cursing. It scared me to death, thinking Jack must have come back and I hadn't known it, and now he'd fallen down the stairs because I turned off the light. I was in a panic when I opened the door, but it wasn't Jack. It was Jared Bedford, cursing me, telling me what he was going to do to me. I slammed the door shut, turned the lock and turned the light back off, and ran. I heard a loud crash, and then footsteps running behind me. He was already bloody and furious from falling down the stairs. I knew what would happen if he caught me. Trey's appearance was a miracle. He'd just gotten off a flight from Phoenix. I knew his flight had probably landed, but feared he would be too late to save me. Only he wasn't."

She took a slow, shuddering breath, clutching Trey's arms as he held her even closer.

"Where exactly is this attic?" Officer Dewitt asked.

Trey pointed down the hall, where the broken door was standing ajar. "Jack and I were just up there a couple of days ago. Marley, honey, will you be okay for a bit? I won't be long."

She nodded. "I called Jack and Wanda. They'll be here any minute." Then she explained who they were to Dewitt. "Jack and Wanda Wallis are like parents to me. They've worked here for years. When they get here, please let them through."

Dewitt nodded, radioed the officers still outside, and then stood. "After you, Mr. Austin."

"Call me Trey," he said, gave Marley a quick glance and then took Dewitt up to the attic. It was easy to see the bloodstains on the stairs and on the walls where Bedford was grabbing for air as he fell.

"Sidestep the bloodstains. The techs from the crime lab will be here to gather evidence," Dewitt said, so they took care to miss them as they went up.

The first thing they saw was a mattress on the floor by the chimney, and a quilt wadded up on top of it.

"Wow. Looks like he'd been up here a while," Dewitt said, seeing the empty bread wrapper, pop cans, and the container the lunch meat had been in.

Trey pointed at the mattress and quilt on the floor. "About three days ago, that mattress was leaning against the wall over there and covered with that quilt. It's part of the bedroom suite Jack and

I brought up. The son of a bitch just made himself at home while waiting for everyone to leave," he muttered.

"Okay for now," Dewitt said. "I'll get the techs up here later to gather evidence and take pictures. Might need it for trial if he doesn't man up and cop to what he did. I saw security cameras outside. We'll be needing copies of the footage."

"The system is in her office. One of your techs can retrieve what they want from it," Trey said.

They went back downstairs to find Jack and Wanda had arrived. Marley was filling them in on what happened as Trey sat down beside her. When she leaned her head against his shoulder, he put his arm around her. The rage on his face was for what she'd endured and what he'd seen in the attic, but his voice was soft, and his touch was gentle as he pulled her close.

"Are you still cold, sweetheart?"

"I can't quit shaking, but it's not from cold," she said.

Trey took the afghan blanket from the back of the sofa and wrapped her up in it, then pulled her onto his lap. "It's shock from the adrenaline rush. Better?" he asked.

She nodded.

Jack was livid. "I know who he is. I can't believe he laughed because Dan and Lisa are dead. She told me about him manhandling her in the supermarket. I could have ended it before this could happen, but Marley told me to let it go. The deal is, he was part of the reno crew while she was gone. He had plenty of time to see the whole layout of the lodge, including a hiding place," Jack said.

Marley shuddered. "I just thought he was being a jerk, and angry because I rejected his advances. I didn't know he was a bubble off plumb."

Trey grinned. "A bubble off plumb?"

"'Crazy off his rocker' sound better?" Marley asked.

"Fits better, that's for damn sure," Jack said.

"Well, the attic door and the door into the family quarters

are always locked when the lodge is up and running, so there's no danger of this being repeated. And we lock the lodge after midnight every night and unlock it by 6:00 a.m., or earlier if a guest has an earlier flight," Wanda said. "Is there anything we can do? Anything that needs cleaning up?"

"We don't do anything until the police are through here. Officer Dewitt said something about techs from a crime lab on the way, so we don't go in the attic until they've taken pictures and collected evidence, but you're going to need a new door," Trey said.

Jack nodded. "Easy enough," he said, then glanced at Trey as if he'd never seen him before. "Bug said you took him out at the knees."

Trey nodded.

"With a crowbar?" Jack added.

"They cracked like treefall in the woods. He'll never walk right or pain-free again, and it's more than he deserves," Trey muttered.

"Damn, boy. There's more to you than meets the eye," Jack said. "Listen, Wanda and I are going to drive into the city and pick up some food for you. Is pizza okay?"

Marley was still shivering. "It's fine, but you don't need to—"

"Yes, we do," Wanda said. "Sometimes when you can't fix the awful, terrible, frightening things life hands you, a little food goes a long way in resetting your clock. We won't be long. Trey, just take care of our girl until we get back."

"She's my girl, too, and I plan to spend the rest of my life making sure shit like this never happens to her again," he said.

After they were gone, Marley broke into sobs. "I thought I would die. You promised you'd be back, and you came. You saved me."

He held her closer, hugging her tighter, as if love alone could put her back to the way she was before—before a psycho destroyed her sense of safety.

"No, baby, I'm not the hero. I just followed the blueprint the angels gave me. *Don't linger. It will matter.* I thought about it constantly after you told me. I thought about it when the movers came early, like they were helping make sure I didn't miss that flight. And then the plane had a good tailwind and we arrived about fifteen minutes earlier than scheduled. It's what I was thinking about when I put my suitcase in the Land Rover, and looking back, I guess it's why I picked up that crowbar lying by the wheel well and put it in the front seat with me. After I got in the car and saw it, I wondered why *did* I do that? Because it was going to matter. Your angels used me to save you, and I will never doubt their presence again."

She was still crying when she turned her face against Trey's chest and cried herself to sleep. She was still sleeping when Jack and Wanda returned. They left the pizza in the kitchen, blew them a kiss, and slipped out.

The police were still outside, but it was dark when the techs arrived. Dewitt took them to the attic, and to Marley's office to get the security footage, and then came back to fill Trey in on what was happening.

"Jared Bedford is in surgery. He'll be released to a prison facility for further care. After that, he'll go through arraignment and back to jail, unless he pleads out to a judge, which means serving his time without a trial. We found his car parked up the mountain in a lay-by. Our men followed his tracks all the way from the car to the lodge and then found where he sheltered until he took advantage of the unlocked door and slipped inside. He planned this. It was sloppy, but he planned it. Just know that there's not a lawyer in the state who could get him off of this rap."

"Thanks for the update," Trey said.

Dewitt nodded and went back to the attic. It was the bumping and thumping Marley heard that woke her. She sat up with a jerk.

"What's happening? Who's upstairs?"

"Techs from the crime lab. They'll all be gone soon. Why don't you go wash the tears off that pretty face? There's cold pizza in the kitchen."

She wrapped her arms around his neck and kissed him until his heart was pounding, and then she got up and disappeared into the family quarters.

Dewitt and the crew from the crime lab were gone by the time Marley came out. Trey brought in the suitcase he'd left in the car, then locked the door to the lodge when he came inside.

The security lights were on outside, and Marley would set the alarm before they went to bed. Right now, he was concerned about getting some food in her so she could take some pain relievers. She'd cried so hard for so long that she'd almost made herself sick.

"My head is pounding," she said as she downed a couple of over-the-counter pain relievers. "But probably not as much as Jared Bedford's knees. You have a really good swing. Did you ever play ball?"

He nodded as he was making them something to drink. "At the boarding school and on an intramural team in college...for the fun of it, in between writing stories."

"You wrote while you were in college?" she asked as Trey handed her a plate and then opened the pizza box.

He nodded. "I wrote the first two Chapel Hill books while I was still in college, but didn't try to sell anything until I met my agent, Meredith Bernstein, at a creative writing class my junior year. Apparently, the instructor had mentioned my name as a promising writer. She asked me to send her something. I did, and the rest is history. Now, I write a book every nine months, and they release a new one every nine months, as well."

"So, you're always a book ahead?" she asked.

"Sometimes two ahead, if the story comes easy. Others I can struggle with a bit." He scanned the pizza, then took pains to pick out just the right piece.

Marley laughed. "Are you looking for the biggest one?"

"No. Looking for the one with the least number of black olives."

"Another facet of you that I am filing away. Now I know you don't like matcha tea or black olives."

"Truth, but I do like making love to you. Immensely so, in fact."

"My sweet-talkin' man," she said. "It's mutual." She quickly polished off the piece of pizza and went for one more. But she'd barely taken a bite before her eyes welled.

He was immediately concerned and reached for her hand. "Baby, talk to me."

She shook her head. "I'm okay. It was just a momentary flash of what-if. All I'm saying is I am so grateful I lived to have a life with you. Are there any packets of red pepper flakes?"

He pointed to the condiments in a little pile off to the side. "Pepper flakes. Parmesan cheese. Salt and pepper."

She tore open a packet of the pepper flakes and sprinkled a few lightly on her slice, then took another bite and gave him a thumbs-up as she ate.

He got up once to refill their drinks. They finished what they wanted, then put the leftovers in a smaller container and the pizza box in the trash. Marley was putting their plates in the dishwasher when the lodge phone rang.

She frowned at the time, then wiped her hands and went to answer.

"Corbett Lodge. This is Marley."

"Marley, this is Farrah Welty. We just learned of the attempted assault and were wondering if—"

"No," she said. "Get the police report," and she hung up.

"Who the hell was that?" Trey asked.

"Farrah Welty."

Trey frowned. "They never quit, do they?"

That's when she remembered the call from *USA Today*. "Oh, while you were gone, some reporter from *USA Today* called, wanting to interview me. Let me think… How did they preface that request? Oh yes… They wanted an interview with the woman who'd saved the life of the heir to Austin Enterprises. Of course, I said no, and then told him if he wanted information to watch the interview we'd already given, and hung up. Can you believe that angle they were going to take? It wasn't you that mattered. It was who you were related to. Just so you know, I am insulted on your behalf."

Trey was shocked and then silent. It took him a moment to get his emotions in check.

"And now you know why I never wanted anyone to know I was Chapel Hill. In the eyes of the world, the public would have assumed I got published because of my family connections. Publicly, I still don't matter. Only the name holds the power."

"What's going to happen when they finally do find out?" she asked.

He frowned as he considered that. "Honestly, I think my record and books will stand on their own now. I sold my books to publishers without being an Austin. Chapel Hill became famous without being an Austin. And now, hopefully, I'll be the Austin rebel who said no to my dad's massive combine—the one that eats other little businesses alive."

"Proud of you, love, and everything you stand for. And I feel like I've been run through the proverbial wringer. I need to soak in the tub until I feel cleansed from this day and then crawl into bed beside you."

"I can make that happen for you, but first, show me how to set the security alarm. I am no longer a guest in this place. This is home."

While Marley was in the tub, Trey slipped the ring he'd borrowed back into her jewelry box, then unpacked the suitcase he'd brought with him, tucking away the ring he'd bought for her at the back of a drawer behind a stack of T-shirts.

He showered and shaved while she was in her soaking tub, enveloped in lilac-scented bath salts and admiring the view of his soapy back and how the water ran in rivulets down his long, lanky body.

But she was moving on autopilot by the time Trey got her into bed.

"I'm so tired, and I don't know why," she said.

"It's the aftereffects of a huge adrenaline surge. You were running for your life when I drove up. Rest easy now, darlin'. It's all good."

She rolled over onto her side as he slipped in behind her, spooned her up against him, and kissed the lilac-scented spot just behind her ear.

"Love you forever," he whispered.

Marley heard the words and felt his breath on the back of her neck as she was falling into the void.

"And a day," she mumbled.

He smiled. She didn't forget a thing. Forever and a day was the bargain, and he was a man of his word.

When they woke the next morning, they soon discovered they were the lead story on all of the local TV stations, and when Jack and Wanda arrived later with a copy of the local paper, and a new door and doorknob set, the incident was the headline.

LOCAL CINDERELLA ESCAPES ATTEMPTED PREDATOR ASSAULT

She took one look at it and handed it to Trey. "I don't even want to read it. God only knows what they wrote."

Wanda sighed. "It was right along the lines of what you told us, Bug, and Trey is now 'the hero' for saving you."

"They sure tore through Jared Bedford's reputation…or what's left of it," Jack added. "Something we didn't know before. Jared got fired for stealing from his boss the day before he came after you. Sounds like he was just pissed at the world and decided you were an easy target to take it out on."

Marley frowned. "No. He's been a creep for as long as I've known him. I heard every word of what he said he was going to do to me. If Trey hadn't come home a day early, you all would be combing the woods today looking for my body."

Trey shuddered. "Sweet lord, Marley. Don't."

She put the palm of her hand on his chest. "Truth is truth. You acknowledged my part in keeping you alive. Don't ever discount what you did for me."

He took a deep breath. "Understood. Now, what needs to be done today?"

"I need to verify that the commercial cleaning service is coming tomorrow. They come weekly when the lodge is open, but they haven't been here since the renovation was finished," she said.

"What do you want me to do, Bug?" Wanda asked.

"Would you do an inventory of the stores and the pantry for me? I started a running list a few days ago, and you know what we need. The first overnight guests will be partygoers here for New Year's Eve. New Year's Day is when regular guests with reservations begin again."

"Are our sous-chefs back on schedule then, too?" Wanda asked.

"And the housekeepers?" Jack added.

Marley nodded. "Nobody moved. Nobody quit. I've already heard from all of them. Everybody is coming back."

"Is there anything I can help with?" Trey asked.

She smiled. "My dear knight in shining armor. You have your own agenda already. Just watch for those movers who are due with your stuff, then when they're gone, have fun setting up the best office ever in your new space, because that's where you shine. I promised you peace and quiet to do your work, and there's no such thing out here when we're back up and running. So, take advantage of the lull before the storm."

"Sounds like a plan, and we'll weather this media storm just like we did before. One of these days, we'll be old news and life will find its own level again," Trey said.

"Lord, I hope," Marley said.

Suddenly, Jack interrupted the conversation. "I hear a truck."

"Hopefully it's the movers," Trey said, and left the kitchen with Jack right behind him.

"That's one way to get Jack out of my hair. I'm off to the pantry and then I'll be down in the basement for a bit," Wanda said.

"I'm going to the office to confirm cleaners and florists, and then I'll come help you," Marley added.

Within moments, the only thing left in the kitchen was the newspaper, and it was already old news.

Chapter 14

Anders and Gloria were back in New York City. After missing a flight connection, it had taken an extra day for them to get home, and today they'd finally awakened in their own bed.

Anders immediately got up and headed for the shower, while Gloria buzzed the kitchen and asked for coffee to be brought to their suite. She'd long since gotten over the luxury of having what she called "help," and now took it for granted.

Anders was still in the bathroom, and she'd propped herself up with all the pillows and was watching TV when there was a knock at the door.

"Come in," she called, and then pointed to the table near their sitting area. "Just put it there," she said.

The maid nodded. "Yes, ma'am. Chef wants to know if you'll be having breakfast."

Gloria glanced at the clock. It was already almost 9:00 a.m. "Tell him we'll be down for brunch in about an hour."

"Yes, ma'am. Thank you, ma'am," the maid said, and slipped out, quietly closing the door behind her.

Gloria got up, poured herself a cup of coffee, stirred in all the extras she enjoyed, and sat down to continue watching the morning news. She was absently scrolling through her phone with the TV in the background when she heard a name mentioned with the lead-in to the next story, glanced up in shock, and saw Trey's face flash on the screen, and then it went to commercial.

She ran across the room and knocked on the bathroom door. "Anders! Anders! Come quick! Something about Trey is on the news!"

Anders came flying out of the bathroom wearing nothing but the towel wrapped around his waist. Half his face was shaved. The other half was not.

"What's happened?" he asked.

"I don't know. It was the lead-in to the next story and then they broke for commercial."

"Damn it, what now?" Anders said, and plopped down beside Gloria, poured himself a cup of coffee, and waited with her.

Moments later, the newscast resumed, and the news anchor began the story, starting with a few comments about the Search for Cinderella man, and then went into the immediate story, of how he'd just repaid the favor by saving Marley Corbett's life.

Gloria gasped, and even Anders was shocked at the thought of a psychopath hiding in an attic, waiting for a chance to strike.

"Oh, Anders, she was alone! Can you imagine how horrifying that must have been?" Gloria said.

Anders shook his head, but he was thinking about the fact that Trey had given up his home in Phoenix to go live with this woman. He'd promised Gloria he wouldn't make a scene, but he was even more convinced now that he needed to meet this woman face-to-face and talk to Trey. He knew they didn't have to like it. He knew it was none of his business. But Trey Austin's business, whatever it was, could rub off on him, and Anders hadn't spent his whole life chasing the almighty dollar just to have his good name slandered in any way.

"We have to go there," he said.

Unaware of what he was thinking, Gloria agreed. "Yes, I'll call Trey shortly and see if they'll talk to us."

Anders stood abruptly, then grabbed the towel to keep it from falling off. "I'm not about to beg an invitation. I'm flying there today."

"But what about tickets? We might not be able to get a flight at such short notice," Gloria said.

"I don't need tickets for the company jet. I'm calling the pilot. Even if it's a hit-and-run visit, I'm still going," he said, and went to finish shaving.

Gloria sighed and went to get dressed. So much for brunch. They may not be welcomed, but she needed to be there, if for no other reason than to make sure Anders didn't get into a fight with his own son. That would certainly wind up as news they didn't need.

The moving van was gone, and Trey and Jack were in the family quarters setting up his office.

Wanda and Marley had finished the order list and inventory and were now in the primary bedroom putting up Trey's clothes. Every so often Wanda would notice Marley pause and run her hand lightly down the fabric of one of his jackets or straighten the collar on a shirt.

"It's a woman thing," Wanda said.

Marley blinked. "What's a woman thing?"

"Taking pleasure in the sight of your man's clothes hanging next to yours. Knowing you are now responsible for the welfare of each other, and doing it out of love," Wanda said.

Marley's eyes welled. "That's so beautiful, Wanda. I never thought of it like that. I do love him so much."

Wanda hugged her. "We know, Bug. And the best part is how much he loves you back."

Marley sighed. "Who knew a search for a chocolate gravy recipe would lead me to the love of my life?"

Wanda burst out laughing, which made Marley giggle.

Trey and Jack were down the hall in the office when they heard the laughter. "Something was sure funny," Jack said.

Trey set down the printer he'd just unboxed. "Five dollars it was something Marley said."

Jack grinned. "You're on!" he said, and bolted out of the office and up the hall into the bedroom. "Okay, you girls are having way too much fun! What's going on?"

Wanda frowned. "Nosy britches. Can't we have a girlie moment without an audience?"

"Oh, it was nothing," Marley said. "I just made a comment about the irony of how Trey and I met."

Jack glanced at Trey and the grin on his face, knowing he was about to lose that bet.

"What did you say?" Trey asked.

"I just said, 'Who knew a search for a chocolate gravy recipe would lead me to the love of my life?'"

"Dang it," Jack muttered, and fished a five-dollar bill out of his wallet and slapped it in Trey's outstretched hand.

"What's going on?" Marley asked.

"When we heard the laughter, I bet Jack five dollars that it was because of something you said, and he just lost the bet," Trey said, and then put the five dollars into Marley's hip pocket and kissed her. "And thanks to the both of you for unpacking my clothes."

Marley patted her pocket and blew him a kiss. "We've actually finished. We keep the luggage in the attic, but I'm not ready to go up there just yet."

"We'll go," Wanda said, and grabbed one bag, while Jack picked up the other two and left.

Trey couldn't bear the haunted look in Marley's eyes. Without saying a word, he just wrapped his arms around her and held her.

Marley locked her hands around his waist and held on as if she was about to blow away. He'd become the anchor she hadn't known she needed.

"I am so glad you love me," she whispered.

He sighed. "Ah, my daring, darling Cinderella… You gave me no choice."

Wanda and Jack left for the day, with a caution to call if anything came up that Marley needed help with, and finally, Trey and Marley were alone. He'd finished setting up his office, and Marley was in the family quarters with him, curled up on the sofa with her book.

It was nearing two in the afternoon when someone began ringing the doorbell at the entrance to the lodge.

Marley sighed, put a marker in her book, and called out to Trey. "Be right back. Someone ringing the doorbell."

He bolted out of the office and followed her partway, just to make sure there were no ugly surprises at the door. Then he caught a glimpse of the man standing just outside the entrance and frowned.

"You just couldn't let it alone, could you?" he muttered, and lengthened his stride to catch up.

Marley saw the well-dressed couple standing on the porch and first assumed they were guests hoping for a room without a reservation.

She opened the door. "I'm sorry, but we're closed until New Year's Day."

"We're not here for a room. We came to speak to our son, Trey."

She lifted her chin. "Ah…I see a vague resemblance now that you mention it. But let's be honest. You didn't come to talk to Trey, because you've never bothered to do that before. You came to look at me."

Anders blinked. Forthright wasn't something he'd expected.

Marley frowned. "Well? Are you coming in, or are we doing this out in the cold?"

Trey hadn't heard much of what was said, but was shocked to

see his parents scuttling inside in silence. God. Whatever she said had just taken the wind out of the storm that was his father. Where was Marley when he was growing up?

Marley closed the door and then saw Trey as she turned around. "Ah, Trey, your loving parents have come to inspect me. Wanna watch?"

"You do you. I've got your back," he said.

"Follow me," Marley said. "We'll sit by the fire. Despite the sunshine, it's cold enough to freeze the balls off the devil."

Trey grinned.

Anders was dumbstruck. He'd expected a simpering, clinging blond.

Gloria was intrigued, both by the woman and her vocabulary. It reminded her of where she'd grown up, and anyone who'd just rendered Anders Austin mute had her attention.

Marley couldn't see herself through other people's eyes. She was just being herself. All five feet, four inches of her in skinny jeans and a blue cable-knit sweater, padding through the lobby into the great room in her fuzzy black socks with gripper soles.

She plopped down in her favorite chair, knowing Trey would sit down on the arm of it beside her and slide his arm across the back of the chair, like he always did. It was just him being protective of her, but in this instance, she knew his parents saw it as a united front against the enemy (them), and that was fine with her.

"Okay, we're here. You're in my world uninvited, so we'll get the nasty details out of the way first. How's that sound to you?" But she didn't wait for an answer. "I did, by accident because you were shouting, overhear your conversation with Trey about me being after your money. And we both know you weren't worried about Trey. You were worried about yourself. So, Anders Austin the second. Look around you. All this and a good portion of the land around it is all mine, and business is good, and my reputation is stellar. But I know you understand how this works, because you also inherited what your father created, just as I inherited what my great-grandfather, my grandfather, and my father created. Four generations.

"And of course, you have grown your holdings, because in your mind, you'll never have enough. While as I continue to build the business, which is amazingly sound, I want for nothing. I have all the money I'll ever need. I own the lodge, which is also my home. So, our situations are exactly alike…aren't they? Oh…except for the greedy part. Now, that's all you and I have to say to each other, unless you two came to thank me for saving your wonderful son's life. And while you're at it, try to see him as the brilliant, amazing man that he became without anyone's help. And know that yesterday he saved my life. If it hadn't been for him, they would still be looking for my body."

Her voice was shaking now, and Trey knew it was taking everything she had to get this said, but she was the one they'd come to crucify, and he wanted them to see her as he saw her. When she was done, he would happily peel the hide off their pretense and send them packing.

Anders cleared his throat. "Yes, we heard about what happened yesterday."

Marley waited, then shifted her focus to Gloria. "Are you allowed to speak, or…"

Gloria nodded. "I am. But I have been basking in the guts and glory of the woman you are. Trey has no right to forgive us. And you have no obligation to us whatsoever. If I read the room correctly, and I'm usually very good about that… I'd say you are the perfect woman for any man to love, and that my son is most fortunate to have found you. I came along for the ride to make sure Trey's father didn't make another ass of himself."

And then Gloria looked straight at Trey. "Everything you said to us was painfully true, and I am ashamed to admit I never once thought about how you felt regarding the decisions we made for you as a child. Knowing it now, I will regret it for the rest of my days. I didn't come to beg forgiveness or hope for any kind of reconciliation. You just deserved to hear your truth acknowledged. I don't know what you're doing with your life, but I know whatever it is, you earned it all on your own, and I am proud of you."

Trey was silent for a moment, reading her steady gaze as being as truthful as she knew how to be. Finally, he nodded.

"I don't have any gushing gratitude to give you, Mom. But thank you for the honesty."

Gloria blinked back tears. He wasn't being rude. He didn't even have enough emotion to be cold toward her. She was the stranger who'd given birth to him and given him up to others from the day that he was born. There was no maternal bond. No familial bond. In truth, no bond at all. But it was done.

And yet she knew from the way he looked at Marley Corbett, and the way she looked at him, there was an emotional bond between them, and for that she was grateful. At least she and Anders hadn't destroyed the man. Just their relationship with him.

Anders sat staring at the floor. Now the onus was on him to speak or remain the monster in the closet.

"I did what I thought was best for you," he finally said. "I thought I was supporting you by making sure you had money, only to find out you not only hadn't spent it, but that you sent it back with the interest it had accrued. So now I wonder how you've been making a living."

"It's entirely legal, if that's what's been bothering you," Trey said. "And everything I am, and all that I earn, I do without the auspices of your power, or your name, or your help. You own nothing of me. I owe nothing to you. Understand?"

Anders glared.

Trey stared back without blinking.

Anders shifted focus to Marley. "I suppose you know what he does?"

"Of course, I know. What an absurd thing to ask of me. Am I going to talk about it? Absolutely not. Not my business to tell."

Anders stood up, but before he could open his mouth, Trey was standing between them, so close to his father that he could see his own reflection in Anders's eyes.

"Don't you do it! Whatever it is you were about to say to her, suck it up now. Yesterday, I took out a man with a crowbar whose sole intent that day was to destroy her. So, know that I will lay you out before I'll stand by and let you bully her like you used to do me."

Marley wasn't surprised by Trey's reaction, but she hadn't seen it coming, and then before she could react, she heard the voices.

The first was the worst. Say it.

"The first was the worst," Marley said.

Anders paled, staggered backward, and sat down with a thud.

Trey didn't know what was happening. His father looked like he was going to pass out from what she'd said. He turned and looked at her.

"What does that mean?" he asked.

"I don't know. The angels told me to say it."

Gloria frowned. "Angels? What are you talking about?"

"They talk to me," Marley said. "I've always heard them. It's because of them that I even found Trey in the wreck. Everyone who knows me knows it. It's not a secret." And then she heard voices again and tilted her head slightly to catch all the words. *Afraid he'd repeat it.*

Marley looked back at Anders. "Afraid you'd repeat what?"

Anders couldn't quit staring at her. "How did you… Why did you… You couldn't possibly…"

And then Marley's understanding dawned. "Your father physically and emotionally mistreated you, didn't he? You were afraid to be a father for fear of repeating it. Weren't you? You kept Trey at arm's length for fear you'd become the monster like the man who raised you."

Gloria gasped, and Trey turned, staring at his father as if he'd never seen him before.

"Dad. Is this true?" he asked.

"I'm not talking about this," Anders whispered, but Gloria was at his side, clutching his hands, and Trey was looming over him like an avenging angel, and for the first time since his youth, Anders wanted to hide.

Trey sat down, and when he did, Marley scooted up beside him. At this moment, her presence was everything.

Nobody spoke. It was like sitting vigil beside a body waiting to be buried. And then Marley heard another message.

All is forgiven.

Oh man…he's not gonna like this, Marley thought, but she knew better than to ignore the messages.

"Sir…they said to tell you, 'All is forgiven.' I would take that to mean your father has been forgiven his trespasses. And God has already forgiven you, even as you still repeat them." And then she laid her hand on Trey's knee. "Trey doesn't hold the key to your happiness. He isn't the answer to your emotional needs. He'll do what he feels right for him, and that may not include being the crutch for either of you."

"Look at her. Both of you. She's brave and strong and gutsy and the funniest person I've ever known, and she freakin' talks to angels," Trey said. "I'm the living proof. She is also the love of my life. She is who I choose. And lord love her, she chose me, too. So, you came, you saw, and now just go on about your lives as you've always done. Be happy with each other. You don't need me to do that. You never did."

Marley got up, moved the fire screen to stir the embers, and added another log to the fire, then slid the screen back in place and dusted off her hands, while Anders and Gloria watched her perform a task that neither of them would have lowered themselves to do. But Marley didn't care what they thought about her.

"Trey, my love, I'm going to make coffee. Your dad is going to need a little caffeine to be able to get up. I won't be long. Gloria, would you care to join me?"

Gloria hadn't been asked to help do anything since she left the Ozarks, but she didn't have the guts to tell this woman no.

"Of course," she said, patted Anders's knee, and then followed Marley out of the room, leaving Trey and Anders alone.

Anders finally looked up. "I have this rage I can't control. I couldn't fight back then, and I carried it into life, thinking I had to fight for everything or be lost again."

Trey listened without comment, never taking his eyes off his father's face as he kept talking, and all the while, the lack of emotion in Anders's voice was almost as scary as what he was saying.

"He walked with a cane…my father…and used it as a weapon. When he didn't beat me, he locked me in closets. In the basement. In the attic. He refused me food, but in public showered me with everything. I loved him. I hated him. I feared him. When I was twenty-four, I married your mother. She was my escape from the main house. He died before you were born. But the day I saw you in the hospital, I saw my reflection in the nursery windows and saw him instead. I feared I would turn into him, and so I abandoned you to hired help and felt like I'd done the right thing. I don't want your forgiveness. I don't deserve it. But I will forever believe that I saved you from turning into me. Be happy, Trey. Love her hard. I think she's worth it all."

Trey nodded. "I know she is. Go to counseling, Dad. You have demons to banish."

Anders shrugged. "No counseling. No sign of weakness. Austin Enterprises would sink at the first sign."

Trey shook his head. "You're still doing it…putting power ahead of sanity. It's your funeral."

Before Anders could say more, Gloria came out of the kitchen. "Coffee is ready. You come to it. It's not coming to you."

Trey grinned. "Marley said that, didn't she?"

Gloria nodded. "She has hand pies. I haven't had hand pies since I left home. She said she made them."

"Oh, she's also an amazing chef as well," Trey said. "So far, the only thing I haven't seen her do is fly, but I swear she could if she wanted to. I'm pretty sure I've seen wings."

Gloria tilted her head, smiling as looked at Trey. "You have quite a way with words. I don't think I knew that about you."

"In the months to come, you'll learn all kinds of things about me," Trey said. "In the meantime, we are going to have pie and coffee. And then you two will go back to New York City and tend to your business, and leave Marley and me to ours."

It was dark by the time Anders and Gloria left. But there was no rush. No scheduled flight to catch. The jet had been refueled and was sitting off-site at a private runway, and the pilot was already in the plane, waiting for their arrival.

Anders was silent as they drove away from the lodge, but Gloria hadn't stopped talking. She knew he'd told Trey things he may never tell her, but she'd lived with Anders Austin long enough to know that he would feel ashamed to be weak in front of her, and that was the last thing she wanted.

And at least Trey had given them the space to unburden themselves. The fact that he still held his secrets close to his chest was fair. She was proud of him, and in awe and just the tiniest bit afraid of the woman in his life.

By the time they drove into the city and headed for the airport, she'd fallen silent.

"We're still good, aren't we?" Anders asked.

Gloria reached across the seat and patted his knee. "Yes, dear, we're good. As long as you're happy, I'm happy. Will you hang my clock tomorrow?"

He nodded. "I will hang your clock."

The last of a huge weight had been lifted.

Within the hour, they were in the jet and taxiing down the runway. When they lifted off, Anders glanced down once into the lights of the city below and then up at the mountain. He fancied that he saw a glimmer of the lodge's security lights outside, but it could also have been a reflection in the glass from the lights on the jet, and then they were gone.

Chapter 15

THAT NIGHT WHILE MARLEY WAS SOAKING IN THE TUB, Trey walked into the bathroom naked.

"Move over, darlin'. Incoming," he said, and swung one long leg over the side of the Jacuzzi and then the other, and slid down into the bubbly water, facing her.

Without asking, she sat up, grabbed one of his feet and pulled it across her lap, and started massaging it. He slid deeper into the water and gave way to the joy of the unexpected foot rub.

"You know you've ruined me forever," he growled.

She glanced up, watching little bubbles catching and bursting within the black hair on his chest, and thought of the years to come.

"Just forever? Dang it, Trey. Don't think for a moment you're going to cheat me out of our bargain," she said.

He laughed, his voice booming and echoing within the confines of their tiny marble palace. "Once again, my deepest apologies. Forever and a day, my love. Forever and a day."

When the cleaning service arrived bright and early the next morning and Trey witnessed Marley going into overdrive with orders, he did her a favor, told her he was going to work, and made himself scarce.

Once Marley had the cleaning service started, she and Wanda and the two regular sous-chefs went to work prepping the hors d'oeuvres for the party two days hence. It was almost New Year's Eve. And since it was all finger food and wine, the stress of serving a meal to the expected crowd wasn't there. It would be lots of noisy fun and all twelve rooms upstairs booked for the night.

Silver service trays were being polished. Wineglasses came out of storage, and the cleaning crew were on ladders dusting the huge beams that ran the length of the great room, polishing floors, ironwork, and woodwork. The lodge was beginning to smell like lemon oil and cedar.

Even with all the commotion, the quiet within the family quarters was surprising. Thick log walls separating the old lodge from the newer part were excellent insulation.

And since Trey was at the far end of the old lodge, he heard nothing but the faint hum of a computer fan now and then, and the constant *click, click, click* of the keys on the keyboard as he typed.

It was nearing noon when he finally stopped to take a break. He stretched, wondering what was going on in the real world, and wandered up the hall and out of the door into the main lodge.

The cleaning crew was down to polishing the floors, and working their way out of the lodge as they went, so he slipped up the hall and into the kitchen, causing a little stir with all the extra employees he had yet to meet.

Marley heard a giggle and a gasp and looked up, then smiled.

Trey was in the house.

"You can look, but don't touch," she told the girls, which made them giggle even more.

Trey wound his way through the kitchen, introducing himself as he went, and ended at Marley's station and gave her a quick kiss.

"I just came to make a sandwich. I promise I'll stay out of the way," he said.

She glanced at the clock and then stopped and wiped her hands.

"Oh gosh! I had no idea what time it was. Lunch break, everybody. See you back in a while, or you can make yourselves something here and join us."

"I need to pick up some meds to take to my mother," Toni said.

"And I promised my husband I'd lunch with him if I could," Angela added.

"Then off you go," Marley said, and opened the refrigerator as they left. "Cold cuts okay?"

"Absolutely," he said.

"Good. There are hoagie rolls or sandwich bread. What's your pleasure?"

"Well, that would be you, but since I only have bread choices, I choose a hoagie."

Marley grinned. "We can renegotiate tonight."

He gave her a thumbs-up. They made lunch together and then made three extra sandwiches, knowing Wanda and Jack would be wandering through at any moment, which they did.

Soon, they were all sitting down together, talking about the weather report for New Year's Eve and arguing the finer points of yellow mustard versus whole-grain mustard, when the phone rang.

Marley got up to answer, and when she did, they all stopped talking so as not to interfere with the call.

"Corbett Lodge. This is Marley."

"Miss Corbett, this is Adrian Barlow from the ABC affiliate here in Colorado Springs. We'd like to get your side of the story about the assault and—"

"What do you mean, my side of the story? You can't possibly be trying to make an exposé out of a failed murder attempt! I'm not the least bit interested in talking about what happened, and being hounded about it makes me feel like vulture bait. Since nobody's dead here, and vultures only feed on carrion, I don't see that story anywhere in your future. I do, however, wish you all a Happy New Year. We're opening back up New Year's Day, so if you're ever in the mood for some great food, our noon buffet runs from 11:00 a.m. to 2:00 p.m. every day, and breakfast brunch Sunday from eleven to two. Thanks for calling."

She hung up the phone and turned around.

Jack was grinning.

Wanda was big-eyed.

And the moment she hung up, Trey doubled over with laughter.

"You did not just call the TV station vultures!" Wanda gasped.

Marley frowned. "No, no, I don't think I did. I said they made me feel like vulture bait. They can draw their own conclusions as to how I came to that impression."

Trey raised his hand as if asking permission to speak. Marley threw a corn chip at him. He laughed and swatted it away. "You rolled all around yellow journalism without ever calling them out, and then the best part was sliding right into a plug for the lodge. In another life, you could have worked in repo and made the people losing their cars apologize for your inconvenience. 'Vulture bait.' Oh my God, Marley! You are a treasure."

She sat back down and then waved her fork at all of them. "I'm not discussing this further," she said, and pointed to the pickle on Trey's plate. "Are you going to eat that?"

He immediately pushed his plate toward her.

"Thank you," she said, and forked the pickle onto her plate. "Bread-and-butter pickles are my favorite."

"Duly noted, and you are so welcome," he said. "You know… the irony of you scavenging off of my plate is not unlike the behavior of the birds that shall not be named."

Jack roared. Even Wanda was grinning.

Marley blinked, then crunched the pickle between her pearly white teeth, chewed, and swallowed. "Tasty little morsel, and it wasn't even roadkill," she said.

Trey just shook his head. "What is that word they used to say in the old days when someone had just been soundly beaten and wanted to give up?"

"Uncle! You cry, 'Uncle'!" Jack said.

"Yep, that's it! So, Uncle, Marley! I give. You will always win the zinger contests."

She smiled sweetly. "Don't feel bad. Remember, you're the man with all the pretty words."

A couple of hours later, Trey was back in the office when he got a text from Meredith.

> Check your email. They sent the contract within the timeline I asked for. I've looked it over. You read it, and unless you want something changed, it's ready to sign. When you do, they'll be contacting you about the big reveal, because they are going to publicly announce their coup. Your name and face, and Chapel Hill, are likely to wind up on Entertainment Tonight.

He sighed. The sweet smell of success was going to come with a price.

> I'm fine with the reveal, but they need to know that any "appearances" I make for a while will be via Zoom. Someone tried to kill Marley yesterday. I've been gone, and this psycho snuck into the attic and lay in wait for the workers to leave. I took an early flight home. My plane landed, and I drove straight back to the lodge just as she came running out screaming, with the man only a few steps behind her. I took him out at the knees with a crowbar. He's not going anywhere for a long time, but she's still pretty rattled. So, there's that.

> The contract is good news to sleep on tonight. I'll read it, but I'm sure you've already covered all my bases. I'll sign it before the night is out.
> Trey

He hit Send, and within minutes, had one more message from her.

> Oh my God! The attic! A woman's worst nightmare. You were the hero she needed. I need to meet this woman one day.
> M

Trey set the phone aside, went to his laptop, and began reading through the contract. After reading it twice, he was satisfied with the language, e-signed it, and hit Send, knowing it was now in the hands of the people with the money and the plans.

Chapter 16

It was the day before the party. There was nothing left to clean or decorate. Bar-height tables had been strategically placed throughout the lodge. Music had been chosen for the piped-in sound system. Food was ready, either waiting to be heated or served cold.

Marley was standing in the middle of the space, eyeing everything in sight, looking to see what they'd missed when Trey came up behind her, slid his arms around her shoulders, and gave her a hug.

"It looks beautiful. You're beautiful. The world is beautiful. Time to relax now. Tomorrow is the party. The day after, you reopen. When that happens, I want you to forget that I'm on the premises and do what you always do. I won't need tending to. I won't feel abandoned. Because I know who I love and who loves me, understand?"

She turned within his arms. "Yes, and know that when I'm up to my eyes with the fuss and bother, I'll always know who anchors me and where you are."

"Having said all that, there's just one more thing I need to do," Trey said.

"And what would that be?" she asked.

He pulled out the ring he'd purchased in Phoenix. "Despite

the fact that this is already a given, you deserve to hear me say the words. Marry me, Marley." When he opened the ring box and took out the engagement ring, she gasped. "Will you be my wife… forever and a day?"

"Yes, yes, yes," she cried, and when he slipped it onto her finger, she sighed. "It fits perfectly!"

"Just like us," he said, then cupped her face and brushed his lips across her mouth.

Marley was laughing and crying as she threw her arms around his neck, and then her feet were off the floor, and he was swinging her around and around beneath the crystal chandelier.

That night when they went to bed, the only thing Marley was wearing was the ring. And the only thing on Trey Austin's mind was the woman wearing it.

The party was in full swing. Guests who were spending the night had already been to their assigned rooms and were back down in the midst of it. Other guests were still arriving in Ubers. A small room across from the public restrooms had become the designated coat room.

Waiters in white shirts with black vests moved through the guests with trays of hot and cold hors d'oeuvres and glasses of wine, both white and red.

The guests were wearing their best, and flashing jewelry and big smiles. Every so often someone would burst into laughter, and heads would turn to see who it was and wonder what was being said.

Trey was at Marley's side from the beginning, charming everyone who entered. His reputation had preceded him, and he'd turned a simple black tuxedo and bow tie into a Prince Charming fashion statement. But it was the fitted red sparkle cocktail dress and the three-karat oval-cut diamond on Marley's ring finger that had turned her into the ultimate Cinderella at the ball.

She was the light among them, beaming from the joy and happiness within her, and the man at her side had eyes only for her.

As was the way of the world, women envied. Men coveted. And the party went on.

Jack and Wanda were in the background, keeping everything organized in the kitchens and the wine flowing.

It was nearing midnight, the time to ring in the New Year, when a man Trey had been introduced to earlier finally cornered him near the Christmas tree.

"Say, Trey! I know this is asking a lot, but I've been trying to get in contact with your father for almost a month. We were talking about a merger, and then nothing."

"I'm the last man you should be talking to. My father and I don't communicate. I have nothing to do with Austin Enterprises... by choice."

"But surely you..."

"No sir, surely I don't," Trey said, turned his back and walked away.

Within seconds, Marley was beside him, still smiling, but the tone of her voice was anything but.

"What did he say to you?" she asked.

Trey shrugged.

"Who is he? I don't know, but I can find out. He came as a guest of one of the locals."

"Let it go," Trey said. "He just thought I'd be his inside contact to my father."

"Oh, for heaven's sake. Well, we all have our crosses to bear," she said.

He started smiling, and then he laughed. "You always put everything into perspective."

"It's what I do," she said, and then glanced at the time. "It's almost midnight. I need to find Jack. We can't ring in the new year without 'Auld Lang Syne.'"

"There he is," Trey said, pointing toward the fireplace. Jack waved his hand and then gave Marley a thumbs-up.

"I guess he's already on it," Marley said. "How's your singing voice?"

"We're about to find out," Trey said, and clasped her hand as the clock began to strike.

The room went quiet. Jack started the countdown, picking it up at ten.

"Ten! Nine! Eight!"

The guests joined in. "Seven. Six. Five. Four. Three. Two. One! Happy New Year!" they shouted.

The music of "Auld Lang Syne" began to spill out into the room, and as it did, the words of the song rose among them.

Trey felt the past fading, fading, and there was only Marley and all their tomorrows.

"Happy New Year," he said.

"The happiest ever," Marley said, and kissed him.

Trey was dreaming about the blood on the snow beneath Jared Bedford's legs when he heard Marley's feet hit the floor. Before he could turn over, she was disappearing into the bathroom. He glanced at the clock. Barely 5:00 a.m. He lay there, waiting for her to come out, then heard the shower come on. Obviously, she was up for the day. Less than five minutes later, the shower went off. A drawer banged, and then silence.

Minutes later, she shot out of the bathroom without a stitch, saw that he was awake, and blew him a kiss.

"Good morning, love," she said, then grabbed underwear from a dresser and bolted to the closet.

He'd never seen a woman get dressed as fast as she did, and a few moments later, she shot out of the closet, paused long enough to throw herself on top of him on the bed and kiss him senseless. Before he could think, she was out the door.

"If this happens every day, there's no chance of ever oversleeping," he said, and went to shower. *Better make it a cold one,* he thought as he turned on the water, stepped beneath the flow, and braced himself against the shower walls until the ache she'd awakened had gone away.

Marley's haste was all due to the overnight guests at the lodge. She knew they'd all be checking out this morning, and was getting ready to put out a continental breakfast when the first guests came down the stairs, headed straight for the coffee, and rejected the idea of food, which was fine with her. Obviously, they were still hungover from the night before and minus an appetite, so Marley slipped behind the counter, greeted them all sweetly as she checked them out, and gave them coffee to go as they went to the front lobby to wait for their rides.

She was immediately on the phone with Carol and Sue, the housekeepers who cleaned the rooms. "Girls, the last guests have checked out, so head up to do the rooms. We have two reservations checking in after 10:00 a.m., and the rest with scheduled arrivals after lunch."

"On it, Marley," they said, and headed up in the elevator with their cart full of cleaning supplies and fresh linens.

Next, she slipped into the kitchen to talk to Toni and Angela about today's lunch menu. They already had their heads together, reading over the menu she'd left last night.

"Morning, girls. No worries about breakfast today. Everybody's already checked out with hangovers. Too much party last night. So, let's go over the lunch menu before I get busy. We have to have black-eyed peas for good luck, and I kept the ham bone from Christmas dinner, so add it to the pot for extra seasonings," she said.

"Yes, ma'am," Toni said, and made a note.

"I need someone to make a quick breakfast for Trey. An omelet and toast will be perfect. Let me know when it's done. I'll text him to come get it."

"He can eat in here with us," Angela said, and then smiled.

Marley grinned. "I'll let him know he's invited, but I'm not sure what his morning looks like."

After a few alterations, the menu was set, and the sous-chefs began prepping. Angela made the omelet while Toni went to get the leftover ham and bone from the commercial cooler and put it on to boil. It was already cooked, but they wanted the flavor of the bone and the ham in the juice with the peas.

Satisfied that everything was under control, Marley went back to the lobby. A few minutes later, Angela came out with Trey's food.

"Thanks," Marley said, then set it down on a nearby table and sent Trey a text.

> Your breakfast is on a tray by the checkout. Come and get it before Jack gets here, or you'll be having leftovers.

A few moments later, Trey waved at her as he picked up his tray and went back inside.

Jack and Wanda arrived by seven, and their routines began.

During the day, guests continued to arrive. Marley was checking them into the hotel and showing them to their rooms, while the staff was getting food ready for lunch.

Besides the new attic door, there was another addition to the lodge, and it was hanging on the wall behind the front desk. It was a framed shadowbox with a newspaper clipping of Trey's Search for Cinderella and the famous shoe.

People were taking pictures of it, and of her, and when Trey wandered through the dining area at lunch, he became part of the story once again.

"Can we get a picture of the two of you together?" people would ask, and of course they obliged, but once Trey got a plate of food, he went back to the office and, at Marley's instructions, locked the door behind him.

As the noon rush began to subside, and the last of her guests with reservations had checked in, Marley began to breathe easier.

Trey had been right. Nothing had changed, except her knowledge that he was under this roof and within the sound of her voice.

But on the same day, Trey's life was changing fast. He was researching how many cartridges were in a Glock clip when his phone rang. He pushed back from the computer to answer.

"Hello."

"Mr. Austin?"

"Yes."

"I'm Morris LeHigh. Maybe your agent, Meredith Bernstein, has mentioned me?"

"I saw your name on the contract I signed," Trey said.

"Excellent! I'm also your liaison with the media and am in charge of the big Chapel Hill reveal." Morris was just short of gushing as they spoke. "This is an exciting venture for us, and revealing the identity of Chapel Hill is not only going to up your sales, but also generate a whole lot of interest for moviegoers. Especially when they learn that Trey Austin, the Cinderella Man, is also Chapel Hill, and that Marley Corbett, the woman who saved you, is now your fiancée. Yes, I know. Meredith told us. And you need to prepare Miss Corbett for an onslaught of media, as well."

"We've already had plenty of that. She runs her own business," Trey said. "I don't need to prepare her for anything. She's fully capable of handling anything that comes her way."

"Excellent," Morris said. "Maybe we could get her included in the Zoom?"

"Not right now," Trey said. "She's incredibly busy at the moment. Things will slow down for her some in the days to come, but this is reopening day after a shutdown for renovations, and there's no stopping place for her."

"That's fine," Morris said. "So, four this afternoon, your time? I'll send you a link right before. I've emailed you a series of questions so you won't be caught unaware, and if anything is off-limits, just say so."

"I can tell you right now, absolutely no references to my father. I did all of this on my own, and anonymously, because everyone would immediately assume he got me where I am today, when the truth is he still doesn't know what I do."

"Wow. Oh. Okay, then ignore the last three questions on the list," Morris said.

"Thank you," Trey said.

"No problem. I'll send you a new list and change the tone of some of the questions, okay?"

"If you want an interview with me, that's what it's going to take," Trey said.

"We just want to make you happy," Morris said. "Ignore the first email. I'll revise the question list, and then about thirty minutes before the Zoom, I'll send you the link."

"I'll be ready," Trey said, and disconnected.

He sat for a few moments, thinking about what was going to happen. He was opening Pandora's box of trouble by revealing his identity, and whether he liked it or not, he was going to have to deal with it. Politely. Nicely.

He deleted the first list of questions and waited for the new list to arrive. After they did, he read them through and laid them aside. It was a good two hours before the call. He needed to talk to Marley.

They were cleaning the dining area after the lunch service as he entered the main lodge.

"Hey, Jack, do you know where Marley is?" he asked.

"She went that way," he said, pointing to the elevator leading up to the guest rooms.

Trey nodded, then sat down on the stairs to wait. Either she'd come down the stairs, or he'd see her when she got out of the elevator.

Within a few minutes, he heard footsteps behind him, turned, and looked up.

"Trey, honey, what are you doing on the stairs?" Marley asked.

"Waiting to talk to you. Do you have a minute?"

"For you, always," she said. "Let's sit over there where it's quiet."

As soon as they sat down, he unloaded. "I just took a call from Morris LeHigh, the man in charge of the 'big reveal' as he puts it. I'm doing a Zoom call with him in a couple of hours, which he will incorporate into the statement they're releasing via *Entertainment Tonight*."

Marley grabbed his hands. "This is so exciting! Are you anxious about it?"

"A little. I've already nixed the first list of questions they sent for me to review. No surprises, et cetera, but some of them kept referring to Dad, so they sent me a second list. The questions are fine, but he warned me, this is likely to stir up some measure of interest and to prepare you for that. There could be any number of people showing up here because of me, but—"

She shook her head. "I already told you that's never going to be an issue. I already have Jack scheduled to build me a bookshelf so we can display all of your titles for sale. And, since I only have twelve guest rooms available to rent at any time, it's not like we're going to be inundated with fans hanging out forever. They'll come. They'll want pictures with you. That won't interfere with anything. I'm in the business of food and rooms. You're in the book business. And you're all in my business every night, so…"

He grinned. "So, I'm all in your business, am I?"

She blinked her big blue eyes. "Oh yes...in a very *big* way."

He grinned, gave her a quick goodbye kiss, and headed back to work, leaving Marley sitting with a self-satisfied smile.

Two hours later, Trey was deep in the middle of the interview, smiling, talking about the books and how he'd begun writing the first two in college. How he'd met his agent and praised her highly for understanding his desire for anonymity. And then, despite his request not to have his father mentioned, the interviewer's last comment was, "Your parents must be very proud of you."

His smile disappeared. "This will come as a shock to both of them. They know nothing of what I do."

There was a long moment of silence, and then the interviewer suddenly realized Trey wasn't going to say anything more about them and picked up the slack by thanking him.

The call ended, and Trey disconnected.

Seconds later, his phone was ringing. He glanced at the caller ID. It was Morris LeHigh.

"Hello."

"Trey! My apologies. She did not have permission to go there. We can edit that out if you wish."

He sighed. "No, it's okay. Leave it. Maybe it will discourage anyone else from trying to weave either of them into my life."

"Okay, but again, I apologize. This will air on *Entertainment Tonight* tomorrow, and then I expect it to go viral after that. Does your publisher know this is happening?"

"Meredith will tell them. I've never talked to them."

Morris was shocked. "Never? Not even over the phone?"

"Never. Everything went through her. Messages, edits, the whole thing. She's the real genius in this story, figuring out how to make it happen and being considerate enough to allow me this freedom."

"And now you've given it up, haven't you?" Morris said.

"I guess, but I'd do it again, just for the satisfaction of seeing my books made into movies."

The call ended, and Trey walked out.

He was over this day.

Done. Finished.

The end.

The only business he had on his mind was Marley.

The next morning, Marley was already at work in the kitchen and about to go out and check the steam pans on their breakfast buffet when the phone rang.

"Corbett Lodge, this is Marley," she said.

"Marley, this is Officer Dewitt. I don't know if you remember me, but I worked your assault case."

Her heart skipped. "Yes, I remember you. What's wrong?"

"Oh, nothing is wrong. I just thought you'd like to know that Jared Bedford has pled guilty to all charges, and when he's well enough, he will stand before a judge to be sentenced."

"That means I don't have to go to court, right? I don't have to see him again?" she asked.

"Yes, ma'am, that's what it means."

"Thank you so much for letting me know. This is a big relief."

"Yes, ma'am. Happy New Year to you and Mr. Austin," he said, and disconnected.

Marley hung up the phone, then went out to check the steam table and popped her head back in long enough to say, "Go ahead and put out that other tray of biscuits and refill the chocolate gravy. Also, if there's more bacon, put it out. If there's not, the sausage that's left will suffice. There are still a few guests who haven't made it down, but they also know breakfast isn't available all day."

"On it," Angela said.

Marley let the door slam shut on her butt as she turned around and headed for the family quarters. She unlocked the door and, after she went in, turned the lock behind her.

All of the horror from the attack.

All of the panic.

All of the nightmares.

All of the stories in the press.

It was finally over.

And she was coming undone.

Chapter 17

Trey heard the door open, and then a lock turned. He sat, expecting Marley to call out, and when she didn't, he got up and started walking toward the front of their home.

When he saw her standing in the living room, trembling from head to toe, he bolted.

"Marley! Sweetheart…what's happened? Are you okay? Are you sick? Did someone get hurt?"

She couldn't cry; she just couldn't stop shaking.

"Jared Bedford pled guilty to all charges. I don't have to go to court. I don't have to testify. I don't have to face him ever again."

He wrapped his arms around her, holding her close. "Oh, baby, I am so glad. This has to be the biggest relief of your life. You never said anything about being worried that might happen. I didn't realize how heavily this was weighing on you."

"I didn't know it either until I heard the words."

"Come sit," he said, and sat her down on the sofa, then went to the liquor cabinet and poured her a shot of whiskey. "Drink it. It'll either settle your nerves, or you'll pick a fight with someone later. Either way, you won't be dealing with this fear."

She grimaced, downed it like medicine, and then leaned back

and closed her eyes as the heat of the whiskey rolled down the back of her throat and into her belly.

Trey sat down beside her, reached for her hand, and held it.

They didn't speak. There was no need. He was there when she needed him, and that was enough.

A few minutes later, she got up, went to wash her face, and came back with her hair brushed and fresh lipstick.

"Are you okay?" he asked.

She nodded. "I just needed to see you. Thanks for the shot, the hug, and the kiss. I think I'm good."

"I'm gonna walk you out," he said.

She leaned against him as they went. "You just want to see Angela and Toni ogle you for a while."

"Whatever. I'm still doing it," he said.

"Got your key?" she asked.

"Always in my pocket," he said.

They left together, and before they'd even reached the front desk, someone approached them for a picture.

"Smile, darlin'," Trey said, and put his arm around her just as the guest snapped the shot, then thanked them, ran back to her table, and immediately sent it to Instagram.

"Trey, Jack is in the shop building that bookshelf, but I don't know if he measured the size of the books before he began," she said.

"How about I borrow one from your stash and take it to him to measure."

"Don't let him keep it," she said. "He's just as likely to use it for a doorstop later."

"Understood," he said, then pulled a Chapel Hill book from the shelves and went out the back door.

"Coat!" Marley shouted.

"Not an idiot!" he shouted back as he snagged an old one from the hook.

She laughed.

It felt good.

Trey didn't know it, but Meredith had demanded to see the final version of his interview before it aired, and Morris LeHigh had agreed.

When she got to work the next morning, it was in her email. She made herself a cup of hot tea and checked the bank to see if her fifteen percent of the five million had been deposited, because if it had, then that meant Trey had been paid on signing, too, which had been part of her demands.

When she pulled up her account and saw the pending deposit, she smiled, then sat down at her desk to watch the interview, and when it was over, she leaned back in her chair with tears in her eyes.

She'd always dreamed of having a client who'd made it big, really big. When she'd first accepted Trey as a client, she would never have imagined it would be him. But the mystery of his identity had been the hook needed to suck readers into his stories, and now they were as invested in the books he wrote as they were about the secret.

But what had touched her so deeply about the interview was the recognition he'd given her for being the wall between him and the anonymity he'd desired. She rewatched it twice over, just so she could get to hear him saying, "Were it not for Meredith Bernstein, none of this would have happened. She made it easy for me to be me."

Satisfied with it, she sent a thumbs-up to Morris, then started making phone calls.

Jack finished the bookshelf Marley wanted, and stained it. He didn't know what it was for, but he didn't argue with the boss. Just as he was getting ready to leave, Marley caught him at the back door.

"Tonight, you and Wanda be sure to watch *Entertainment Tonight*."

"Why?" he asked.

"You'll find out when you watch it. Can't say more. It would ruin the surprise."

"If you say so," he said, and put on his coat and gloves and left.

Then Marley sent Wanda a text with the same instructions, knowing Jack would forget, and she wouldn't.

Trey and Marley ate an early dinner and then bolted for the TV in the great room. A couple of guests were at the jigsaw table, and a single guest was scrolling through his phone by the fire.

Trey reached for the remote as soon as he sat, while Marley scooted onto the cushion beside him. He glanced down at her and grinned.

"Here goes nothin'," he said, pulled up the guide on the TV, scanned until he found CBS, and then keyed in.

Moments later, the show began with a lead-in telling viewers to stay tuned for an important announcement. That a long-awaited big reveal was coming tonight, and it was going to rock the publishing world.

She leaned over, whispering in his ear.

"You're about to set a whole lot of people's hair on fire."

He grinned. Hers might be smoking in a minute, too, when she realized the Santa Claus picture she'd given to him for Christmas was in the background of his interview.

Wanda herded Jack to the television, listening to him complain all the way.

"I don't see why we need to watch *ET*. I wanted to check my chickens before dark."

"You missed that window of opportunity," Wanda said. "It's already dark. If Bug wanted us to do this, then she has a good reason. Sit yourself."

Jack flopped down, put his feet up on the coffee table, and leaned back against the sofa as Wanda slid in beside him.

Gloria Austin always watched *ET*. She felt obligated to keep up with the pretty people, and the famous people, and who was getting divorced, and who was dating who.

Anders came out of his office and saw where she was sitting. Right beneath the cuckoo clock he'd hung on the wall. He knew about her penchant for keeping up with the rich and famous, and when he heard the hosts talking about a big reveal in the publishing world, he got curious and sat down beside her.

"I wonder what the big news is," Gloria said.

Anders shrugged. "We'll soon find out."

Like every night, a huge portion of the nation tuned in to *ET*, and for most, this day was no different from any other. But Meredith was hosting a little soiree at her apartment for a few of her agent friends, and for a few editors from local publishing houses.

Canapes were serve-yourself, and wine was flowing. She was the consummate hostess, and tonight, she'd dressed for the occasion. In the middle of industry gossip and conversation, Meredith suddenly quieted the room.

"Find a place to sit," she said as she turned on her TV. "This is why you're here—to help me celebrate a bit of good news." And then the lead-in regarding a bombshell reveal within the publishing world had their attention.

Meredith took a seat in the middle of the sofa as some of her friends crowded around her. She upped the volume as the show began.

The first guest was familiar to everyone in the room. Even if they didn't know him personally, they knew who he was. One of the agents suddenly pointed toward the screen.

"That's Morris LeHigh with Vyjack Productions! He's out of LA. Maybe they're going to make a film about some actor's memoir."

"Gawd, I hope not," another agent muttered.

Entertainment Tonight host Kevin Frazier and cohost Nischelle Turner were all smiles as they began their broadcast.

"Hello and good evening. Wow, do we have a scoop for you tonight," Kevin said.

"You're hearing it first on *ET*, and to lead off our story, our first guest is Morris LeHigh, head of production with Vyjack Productions in LA," Nischelle said. "So, what's going on, Morris? We're all ears."

The camera cut to LeHigh, a short, balding man in his midfifties who couldn't seem to stand still.

"Thank you, *ET*, for the opportunity to break our big news here," Morris said. "The news is exciting, but we have an even bigger reveal along with it. We are proud to announce that Vyjack Productions has optioned the film rights to the first twelve Chapel Hill mystery novels. We're already in discussion as to which book we'll turn into a film first!" Morris said.

"Oh wow! How did you make this happen when the writer is an anonymous entity?" Kevin said.

Morris shook his head. "That's our next big reveal! He isn't anonymous anymore! We just filmed our first interview with Chapel Hill. You might recognize the headshot. He's been in the news quite a bit lately, but for another reason altogether." The screen flashed on a still shot of Trey Austin. "We're about to roll the footage on the first-ever interview."

"But that's the Cinderella Man," Kevin said.

"Yes, but he's also the writer behind Chapel Hill," Morris said as they cut straight to their interview. "Jessica Hartley, with Vyjack, conducted the interview."

The next image that popped onto the screen was Trey Austin, kicked back in a chair in his office.

"Good afternoon, Trey. I'm Jessica Hartley with Vyjack Productions. Thank you for taking the time to speak with us."

"I guess it's been a long time coming," Trey said.

Jessica laughed. "Indeed. First, would you please tell us a bit about how you got started? What made you want to write, and why mysteries?"

"I was a lonely only child," he said, and then grinned. "How does that sound for an excuse not to admit that I'm something of a loner? That I fully expected to become a hermit by the age of fifty?"

Jessica laughed. "Okay, I get that. We all have those days, I think. So why mystery?"

He didn't hesitate. "To me, life *is* the mystery. Why not tell the stories? You wonder as a child, why people act the way they do, but you don't have answers. You wonder how the stars stay up in the sky without falling. You wonder why getting older makes a body start coming apart." And then he chuckled. "As a child, that's what I thought was happening when I'd see old people take out false teeth, or watch them growing bald and getting wrinkles where once there were none. And wondering why good people die, and evil lives on? Some people grow out of childish thoughts. Writers grow up with them and turn them into stories. Everything is fair game to us. Make an enemy of me and you'll become the bum in my next book, or the murder victim. No one but me will know it's you, but that's the satisfaction I get from giving you my own brand of justice. That's where the mysteries come from."

"Fascinating," Jessica said. "So, why anonymous? Most people want the recognition of success."

He shrugged. "And lose their personal freedom in the process? It never much appealed to me."

"What meaning does Chapel Hill hold for you? It must mean something. You've hidden behind the name for what…ten years now?"

"Actually twelve years. I wrote my first two books while I was still in college. That's where I met my literary agent, Meredith Bernstein, the woman who helped hide me from the world. I couldn't have done any of this without her. She found a way to let me be me and still write. But she's also the one who finally convinced me to give up the secret. As for the name, Chapel Hill, that was a place just off my college campus that had a reputation as a lover's lane…a place for secret liaisons. Ironically, it was located on a wooded hill behind a church."

"Are you a churchgoer?" Jessica asked.

"Not in the sense you mean, but I have learned to believe in angels and in a higher power, thanks to my own Cinderella, Marley Corbett, who saved my life a little over a month ago. Were it not for her unbelievable courage and bravery, we would not be sitting here."

"We understand you two have become close friends," Jessica said.

Trey grinned. "Close enough that I put a ring on her finger."

Jessica gasped. "You're engaged! Oh wow! So, Cinderella got her Prince Charming. By any chance, did you actually put that shoe on her foot when you found her?"

"I did, and it's hanging in a shadow box at the lodge now. A reminder to the both of us how random life can be, and how blessed we are."

"I love stories with happy endings," Jessica said. "What's next for Trey Austin, now that you've outed yourself?"

"A little travel now and then for Vyjack Productions. Continue working on the new novel in progress, and whatever my Marley wants and needs."

"I couldn't help but notice that charming picture behind you of the pretty blond sitting on Santa's lap. Is that her?"

"That's her. My own personal guardian angel."

"So, what do your parents think about your work?"

Trey froze.

Jessica took a quick breath. The look he'd just given her was frightening. She'd been told not to mention his family, but she'd thought, nothing ventured, nothing gained, hoping for a little scoop about being the heir to Austin Enterprises.

Trey's whole demeanor shifted. "They know nothing of what I do. They will likely be shocked by the news."

It wasn't the answer Jessica expected, and now there was dead air between them.

"Thank you for speaking with us tonight. We'll be seeing more of you in the future," she said, and then it faded back to the hosts at *ET*.

"Wow, who knew?" Kevin Frazier said. "The man flies under the radar for most of his adult life, and then look at how his life has changed, and all within the last few weeks!"

"I wouldn't mind being his Cinderella. He's a handsome, charming man," Nischelle said, and then the show went to commercial.

Gloria and Anders were in shock, and their phones were already buzzing with text messages they were already ignoring.

"I can't believe it! I own three of those books. My own son wrote them, and I never dreamed. Oh my God! Vyjack Productions! All twelve books optioned. But why on earth did he keep all this a secret?" she cried.

"Because everyone would have assumed I'd bought his way into the business," Anders said.

"If you'd known he wanted to do this, would you have done that?" she asked.

He sighed. "Probably."

"Why?" Gloria asked.

"I wouldn't have believed he had the skill to do it on his own. I wouldn't have wanted failure of any kind associated with me. He did the right thing. Again. Despite us."

"Well, I'm excited," Gloria said.

Anders sighed. "Fine, be happy for him. But we don't take credit for anything. We never saw this skill in him. We don't have a relationship with him. Don't claim one now. Don't take the shine from his star. It's his alone."

Gloria blinked, and then her eyes welled. "Of course. For a moment, I was so wrapped up in the news that I forgot. We never talked about him before. We don't have the right to do it now."

Anders nodded.

"Are you going to call and congratulate him?" Gloria asked.

"You saw the look on his face at the end of the interview when the woman mentioned us. What do you think?"

"I think, no," Gloria said. "So, what do we do about all the texts we've been getting?"

"Ignore them. We don't owe anyone explanations for our personal lives."

Gloria nodded. "You're right. We don't."

The moment the interview ended, Meredith's guests began congratulating her and quizzing her on how she'd managed to keep his identity secret.

"I just did what I promised and said nothing to anyone. I never even told a soul that Chapel Hill was my client. The publisher knew I spoke for Chapel Hill, and they wanted to keep him with their house, so they didn't push the issue," Meredith said.

"What's he like?" one editor asked.

"The nicest, sweetest man on the face of the earth," Meredith said.

"Have you met Marley Corbett?"

Meredith shook her head. "Not yet. But I'm invited to the wedding…whenever that happens."

"What's the deal about not communicating with his parents?" one of the agents asked.

"I don't talk about his personal business. I just honor his decisions," Meredith said. "Come! Eat up. Who wants more wine?"

As soon as the interview ended, Trey turned off the TV. "So, what did you think?"

Marley was beaming. "I think you were marvelous. I think a million women are going to fall in love with you. I think your book sales are going to skyrocket. I think you snuck my Santa picture into the background. What do you think?"

"I'm all for the rocketing book sales, and I suspect you'll never have an unrented guest room again," he said.

"That won't hurt my feelings. If business becomes all that, I might have to hire more help," she said.

"And maybe sneak in a quick weekend trip with me when I have to travel?" he said.

"Maybe so," Marley said. "It would be a delight to ride your coattails. This calls for a celebration. I have a bottle of champagne that I've been saving for something special. I think this is it!"

She left on the run and came back the same way, with two champagne flutes in one hand and a chilled bottle of champagne in the other.

"Would you do the honors?" she asked as she handed him the bottle.

Trey did the deed. The bottle opened with a pop and then bubbled over.

She squealed, then laughed as Trey poured the bubbly liquid into their flutes, then handed one to her before picking up his own.

"To Chapel Hill, and to the genius behind the stories. To Trey," Marley said as she raised her glass.

"And to us," Trey said.

"To us!" she echoed.

They were still sipping and talking when Marley's phone rang. She glanced down, then answered.

"Hello, Wanda, I'm putting this on speaker. Trey and I are celebrating."

"Oh, my freaking word!" Wanda said. "Huge congratulations to you, Trey! What a wonderful opportunity. And movies! I can't wait! Here's Jack. He wants to say something, too."

"Trey, we're real proud of you and so happy for you and Marley," Jack said.

"Thank you both for having faith in me from the beginning and trusting me with your girl," he said.

"See you both tomorrow," Wanda said.

"Tomorrow," Marley said, and disconnected.

At that moment, headlights swept across the room. The guests who'd gone into the city for dinner were returning. Moments later, the two couples came in laughing and talking and headed for one of the seating areas at the fireside.

They saw the champagne and Trey and Marley's smiles. "Celebrating tonight?" one of them asked.

"Indeed," Trey said. "There's plenty here to share. How about a champagne nightcap?"

"Oh, what fun. We'd love to."

"I'll get the glasses," Marley said, and bolted, then came back with four more.

Trey poured, and they finished off the bottle with Trey and Marley, without knowing what the celebration was all about.

Hours later, the last guest had returned to the lodge and Marley was locking up behind him.

"Sleep well," she said as he headed up to his room.

"Thank you," he said, then paused and turned around. "This place is magic. It's so low-key and comfortable. What a gift it is that you get to wake up to this every morning."

"Thank you," Marley said, but the man was already up the stairs and headed to his room. She waited until she heard him close his door, and then she turned out the last overhead light, leaving the lodge bathed in soft, blue night-lights, and went to join Trey, locking the door to the family quarters behind her.

She could hear the deep rumble of his voice down the hall and guessed he was on the phone. She paused in their kitchen long enough to get a bottle of water and then carried it with her to the bedroom.

Even as she was getting in the bath and sinking down into the bubbles, she heard the voice.

And so it begins.

The big reveal had forever changed their world. Trey's fans and followers would be coming. She needed to be ready for the onslaught, and the first thing to come down the next morning was the Christmas tree.

All four of them, Marley and Trey, Jack and Wanda were busy packing up the precious memories and putting them back in the attic.

Another snowy mountain Christmas marked as done.

Chapter 18

WITHIN THREE DAYS, PEOPLE BEGAN SHOWING UP AT THE lodge, carrying copies of their favorite Chapel Hill books, wanting to have them signed and to have photos taken with the now-famous author.

Trey Austin had already become every woman's dream when he began a nationwide search for his Cinderella, but finding out he was also the mysterious author of the Chapel Hill novels elevated him even more in the public eye.

The number of people who began coming to lunch at the lodge increased dramatically, to the point that some were actually waiting in the lobby for a place to sit, and at the request of local booksellers, Trey went to the stores and signed the copies of his books they had on hand, which helped slow down the flurry of unexpected visitors to the lodge.

One evening after the first week had passed, Trey flopped down onto the sofa beside Marley, took her hand, and kissed her work-worn knuckles.

"You are a wonder. You're taking all this in stride, and I'm looking for a place to hide," he said.

She laughed. "My business has always been about all kinds of people coming from everywhere. You've been holed up on your own in an office for what…the past ten years…answering to no one but yourself?"

He grimaced. "Pretty much."

She ran her fingers through the dark thatch of his hair, feeling the wiry coarseness beneath her palms, and then massaged the back of his neck.

"Trey…sweetheart…this isn't terrible. It's just different. You haven't lost yourself. You're broadening your horizons."

He grinned. "Oh, so that's what it's called."

"I think after the novelty wears off, the rush will subside. After that, a new book release might cause a resurgence. And maybe the film. Morris LeHigh already expects you at the premiere."

"He knows I'll show, but I'm planning to trot your pretty little ass up the red carpet with me."

"That would be something," she said. "Anyway…that's in the far future. Nothing to worry about now. Oh… Five boxes were just unloaded on the front porch. I had Jack bring them inside. They're in the hall. I'm thinking they're the copies from your publisher."

"Oh… I'll check them out. If they are, I'll get the books signed and on the shelves. That bookshelf Jack built is about to be put to good use. Is it located where you want it to be?"

She nodded.

"Then I'm on it. Why don't you take a break? If anybody needs you, I'll send you a text."

"Ordinarily, I'd argue that, but I think I will put my feet up for a bit."

A few minutes later, Marley was stretched out on the sofa and Trey was out in the lodge signing books and putting them on the shelves. They were slowly coming to a place of peace.

Some nights, Marley went to bed wishing her parents were still alive to see this happening. And other nights, she accepted that they were likely watching it all unfold.

They'd set a mid-April date for the wedding, after the snowy season had passed. But neither of them wanted to turn it into an event and decided Marley's Christmas guests and Trey's agent would be the sum total of their guests, because those were the people who loved them.

On January fifteenth, the day of Marley's birthday, she woke up to a pair of diamond earrings sparkling from a little box beside her pillow and Trey coming into the room, bringing her breakfast in bed.

"Trey! The earrings! They're beautiful," she said, and promptly put the little posts on the studs into her ears. "Thank you. You're spoiling me, you know."

"Keeping you satisfied in every way is part of my job."

She laughed. "You're just waiting for me to reassure you that you are indispensable, which you are. And terribly good at what you do."

"Nothing is too good for my angel. And before you panic... Wanda is checking out the guests who are leaving, and Toni and Angela have the kitchen in hand. This is your day, darlin'. I want to give you the world, but I come bringing pancakes instead."

Marley pulled a T-shirt over her head and straightened out the covers as Trey put the tray down in her lap.

"I see there are two forks," she said.

"Your eyesight is amazing," he said, and watched her take the first bite. "Happy birthday, angel mine. Enjoy."

Later in the day, a huge three-tiered birthday cake was delivered to the lodge. Marley was surprised and delighted.

"Trey! It's huge! What in the world are we going to do with all this cake?"

"Put it on the dessert table at the lunch buffet. Everybody loves you. They can have cake with you. Here. I even made a little placard to put beside it."

MARLEY'S BIRTHDAY CAKE. HAVE A PIECE. WE'RE CELEBRATING MARLEY TODAY.

Pieces of cake had already been sliced onto little plates, and one of the servers stood ready to slice more. Every single person who ate with them that day also left her with a birthday blessing.

Marley's life was full and overflowing.

January passed into February. A late snow fell on Valentine's Day and melted off within the week.

February slipped into March without a hitch.

Life was full and busy and hectic, and Trey was up to his ears with the new novel.

Then one morning in mid-March, just before daylight, Trey heard Marley get up. He waited for the sound of the shower to come on, or to hear drawers opening and closing. Something ordinary. Instead, there was silence, and then he heard her being sick and flew out of bed and rushed in.

She had already thrown up and was sitting on the side of the tub with her head in her hands.

"Honey! What's wrong?" Trey asked.

She pointed to the sink without looking up.

He saw a pink-and-white test strip lying on the counter with two little lines running across the little window.

"You're sick!"

"Not exactly. I'm pregnant. No need for a shotgun wedding. We'll just use the one we already planned."

He didn't know whether to laugh at her nonsense in the middle of her misery or cry from the joy of the news.

"Oh my God…sweetheart…oh my God. I am so sorry that you're miserable, but I feel like heaven finally opened the gates to let me in."

Marley's eyes welled. "There you go, talking pretty again," she whispered, and started crying.

Within seconds, she was in his arms, and he was carrying her back to bed. Then he grabbed a wastebasket and pulled it close… just in case.

"What can I do? What do you need?"

She looked up then, laughing through tears. "You already did your part. I just need the world to stop spinning, and I'll be fine, too. So, you're not upset that this happened?"

"Never," he said, and then a thought occurred. "Are you afraid I'll turn into my father?"

"Absolutely not," she said and then closed her eyes again. "Ugh. I need the room to stop spinning. I'm not afraid of anything about you. I was mostly alluding to fatherhood interfering with your newfound fame."

Trey ran to get a cold cloth from the bathroom, then folded it and put it across her forehead.

"Maybe that will stop the spinning. Now, hear me. Fame is fleeting. Life means nothing without you. The baby is ours. The beginning of our family. I can't wait to be a father. I can't wait to hear someone call me Daddy and to be present for every milestone. I will be everything for you and them, in a way no one was for me. The best thing about me is that I already know what *not* to do.

"I have so much love to give, Marley, but before you, there was no one to give it to. Finding you was the most wonderful Christmas gift I'd ever been given, and now you're the gift that keeps on giving."

"Then we're good here," she said. "And just so you know, other than morning sickness, this is the happiest feeling I've ever had."

He took her hand. "I have only one request."

"What's that?" she asked.

"If it's a boy, we do not name him after me. There will be no Anders Allen Austin the fourth. That ends with me. Every child needs to become their own person. Not have to grow up being constantly compared to the other namesakes who came before them."

"I promise. We're starting our own line, making a brand-new Austin."

Trey nodded. "Thank you. Maybe we could name him Corbett Austin, and keep the Corbett name alive."

She smiled. "And if it's a girl?"

"We should probably name her Angel. Just to keep the good guys on our side."

"They're already here," Marley said.

"How do you know?"

"Because if they hadn't shouted at me in my sleep to wake up, I would have probably thrown up in bed."

He laughed, and she laughed with him.

There were balloons and ribbons hanging from the Corbett Lodge sign out on the main road, and a sign taped across it:

CLOSED FOR THE WEDDING

Meredith Bernstein had flown in yesterday. Trey picked her up at the airport. They took one look at each other, smiled, then embraced.

"You are my only guest. By choice. Thank you for coming," he said.

"I wouldn't have missed this for the world. I hear congratulations are in order again. Fatherhood will suit you."

"I know," Trey said. "Let's go. Marley is anxious to meet you."

"And I, her," Meredith said as he walked her to the car.

As soon as they were on the way, Trey began talking. "I can promise you the most amazing assortment of wedding guests you will ever experience. Just know that they were her parents' friends before she was born. They've watched her grow up, and they are her honored guests every year at Christmas dinner. She knows about everybody in the city, and they know her, or at least know of her. But these people are all she has left to call family."

Meredith's eyes narrowed. "If you think you're warning me to be prepared for people who do not mingle within high social circles, there is no need. We all come from the same place. We just wear different clothes and different faces."

Trey glanced at her. "You sound like Marley."

"Excellent!" Meredith said.

He laughed. "You would say that."

A few minutes later, they arrived at the lodge.

Meredith gasped. "This place is amazing!"

"Yes, it is. Wait until you see it inside." He grabbed her bag, then helped her out and up the steps. Just as they reached the front door, it suddenly swung inward and Marley was there, smiling and welcoming them inside.

"Meredith, I'm Marley. I have tried to picture you in my mind as this fierce warrior within the publishing world, and yet you stand before me, this elegant, fashionable New Yorker. So, I assume you use all this feminine elegance to your advantage in negotiations, when in reality your backbone is pure steel, and your tongue can as easily become a sword?"

Meredith blinked. Looked first at Trey and smiled, and then looked back at Marley.

"One look and she read me like a book," Meredith said. "And me, trying to picture this tiny you, dragging this great, big man to safety. I am in something of a state of shock. However, you made it happen, and I am forever grateful you saved him. He is my favorite client, but we don't tell people that. I hope we are going to be friends."

"Of course we are," Marley said. "Trey is going to take you to your room. You make yourself at home here and come find me when you're settled. I'll be in the kitchen." Then she shifted focus to Trey. "Honey, the room key is on the desk. Would you please do the honors and take her up?"

That was yesterday, and today was their wedding.

The florist had come and gone.

The wedding cake was on a sideboard, along with serving plates and silverware.

The threads of silver in Meredith's blue dress flashed beneath the lights, calling attention to the lovely blond highlights in her dark hair. Her jewelry sparkled, but not as brightly as her eyes. She and Wanda had hit it off and were in quiet conversation as they waited for the guests to begin arriving, and when they did, they came in their finest, some of which they'd pulled out of mothballs, and some of which were styles from days gone by.

They came carrying their gifts, some wrapped and some in little gift bags. But they were all as shiny as new pennies, and Meredith was introduced to them all in a sort of receiving line.

Mr. Doolittle and Alvin Smith.

Craig, the woodcutter.

Gert and Mabel Jukes.

Arnie Fitzsimmons.

Patsy and Charlie Barrett.

Shirley Lowrey and Lawrence Atwood.

And Keith Murphy.

It was hard to say who was more impressed—Meredith in the midst of them, or them meeting Trey's famous agent from New York City.

And then a car pulled up out in the parking lot and skidded to a stop. Jack got out, grabbed his passenger, and came flying in the front door with the pastor in tow.

Wanda rolled her eyes. "Better late than never," she muttered, and went back to knock on the door and tell Trey the pastor had arrived, then hurried back as everybody took a seat wherever they were most comfortable.

The pastor took his place beneath the chandelier in the lobby.

Benny, the photographer, who took Santa Claus pictures, was set up nearby to capture it all.

And once the "Wedding March" filled the air, Jack hurried back to sit down beside his wife.

Moments later, Trey and Marley appeared at the far end of the hall and began walking toward the light and the man standing beneath it.

We are with you always.

Marley heard the words and knew her truth.

Trey tightened his grip.

He felt like he was floating, and one thought kept rolling through his mind.

I am a blessed man. Once I had nothing...until her.

Epilogue

Baby boy Austin came into the world screaming, objecting to everything that was happening and indignant that the comfort of his mother's belly was no longer an option.

When they laid him on his mother's chest, and she put her hands on his little bare back, the doctor laughed.

"Did that baby just let out a sigh?"

"I think he was just drawing a breath for the next round," a nurse said.

"He recognized the heartbeat. He's not afraid anymore," Trey said.

Moments later, they were measuring and weighing and typing his blood and he was screaming again. Then finally, as he was still wailing, they swaddled him in a soft blue blanket and handed him to Trey.

"There's my boy. There's my sweet baby boy," he kept saying.

The baby's cries dwindled down to a little squeak and then nothing, and Trey kept talking to him in that deep, rumbly voice, and the baby shuddered, as if ridding himself of the last of his complaints and stared straight up into Trey's face.

"He can't see me yet, can he?" Trey asked.

"They see, but not perfect vision. It takes a while for their eyes to adjust and focus. He doesn't know what he's looking at, but he already knows what he hears," the doctor said.

"He knows the sound of his father's voice as well as he knows mine," Marley said, but she could barely see the look of wonder on Trey's face for the tears in her own eyes.

Before you knew each other, your son chose the both of you.

Marley got chills. Someday she'd tell Trey what they said, or maybe not. Maybe the simple miracle of this baby's birth was enough.

Trey cradled his son against his chest, gently kissed his soft baby cheek, and then whispered in his ear.

"I will love you forever. I will always have your back. And whatever you come to be in this world, it will be enough."

A nurse approached. "Sorry, Daddy. He's going to the nursery for a bit. Have you two picked out a name?"

"Corbett Joseph Austin," Trey said.

"Nice name," she said. "Mama needs to rest, and Daddy needs to start making phone calls to all the family to let them know Corbett is in the building." She was laughing at her own joke as she laid the baby in the little bed and wheeled him out of the room.

Trey kissed Marley's forehead, smoothing the blond curls away from her face. "Rest, darlin'. This may be the last chance we get for the next twenty years. I'll call Jack and Wanda."

"Don't forget to call Meredith," she added, and then closed her eyes.

He stood, watching her sleep, remembering that, just like his son, his first knowledge of her had been the sound of her voice.

Life was a wonderful thing.

Read on for more
small-town holiday romance from
New York Times and *USA Today*
bestseller Sharon Sala

Chapter 1

Jacksonville, Florida

Sixteen-year-old Duff Martin was missing, and his older brother, Allen, and his mother, Candi, were in a panic. His bed hadn't been slept in, Allen's car was gone, and it appeared some of Duff's clothes might be missing.

Candi was hysterical.

"Oh my God! What happened? Is this because of last night? We have to call the police!"

"And tell them what, Mom? He took my car and ran away? So do you want him reported as a car thief? Dad's already in prison. We don't need to send Duff down that road, too," Allen said.

Candi sat down on Duff's bed, her shoulders slumped, tears running down her face.

"It's all my fault. Last night, when we began talking about your daddy going to prison, Duff freaked out. I still don't know what I said that set him off."

"He was just six when Dad was sentenced. How much of all that did you ever tell him?" Allen asked.

Candi shrugged and wiped her face. "At the time? Not much.

He was too little to understand. And then over the years, he never asked for details. He just knew it was for theft."

Allen sat down beside her and gave her a quick hug. "What exactly were you saying right before he blew up? Do you remember?"

Candi sighed. "Lord...I don't know. I mentioned seeing Selma Garrett's obituary, and he asked who she was, and I think I said...she was the woman who accused Zack of stealing her jewelry. And then Duff got this funny look on his face and asked, 'What jewelry?'"

"Oh yeah," Allen said. "And I added they were family heirlooms, valued at over a quarter of a million dollars, that went missing while Dad was painting at her house."

Candi nodded. "Something about that set Duff off. When he jumped up from the table all pale and shaking, then started hitting himself on the head and crying, I knew something was wrong. I should have talked to him last night, but he wouldn't let me in. And now this!"

"But why would that have upset him? After all this time? And what about all that would have made him run away?" Allen asked.

"I don't know, but he's gone, and I'm scared of what might happen to him," Candi said.

"Does he have access to money?"

Candi gasped. "His college fund!"

"Quick, Mom...check his bank account," Allen said.

Candi pulled up their joint account, checked it, and groaned. "There's a thousand dollars missing."

Allen nodded. "Okay, then he's not about to go robbing some Quick Stop for money. Call him to see if he answers."

"Yes, yes," Candi said, and quickly sent Duff a text.

Allen gave her a hug. "Okay. We've reached out. Now we need to wait and see if he responds. The bottom line here is that he's sixteen, so he's a minor. He wasn't abducted, so the cops will call him a runaway. And the only way the police will get involved is if we press charges for him taking the car, and I'm not going to do that. Something is going on with Duff. He's a good kid, and I'm not going to fly off the handle here and make a bad thing worse."

"You're right," Candi said, and then broke into tears again. "But he's just a kid, and we just put up the Christmas tree, and now he's gone."

"So pray, Mama. Pray for a miracle that we get him home."

Duff Martin didn't run away from home, but he was on a mission. Something his mother said last night had triggered a long-forgotten memory. All he could think afterward was *what if it was my fault?* And the only way he could know for sure was to go back to the place where it all began.

So he packed up a bag and headed north, driving out of Florida into Georgia, going back to Blessings, the little Georgia town where he'd spent the first six years of his life. He didn't tell anyone where he was going, because in his sixteen-year-old mind, this was his problem to solve.

He'd snuck out of the house just after 2:00 a.m., arrived in Blessings about 5:00 a.m., and immediately got a room at the only motel. It wasn't the cleanest, but he didn't have money to waste on the nicer bed-and-breakfast he'd seen online, and this place was a roof over his head.

He stretched out on the bed, so tired he ached, but this wasn't the time to sleep. Now that he was here, he was uncertain where to start. He had memories, but they were vague, and he wasn't sure how much of them was real.

He couldn't remember the house they'd lived in.

He couldn't remember the name of the lady his dad had been working for. He'd heard his mother say it, but he was so freaked out about the rest of the story that it didn't soak in. The only things he could remember for sure were being in first grade at the elementary school and the lady who babysat him after school. Miss Margie. He'd called her Miss Margie.

His first instinct was to start driving the streets of Blessings and see what rang true. He wasn't on a schedule, but as soon as the town began opening up, he took off down Main, oblivious to the holiday atmosphere and decorations, and started his first loop through the residential areas, looking for houses and faces he might remember.

When his phone signaled a text, and he saw who it was from, he sighed.

They knew he was gone.

Even without snow, Christmas spirit was alive and well in Blessings. The little town was in full-on holiday mode.

Decorations were hanging from every streetlight on Main.

There was an ongoing storefront-decorating contest and a trophy to be won for the business that had the best Christmas theme, and the upcoming Christmas parade on Saturday with more trophies to win.

Because snow in this part of Georgia was almost always a no-show, Crown Grocers had brought in its own brand of snow by setting up a snow-cone stand at the north corner of the parking lot, next to the roped-off area where they were selling Christmas trees.

Bridgette could feel the magic of the season all the way to her bones as she drove down Main on the way to work.

In the months since she and Wade had become a couple, the only awkward moment between them had been walking back into the home she'd grown up in and accepting it belonged to him now.

Then as it turned out, it wasn't as hard as she had feared. Her brother Hunt had updated and remodeled it to such a degree before the sale that she soon forgot the old house and saw only the one it was today—the one that belonged to Wade. And the first time they made love in that house, in his bed, memories of the old house were no longer visible to her there.

Making love to Wade was passion at its best, but it was feeling cherished that had put the sparkle in her eyes and the bounce in her step. When she thought about how close she'd come to messing it up, she shuddered. He was now, and would forever be, the best thing to ever happen in her life.

She braked at the stoplight, and while she was waiting for it to turn green, it gave her a few moments to check out the decorations going up in the storefronts. They weren't quite on the level of Bloomingdale's or Saks Fifth Avenue in New York City, but they were Blessings's best, and she couldn't wait to see the finished displays.

The day started out cool—right at fifty degrees, but with a promise to warm up to the mid-eighties around noon—and she had a busy day ahead of her with end-of-month reports.

December marked the beginning of a busy season at the feed store, including the new gift section Wade had created a few months ago. Among the items available for sale there were little packs of dog and cat toys, halters and spurs for the locals who fancied themselves cowboys, and colorful bandannas, along with a whole series of country-style Christmas ornaments, and Made in Georgia specialties like peach jams and jellies.

Bridgette had always enjoyed working here, but the fire that gutted the warehouse last year, resulting in the death of a long-time employee, had taken the heart out of all of them. Then Wade came on as manager and changed the vibe to such a degree that the store barely resembled what it had been.

The stoplight turned green, and she drove through the intersection. Once she reached the feed store, she parked and hurried inside out of the cold.

Wade was on his way to the Crown to pick up an order of Christmas cookies for the break room, but he was thinking about Bridgette.

They'd spent the weekend together at his house. The house where she'd grown up was now the place where they played house. Cooking together. Watching movies together. Making love in his bed, and on the living room sofa, and in the shower, and wherever else they were when the notion struck. But she'd gone home after Sunday dinner to do the chores needed at her own place, and waking up alone this morning made her absence even more pronounced.

He was looking forward to work, knowing he'd be spending the day with her, as he pulled into the Crown parking lot. Then he saw Bridgette's brother Junior on the far side of the parking lot and waved as he got out. Junior saw him and smiled, then returned to unloading and setting up the new shipment of Christmas trees.

Once inside the store, Wade headed straight to the bakery.

"Hey, Sue. I have an order of Christmas cookies to pick up."

"Morning, Wade. I just boxed them up," she said and went to get them. He took them up front to pay before heading on to the store.

Bridgette's car was already in her usual parking spot when he arrived. He parked and hurried into the store with the cookies, greeting customers and workers alike as he went down the hall to the office area, then paused outside her office, peering at her through the wreath dangling over the window of her door. She was laser-focused on the computer screen, her fingers flying across the keyboard.

He knocked and walked in.

"Hey, sweetheart! I missed you this morning," he said, and then stole a quick kiss.

Bridgette cupped the side of his face.

"I missed you, too."

"I brought cookies for the break room, but you get first dibs. Take out all you want now, because they won't last long."

"Ooh, yum," she said as he opened the box. "I love iced sugar cookies."

"There are some gingerbread men on the bottom. Dig through and get what you want," he added.

"I'll get some out for you, too," Bridgette said, then grabbed a handful of napkins, laid out a sugar cookie and a gingerbread man for herself, and then two each for him. "There, you can take the rest to the break room. I'll put yours in your office."

A couple of hours later, her sugar cookie was gone and the gingerbread man stashed in her desk. She was almost through with the monthly reports when she realized the total between receipts and deposits was off. There was data in the computer showing sales, but the total of monthly deposits didn't balance out, so she went back over her input again, then pulled up the readouts from the front register until she found the exact amount she was off. The transaction was there, but that day's money deposit was short $532.50—the exact amount of a receipt she had for a feed purchase.

Her heart sank.

Either someone pocketed the money, or gave away the feed and hoped no one would catch it. In all the years she'd worked here, this had only happened a couple of times, and both times it had been theft.

Once a clerk pocketed the money, and the other time, a man working in the warehouse did his buddy a favor, loaded up feed, wrote out a ticket for it to balance out the inventory count, and hoped no one would catch the money missing.

She read the transaction again and saw the register code. It belonged to Donny Corrigan. But that didn't always mean he was the one who'd rung it up. If he'd stepped away from the register to help someone else, any employee could have used it to check a customer out, without keying in their own code. It would be an easy way to take money with no expectation of getting caught.

The next thing Bridgette did was check the time cards to see where Donny was that day, and if he was in the store at that time. She found where he'd clocked in, and then three hours later had clocked out and hadn't come back that whole day.

She frowned, trying to remember why, and then she realized that was the day Donny's wife went into labor with their first baby. He had clocked out, but in his panic, it appeared he had not counted out his till, which left his code in the register, which now made everyone else in the store a possible suspect.

She picked up her phone and called Wade.

About the Author

New York Times and *USA Today* bestselling author Sharon Sala has 140+ books in print, published in seven different genres—romance, young adult, western, general fiction, women's fiction, illustrated children's books, and nonfiction. First published in 1991, her industry awards include the Janet Dailey Award, five Career Achievement awards, five National Readers' Choice Awards, five Colorado Romance Writers' Awards of Excellence, the Heart of Excellence Award, the Booksellers' Best Award, the Nora Roberts Lifetime Achievement Award, the Centennial Award in recognition of her 100th published novel, the Will Rogers Gold Medallion Award, and the CROW National Excellence in Storytelling Award. She lives in Oklahoma, the state where she was born.

Website: sharonsalaauthor.com
Facebook: sharonkaysala
Instagram: @sharonkaysala_

Also by Sharon Sala

Don't Back Down
Last Rites
Heartbeat
Left Behind
The Next Best Day

Blessings, Georgia
Count Your Blessings (novella)
You and Only You
I'll Stand by You
Saving Jake
A Piece of My Heart
The Color of Love
Come Back to Me
Forever My Hero
A Rainbow Above Us
The Way Back to You
Once in a Blue Moon
Somebody to Love
The Christmas Wish
The Best of Me